F
Elmer

Elmer, Robert.

The duet.

Praise for
The Duet

"As sweet and flavorful as Dutch apple pie, Robert Elmer's *The Duet* is a welcome treat. I am so thrilled that Robert is now writing for adults as well as children—and I appreciate this loving look into a music teacher's life and heart."

—ANGELA HUNT, author of *The Debt*

"Robert Elmer's *The Duet* is a charming love story in which backgrounds and traditions clash. If you love music, nostalgia, or a rural setting, then this heartwarming novel is for you."

—RANDY ALCORN, author of *Safely Home* and *Deadline*

"It's never too late for love, and Robert Elmer's first delve into adult fiction conveys that comforting truth with homespun wit and a unique voice. *The Duet* is peopled with characters of many stripes and dimensions, yet they all intersect in the place where grace abounds. Wonderful."

—LISA SAMSON, best-selling author of *The Church Ladies* and
The Living End

"*The Duet* is a delightfully romantic story with real meat on its bones. If I wasn't laughing out loud, I was smiling, and if I wasn't smiling, I was crying. Robert Elmer writes with a charming voice. Truly one of the best novels I've read in years."

—DEBORAH RANEY, author of *Beneath a Southern Sky* and
A Nest of Sparrows

THE DUET

A Novel

ROBERT ELMER

WATERBROOK
PRESS

THE DUET
PUBLISHED BY WATERBROOK PRESS
2375 Telstar Drive, Suite 160
Colorado Springs, Colorado 80920
A division of Random House, Inc.

Unless otherwise indicated, all Scripture quotations are taken from the *King James Version* of the Bible. Scripture also quoted from the *Holy Bible, New International Version*®. NIV®. Copyright © 1973, 1978, 1984 by International Bible Society. Used by permission of Zondervan Publishing House. All rights reserved.

The characters and events in this book are fictional, and any resemblance to actual persons or events is coincidental.

ISBN 1-57856-740-8

Published in association with the literary agency of Alive Communications, Inc., 7680 Goddard Street, Suite 200, Colorado Springs, CO 80920.

Library of Congress Cataloging-in-Publication Data
Elmer, Robert.
  The duet / Robert Elmer.—1st ed.
    p. cm.
  ISBN 1-57856-740-8
  1. Grandparent and child—Fiction. 2. Women music teachers—Fiction. 3. Dairy farmers—Fiction. 4. Grandfathers—Fiction. 5. Widowers—Fiction. I. Title.
PS3555.L44D83 2004
813'.54—dc22   2003019785

Printed in the United States of America
2004—First Edition

10 9 8 7 6 5 4 3 2 1

To Ronda

Chapter 1

All the good music has already been written
by people with wigs and stuff.
—FRANK ZAPPA

So where can I put you, my little man?" Joan Marie Horton parted the white lace living-room curtains with one hand to clear a space for Johann Sebastian Bach. He would fit perfectly on top of the short bookcase the movers had centered under the street-facing four-paned window.

Or nearly centered. But she would fix that later, when her daughter's husband, Shane, stopped by after work. For now she placed the little ceramic bust of the maestro where it could be seen from Delft Street and from her piano, where it would remind her of Jim, who had given it to her for her forty-fifth birthday, just before the accident.

She still wondered if things might have been different had she been a better wife, a better mother. Perhaps *he* would have been helping her unpack in this early summer heat, not their eight-months pregnant daughter, Alison.

"Mom?" came the question from the kitchen. "You want this china put up in the hutch?"

She did. But goodness, after six years one would have thought she'd grown used to the idea of being alone, grown past the tears. Joan tensed her jaw and reached into the box of packing paper to remove a framed eight-by-ten. Wouldn't you know it would be the shot of Jim and their only son, Randy, sitting in the back of the Millers' ski boat at Great Sacandaga Lake, each with a bronzed arm around the shoulder of the other, each wearing the same ridiculous grin.

At the time she had scolded them for ruining the shot. Now? She would set it in the middle of the fireplace mantel, a place of honor in her cozy little rental home for her upcoming sabbatical year. And really, the smiles seemed fitting. After all, it was really no one's fault that Jim had died in the blizzard—not even Jim's. She knew he had been depressed, but she also knew—more than anyone—that he had wanted desperately to make it home. It was just one of those bad things that happened to good people.

All of which was simple enough to say, nearly impossible to live with. *If only, if only.* And up until now she had dealt with it by escaping more deeply into her teaching, her music. That had worked for a time, but she could only go so far before she had to come up for air. Perhaps this move would help her take the first real steps toward putting the guilt behind her and setting her life straight once again.

Step one: Get Randy out of his flea-infested apartment and set him up in her empty Long Island home, with a fully stocked pantry. Who better to housesit? By the time he ran out of things to eat, he would be getting a small paycheck from his new job stocking shelves at the Port Hamilton Market. Of course, at age twenty-four he could certainly land a more promising job. But at least the market was within walking distance so he wouldn't need to drive. And with Randy's license suspended after the DWI arrest, she was pleased their pastor, Tim Jenkins, had promised to look in on him every few days. At least the DWI had forced her to act, pushed her to take...

Step two: Escape New York and move across the country for a year to the small town where Alison and Shane now lived. Reconnect with the daughter she hardly knew, the self-sufficient one whose young life and accomplishments had been passed over during the years when Joan and

Jim were so busy trying to deal with Randy's teenage crises. Could a grandmother now atone for a mother's shortcomings? If only she had it to do over again.

But where did she now find herself? My, the operative word here was *small* town. Because from what she had experienced so far, a crowd in Van Dalen, Washington, meant four people in line at the post office during lunch hour, waiting to mail their letters and packages. Or the families who lined the sidewalk during the Wooden Shoe Fest last weekend when she had arrived in town. Or perhaps the occasional Wang-Li Excursions tour bus that pulled up to the quaint Dutch-styled downtown and disgorged a load of fifty video-toting tourists from Vancouver. Now *there* was a crowd.

This morning, instead of gawking at the lace shops, she had decided to hang a bit of her own over the little window in her front door, just like all the other houses on Delft Street. No matter that she was only going to stay for a year. It would be home.

"So!" She gave the lace a satisfied tug to help it hang just right. "I can look just as Dutch as the neighbors. I'll even change my name to Van Horton." The only other accessory she needed was a pair of kissing Dutch figurines for the front lawn or a foot-high windmill, but she wasn't prepared to plunge quite that far into the ethnic experience.

"Did you say something, Mom?"

No, nothing. But a movement out the side window caught her eye: the lawn service at her neighbors', Fred and Judy Vanderstraat, who had introduced themselves the day Joan's moving van arrived last week. The local father and son gardeners had turned Fred and Judy's front lawn into a putting green with their special rotary mowers, and they were now power edging the corners with a vigor matched only by Bill's Barber Shop downtown. Joan assumed it was Bill who stood on display in his shop window, draping the town's menfolk in pinstripe blue sheets and hand-trimming their heads for $5.25 plus tip. And no, she had never seen anything like Van Dalen lawns anywhere else in the country. Not even in the real Holland, which Van Dalen had done its best to emulate.

In any case the lawns were enough to make Tiger Woods proud. Fred and Judy had assured her this was the way things were done here. Except, Fred laughed, never on Sunday, which had been followed by a generous elbow in his side from Judy. But he was right. Sunday was the day local church doors were opened wide so throaty hymn singing and organ music could waft down Delft Street past all the closed stores. Fred had told her quietly how one of the restaurants had tried to open on Sunday—once—but the resulting firestorm of righteous letters to the editor had put a quick stop to that. He'd heard that someone had posted a little sign on the front doorknob of the place. Something about "Honor the Sabbath Day!" But he hadn't seen it himself, and he thought that was a little extreme, even for Van Dalen. Still, he maintained Sundays were for quiet, and Joan had readily agreed. Van Dalen was just different that way.

Wasn't that part of the reason she was already falling in love with this town? Her little house had probably been built in the 1920s, and its quaint Craftsman style fit in nicely between modest turn-of-the-century Victorians nestled quietly beneath a canopy of full-blown elms lining Delft Street. They paraded up to where the windmill signaled a shift from homes to shops. Everything modest, everything in its place, and above all, everything orderly, from the homeowners' little name-tag signs by the doors to the occasional white picket fence and spit-shined windows.

Joan returned to unpacking but couldn't help picking up the photo once more. And once more she tried to memorize Jim's features, the nose, the eyes. Yet the guilt-laden thought occurred to her that even if Jim were to approach her on a busy Van Dalen street today, six years after his death, she might not be able to pick him out of the crowd.

Well, perhaps he wouldn't recognize her, either. Jim hadn't actually lived long enough to see for himself how many cruel tricks time played on women in their early fifties. For one thing, her thick raven hair had been invaded by stealthy shocks of gray. Even worse, little crow's feet had crept unbidden into her Mediterranean complexion, originally inherited from a vivacious Greek grandmother. Now Joan had been left with missing hormones, frozen emotions, faded memories, and twelve months to figure it all out in a town where nearly everyone was a stranger. At least she still held on to her grandmother's slender build.

The photo, however, slipped from her grasp, hitting the brick hearth with a crack that must have launched her a full three inches into the air.

"Mom?" Alison called from the kitchen, where she was still unwrapping china. "You all right?"

"Just clumsy!" Joan berated herself as she dropped to her knees. She turned her head so Alison wouldn't see the tears and picked up the cracked oak frame by its corner to survey the damage. The photo itself was okay, but wicked glass splinters littered the bricks.

"Oh, I'm sorry." Alison waddled up behind her. "Your favorite photo. Here, I'll help you with that."

"No, no, it's all right." Joan blinked her eyes fiercely, shook the last of the shards from the frame and hurried to set it on the mantel. "You didn't come here to be doing deep knee bends."

"Yeah, I get enough exercise with the aerobics and the ten-mile jogs."

Alison smiled at the look of concern that flashed across her mother's face.

"Just kidding, Mom. But I'm taking vitamins and drinking plenty of local milk. I'll be just fine."

In truth, she probably would. After all, Alison had inherited a good share of her father's square-jawed Teutonic build, not unlovely by any means, but more naturally suited to childbearing than Joan. Even eight months along (and despite the waddle), Joan's only daughter still carried herself like the confident track star she had always been back in high school, back in New York.

"I know *you* will." Joan studied the damaged photo. "Now, your brother…"

Alison followed her gaze, and her voice softened as she slipped her arm around her mother's shoulder.

"Remember all the hurt animals he used to drag home when he was little?"

Joan couldn't help a small smile at the memory: the butterflies, the baby birds, the puppies… Randy, the sensitive, protective one, out to rescue the world. But now Alison's smile had faded, and they both knew where her thoughts had wandered. Now it was her mother's turn.

"It's not your fault, Alison. You've tried to stay in contact. He's made his own choices."

"It's just that he changed so much after Dad died, like he was never able to handle it. It's always scared me, Mom."

You have no idea, Alison. But Joan couldn't voice her own guilt, so she simply tried to think of something encouraging to say.

"I'm praying the next year will be good for him."

"Me, too." Alison bit her lip and nodded…before wincing in pain. Joan's heart nearly stopped.

"Alison? What's wrong? Are you—"

Alison only held up her hand and shook her head. No, she was okay. It was just a kick, and it happened all the time. All she needed was to sit down for a moment, catch her breath. This little one was a kicker.

Even so, Joan would be taking no chances with her only daughter. In fact, she would have preferred that Alison rest on the love seat, had it not been piled high with boxes of sheet music, and had the doorbell not chimed just then.

"Your first visitor?"

Alison steered herself toward the bedroom, and Joan told her to lie down on the bed with her feet up, for goodness' sake. A cheery follow-up knock came at the same time Joan spotted an eager face peering through the lace at her. Joan found a smile to match her visitor's and pulled open the door.

"You are the new piano teacher?" A tall older woman with an enormous sharp nose shuffled right up to the door. "I thought for a moment you veren't here."

"Uh, no." Joan stepped back so the visitor wouldn't step on her toes. "I mean, yes, I am. May I help you with something?"

"Ve're the Van Dalen Velkomvagen."

In the visitor's distinctly Dutch accent every *velkom* started viss a *v.*

"Joan Horton. Please excuse the mess, oh, and the broken glass there."

"Vatch the door, Earl." Mrs. Velkomvagen pointed outside before Joan, still taken aback by the brassy entrance, nearly closed the door on visitor number two.

"Oh, dear, I didn't see you." Joan pushed open the door. "Please come in."

The baldheaded Earl nodded and held out two brimming-full plastic bags, the kind with the cutout hole at the top for hanging inside a car. They were emblazoned with the logo of Hank's Ace Hardware.

"This is for you."

Just four words told Joan that Earl had been born on this side of the Atlantic. But after handing over the free welcome samples, he simply backed into the living room's flowered wallpaper while the missis launched into her presentation. She was obviously quite used to making herself heard in a way that Earl could understand with his dual hearing aids.

"Filling in for Linda Klopstra, I hear?"

Well, yes... They stood between the two pianos in Joan's living room, this soon-to-be music studio. A toilet flushed in the background.

"I've been asked to take her students for a year while she's in Romania."

While Joan continued, the visitor nodded as if she already knew the details, which she undoubtedly did.

"Also my daughter, Alison, is having a baby...I mean, not at the moment, but she's due in two weeks. So I'm helping her while I'm here. I'll be a grandmother for the first time."

"Vahnderful." The woman paused to admire one of the pianos. "I have twenty-seven grandchildren. And your people are from vhere?"

Joan paused and tried to straighten a box of music books on the floor with her foot. Her people? Joan could entertain her with stories of the Sicilian great-grandmother or the shopkeeper grandfather from Athens who was separated from his parents for half a day on Ellis Island...

"Er...I used to teach at a music school in New York, if that's what you mean. We raised our two children on Long Island."

"Ve?"

So the woman wanted the whole story. All right then.

"I'm sorry. My husband, Jim, and I, our daughter, Alison, and our son, Randy. Randy's my baby; well, actually he's twenty-four, and he's living back in Port Hamilton. Long Island. Alison, she's the one expecting. You may know her. Her husband is the county extension agent, Shane Nelson; they live over on Twin Creek Road at the edge of town. Shane was transferred here about a year ago."

"Shane Nelson." Joan's visitor rolled the name around on her tongue with some difficulty. "And vhat does your husband do?"

"Oh. Jim, ah...passed away, was killed in an accident. Storm related. A blizzard."

The catch in her voice surprised even Joan. But obviously the visitor wasn't out for blood, and she wasn't going to ask for all the details about the accident. She finally nodded and stepped around a small pile of sheet music on her way back to the door.

"I'm sorry. I didn't mean to pry."

"That's all right. It's been six years."

Mrs. Velkomvagen mercifully changed the subject. "I hear they're looking for a pianist at Second."

Nothing like moving the conversation along.

"Second?"

"Second Reformed Church. It's just down the street." She pointed. "Around the corner from First Reformed; two blocks from Third. Perhaps it vould be a good way to get involved in the community. I could tell them you're interested."

Joan paused, wondering how to graciously decline.

"That's very kind of you, but I'm afraid I've never attended a Reformed church."

The woman raised her eyebrows, as if she had stumbled across an alien or a pagan. Never? And for one brief contrary moment, Joan considered leaving it at that. But no.

"I was raised in the Church of the Nazarene," Joan went on, "which I suppose is quite a different tradition. My father was a pastor, mostly churches in the Midwest. But I understand there's a small Nazarene fellowship that meets in a Grange hall just west of town."

The visitor took it all in while color returned to her drawn face. This newcomer was not Dutch. Not Reformed. Not Dutch Reformed. And her last name didn't start with a Van. What had she expected?

"Nort' Valley Grange Hall on the Simble Bridge Road. Past the fairgrounds. Isn't that right, Earl?"

That would be *North* Valley Grange Hall on the *Thimble* Bridge Road, of course. Earl nodded politely, but Joan could tell this conversation was over by the way he started edging for the door. Joan thanked them as Mrs. Velkomvagen produced a clipboard and counted several lines with her finger.

"Sree, foor, five. Ve vould stay to chat, but ve have five more homes to visit today for the vagen. So many new people."

Which could be good or bad, depending on one's perspective. Joan nodded and clutched the bulging plastic bags studded with stickers from the Van Dalen Downtown Association. A coupon for a free key at the Ace Hardware fluttered out. Earl picked it up.

"Five more to visit." Mrs. Earl tapped her list again. Maybe she'd gathered all the intelligence she came for. But she paused on the way out, looking over her shoulder.

"Be sure to use the dinner coupon for the Vindmill Grill," she said. "Best hutspot in town."

Joan couldn't be sure if *hutspot* was something to eat or someplace to eat it, but Mrs. Earl assumed everyone knew. Joan shook their hands, thanked them again, and smiled as she watched them totter down the steps and off to their next appointment.

Nice people. Maybe Alison would go with her to find out what a *hutspot* was. "Alison!" As if in answer, her daughter's strained voice drifted in from the bedroom.

"Mother!" This time Alison's voice took on an edge that snapped Joan to attention. "Could you call Shane at work? I think my water just broke."

Chapter 2

Computers make it easier to do a lot of things, but most of the
things they make it easier to do don't need to be done.
—ANDY ROONEY

W hat do you MEAN I've performed an illegal operation? I haven't
performed anything illegal my entire LIFE!" Which wasn't entirely true, but still awfully close. Gerrit Appeldoorn wagged his finger at
the impertinent blue computer screen as if he could threaten it into submission. Well, it had always worked for heifers and weaner pigs.

Show 'em who's boss.

But it didn't matter a fig to this new computer, and it didn't matter a
fig to the e-mail gremlins hiding somewhere inside. They had to be laughing at him, even now. But this invention from the Pit wasn't cooperating
the way his son Warney had promised him it would, and now the computer was blaming HIM? No sir, he wasn't going to sit still for this kind
of insult.

Who were they trying to fool? The black-and-white cowhide-print box
it had come in was just a ruse, a trick to convince gullible country folks like
himself. Yeah, you bet. Make the box look like a Holstein, and we'll think
here's finally a computer rig that'll work for the average dairy farmer.

Make that the average *retired* dairy farmer. As in "put out to pasture,"
left to play with his new one-point-five-gig whatever with extra ROM and
RAM that had nothing whatsoever to do with a male sheep. Which was too
bad, as he might have been able to figure it out better if it did, and he might
have been able to make the e-mail work the way they told him it would.

"You'll be up and e-mailing your kids in minutes." That's what they'd said in the ad. All he knew now was that Warney had told the young gal taking their order on the 1-800 line to include plenty of it. ROM and RAM, that is.

But never mind. It didn't make a fig of difference. No matter how much he threatened this thing, the mail wouldn't "e," the CD wouldn't burn, and now it was telling him something illegal was happening.

And whose fault was that?

He popped a fourth Dubbel Zout into his mouth and began ruminating on the nickel-sized Dutch licorice as it released a comforting wave of eye-watering "double-salt" flavor that non-Dutch folks crudely compared to cow salt. It was nothing like cow licks, which Gerrit had tried once and which truthfully had popped his sky-blue eyes out of their sockets. But people who hadn't been raised on the stuff just didn't get it. Maybe, he admitted, the same way he didn't get this computer. All he knew was that he was a lot more comfy with low-tech instruments like the Philco portable phonograph on his coffee table, spinning low-tech vinyl like his favorite, old Johnny Cash, who was still keeping a close watch on this heart of mine.

"Yeah, I keep my eyes wide open all the time too," he told the Man in Black between chews.

Gerrit had learned that he and the country singer shared a birthday, February 26, though old Johnny had a few years on him. The late legendary performer had once stood head-to-head with Gerrit, though, as evidenced by a Polaroid shot of the two taken right in front of the grandstands some years back when Cash had headlined at the fair. With the years the photo had curled a bit, though in a community of Dutchmen where six-footers were considered short, most everyone still looked up to Gerrit. Literally. His wiry gray hair stood out straight from his head but could not really be called a crew cut. The gray of his once-blond hair only added an extra touch of dignity to his lean frame, particularly since it still sprouted thick enough so he didn't have to comb it across a bald dome, like a few friends he wouldn't mention.

All that didn't help him much with the computer, though. And how was he going to catalog all his records if he couldn't even get it to fire up?

So Gerrit drop-kicked the box across the living room, which he would never have done had Miriam still been alive. But it reminded him (vaguely) how he had once tried a forty-six-yard field goal during the final ten seconds of Van Dalen High School's varsity football game against neighboring Mount Skagit High. People in the north county had talked about that for a long time, as if it had been their destiny to win.

Well, it probably had been. There were, after all, twenty-two Dutch Reformed congregations in this county, the home of many a good Five-Point Calvinist and well acquainted with predestination—even on the football field. And as best he could remember, he had been a little hot under the collar that time too. Only it had been righteous anger, and it wasn't because of a smart-aleck computer. Just a smart-aleck fan with no faith in the Van Dalen Crusaders, who had obviously been foreordained for victory.

But what was that…forty-two years ago? Goodness, he wasn't ready to start talking like a geezer, no, not yet. The box tumbled across the carpet and bumped his little bookshelf, shaking Miriam's eight-by-ten black-and-white portrait (right in front of the photo with him and Johnny Cash).

"Sorry, dear." He lowered his eyes as if she had seen his little hissy fit and would pause from what she was doing to gently scold some sense back into him, the way she always used to do. He might not have minded this time. And he figured she knew him well enough to know he wouldn't forget what Dr. Eubanks told him about not getting excited.

"But what am I supposed to do about it now, Miriam? Have him increase my meds again?"

The little fridge gurgled in reply from the kitchenette. And Gerrit was glad the doc wasn't around just now, or he might have been inclined to call in the boys with the straitjacket. Gerrit was pretty sure other fellows didn't talk to their deceased wives like this. Did they?

"I don't suppose you know anything about setting up computers that come in cow boxes." He paused again as if Miriam would answer. "No, I guess you're not needing any e-mail in heaven. Lucky you."

Lucky wasn't a sanctified word, he knew, since good Calvinists (and especially former deacons from Van Dalen's First Dutch Reformed Church) weren't supposed to believe in luck, just like they weren't supposed to kick computer boxes in anger. But the word had just sort of slipped out, the way lots of things had slipped out since Miriam had gone on to Glory. (Which was, by the way, much easier to say than "died.") But the fact was, a few other things had slipped lately as well.

Housekeeping, for one. With a twinge of guilt he looked around at the tiny living room where he had lived alone since he'd moved out of the big house three years ago, spinning Johnny Cash and Hank Williams records till the needle nearly wore through to the other side. Some old widowers drank themselves silly; he just listened to classic country. Gerrit frowned at the Styrofoam packing strewn across the brown carpet and the rumpled plastic wrap and devilish instruction manuals he had tossed to the side. One instruction book for the computer, one for the monitor, one for the printer, dozens more for all the programs and the system and all that. And instructions, as he had always told his son, were for wimps.

He still believed that. But he sighed.

"Shoot. Looks like I'm going to have to ask Warney for help again."

Which would have been fine if he and his thirty-three-year-old son had been on better speaking terms. Well, they spoke. Most of the time. It just seemed that every time Gerrit opened his mouth, he inserted his boot. As in, "Warney, how come you aren't (fill in the blank)?" And then the hollering started. But in fact, Warner B. Appeldoorn should have been out tedding the hay that gorgeous early August afternoon, giving it a good chance to dry before baling. Instead, well, who knew? He could have been out to one of his county ag committee meetings, talking up a storm about water rights or bST growth hormone legislation rather than tending the farm right here at home. What good did it do to be messing around with all those meetings with all kinds of work waiting? Gerrit had to hand it to his son: Warney was awfully good at getting sidetracked.

Of course Gerrit would have been glad to be out working the tractor himself if it weren't for the doctor and his orders. A little light exercise, but no more stress and no overexertion. Your heart can't take that kind of stuff, Gerrit.

"Not that I'm complaining, mind you." He held up his size-and-a-half hands in mock surrender to the computer, backed up a step, caught the power strip with his heel, and nearly fell over backward. He chuckled for the first time all afternoon when the screen went black.

"Gotcha."

So much for labor-saving devices, which were great in theory. Anybody would tell you he was button-busting proud of the fact that Appeldoorn Farm had been one of the first dairies in the county to install an automated milking parlor, complete with walls painted pastel green to soothe the cows and maximize their production. He might have even added magnetic feeding collars a few years back if they weren't so way-out expensive. Which reminded him how much he had spent on this cowhide computer—at Warney's recommendation. He started gathering up some of the garbage on the floor.

Sure, he appreciated his son's advice. And Gerrit had to admit that living in the little whitewashed guesthouse with the picket fence wasn't all bad, either. Miriam used to call it the Missionary Cottage, and it had been plenty good enough for visiting church folks and family for as long as he could remember, until he'd moved out here himself. Oh well. At least now he stayed out of everybody else's way, arm's length, cushioned from twenty-three years of bittersweet memories haunting the big house where he and Miriam had raised their four kids.

Haunted. Now there was another word that hadn't quite made the sanctified list at First Reformed. And of course he himself knew the Old Testament no-nos against calling upon the dead. Leviticus 20 and Deuteronomy 18. The story of Saul and the witch of Endor. He knew all that, and of course he understood.

But how else could he describe the ghosts? Before Miriam had passed on, their memories had seemed like friendly Caspers that made him grin. Memories of 4-H blue ribbons and prize-winning goats and eating popcorn in the kitchen with the kids. Of her ready laugh and the girlish way she would suddenly run across the backyard to the barn, daring him to catch her. And if he cared to look, he could still imagine seeing Miriam's beautiful face through the kitchen window, calling him to wash up for dinner.

But for the past sixteen years the Caspers had mostly disappeared, faded until he hardly saw them. Faded so much that he even questioned whether he had ever seen them. And he wondered if someone had quietly rewritten the script of Gerrit's past or mysteriously erased his memory of Miriam's face. That was the hardest part, when he caught himself staring at her portrait, trying to rememorize the features. Did anybody else do that? He wasn't about to ask.

But he couldn't remember, and that's what cut his heart the most. The numbness. The trying to remember, but nothing. The blank spaces in his memory that should have been there but had faded, though he would never admit it to anyone, hardly to himself.

"Stupid memory." He would have done anything to reclaim the freshness of her face. The pain he could live with, as long as it kept him closer to Miriam's sweetness.

So it was good that Warney and Liz were trying to fill the big house with their own memories, 'cause he was fresh out. Yet little Mallory was nine getting on ten now, and a fine girl like his granddaughter deserved more brothers and sisters. What was a farmhouse without a passel of farm kids? He'd never imagined his son would make his wife work and then choose to have just one child, though he couldn't help thinking it had something to do with Warney's marrying outside the faith.

Of course no one had asked Gerrit, and it sure wasn't any of his business. Just his opinion, see.

One thing was sure, though: The farm was far too quiet these days. No kids playing hide-and-seek down by the river. Even their 189 head of cattle didn't seem to make as much noise as they used to. Oh, they still gave their all, but milk prices were the same today as they were the day Miriam died.

Lower, actually. And guess what had happened to the price of feed in the meantime, or the price of fuel, the price of a visit from the vet, the price of a new plow...

But enough complaining. If Warney was anywhere around, maybe he could help his dad get the computer demon exorcized. Gerrit tucked in his blue denim work shirt, stepped outside into the warm August afternoon, and headed for the gracious, white two-story frame house his Opa Joost had built in 1899. Actually, Warney and Liz had spray-painted it sky blue last year, after all these years of white, and he still couldn't quite get used to how it looked.

Third house on the Vanderkrans Road, he would tell anyone who asked. White with white trim.

"Warney!" He hollered at the barn, then stopped short in the gravel lane next to his...his son's farmhouse.

"Who drives that kind of fancy car?" He ran his finger along the polished lines of a jet black Volvo, wondering what it would take to trip the car alarm. And he wondered why he hadn't heard it pull up, or why Missy hadn't barked when it did. Of course, the old yellow Lab wasn't hearing so well these days. Spent most of her time sleeping in the sun, snorting and chasing dream chickens with quivering old legs. Or maybe she had heard, and he had just been too busy arguing with the cranky new computer.

But no way could he miss the sound of music that escaped the living-room window. Only this wasn't Julie Andrews, and it wasn't Mallory, neither. It sounded classical, but nothing like the tunes he often skipped past on the radio. More like the kind of stuff his Oma used to play, only this…well, this seemed to pack quite a bit more horsepower than the sweet, simple music that once filled his living room when he was a kid.

Not better or worse, exactly. Just different, and mesmerisingly so. (If *mesmerisingly* was a word.)

This music flowed like Kelsey Creek when the salmon spawned every October, when he would take Mallory by the hand to the edge of their acres past the alderwoods, just to watch the glittering silvers return. And like the creek at spawning time, this music flowed with life. He felt the notes rising and falling, fluttering and tumbling.

For just a second he wondered if dancing salmon knew music. A shame if they didn't. But even though that was about the dumbest thing he'd thought in years, he couldn't shake the sound of the piano any better than he could shake the sweet smell of a fresh cutting of hay. And now this music held the autumn's scent of death and the spring's promise of life in the same watery hand. But mostly life. Mostly tomorrows.

Man, that music sounded sweet. And though it felt sacrilegious to even think it, he knew not even Johnny Cash was this good. Not even Hank Williams.

Gerrit wasn't sure how long he stood outside the window, soaking in the powerful beauty of the piano music as if he were standing too long under a hot shower. But without letting any more Robert Frost fish thoughts jumble his mind, he simply circled around, slipped off his boots, and tiptoed in through the back door. A little closer wouldn't hurt.

Yeah, and that's probably what moths thought when they saw candle-light in the dark.

Chapter 3

You don't need any brains to listen to music.
—LUCIANO PAVAROTTI

*N*ow I've gone and thoroughly embarrassed myself." A woman's warm voice filtered back to the kitchen from the living room. "Believe me, this was not why I stopped by."

"Don't be embarrassed, Mrs. Horton." That was Warney's wife, Liz. "You play gorgeously. I'd twist your arm all over again just to hear those kinds of sounds coming from the old piano."

"Me, too." Mallory giggled. "But I could never ever do that in a million years."

"Never say never," came the strange voice once more. "Mrs. Klopstra told me before she left that you're a very determined girl when you want to be, especially with your 4-H projects. I'm sure you'll be a good musician if you just make up your mind and do it."

That didn't exactly sound like something John Calvin would have said, that self-determination stuff. Gerrit made a mental note to ask Warney just what kind of church this woman attended, if any. But by that time Gerrit knew he should politely clear his throat, kick a chair, slam a cabinet door, announce his presence. Instead, he held his breath and stood as still as his Jersey cows soaking up sun and chewing cud in the south pasture.

"Really, even 'Chopsticks' on this piano sounds beautiful," continued the woman. "I don't think I've ever had the privilege of making music on such an old Steinway upright, before."

Mallory said something about her great-great-grandmother and asked something about how old her piano might be.

"Well over a hundred years old, dear, but even now it's a remarkable instrument to practice on, though it *does* need a bit of tuning. What side of the family was your great-great-grandmother?"

Gerrit couldn't quite make out the next bits of conversation—the small window air conditioner kicked in—except *the fair,* and then Mallory happily added something about her 4-H dairy-cow project, and the teacher replied that of course she would love to see Mallory show the animal. She tried a few more chords as she spoke, as if testing the piano's range. And pretty please would she play just one more?

Gerrit inched toward the living-room entry to hear better as the woman launched into another melody. Only this one chuckled and skipped so that it pulled up the corners of his mouth; he couldn't help it. He peeked around the corner to see the back of the woman's head, bobbing and swaying in time to the music. Her fingertips danced off the ivories as if she were in step with some great, hidden orchestra.

And now Gerrit knew he had never seen, much less heard, anything like this. He knew if he stayed there any longer he would surely start dancing right there on the black-checkered linoleum, so he tried to duck back out of sight before he found himself completely hypnotized. But he couldn't help jumping as Mallory stepped around the corner and pulled up short.

"Grandpa?"

Once more the music stopped, leaving Gerrit staring at his wide-eyed granddaughter, wondering how to explain himself. He sucked air like a goldfish at the fair as Mallory pulled him into the living room.

"Oh, you must be Mallory's grandfather." The teacher stood and held out her hand, but Gerrit's throat went dry at the bright smile and piercing dark eyes. Italian, maybe. East Coast, definitely. Most women around

Van Dalen didn't wear nice navy blue skirts and white blouses with gold pins except on Sundays or at a funeral. And most didn't come at you with their hand out.

But it wasn't every day he ran into a Greek statue. He might have said *goddess,* had that word been in his vocabulary, which it sure as sin was not.

"Oh, right." He cleared his throat and tried not to stare. "That's me."

"I'm Joan Horton." And the more she spoke, the more she betrayed she was not from around here, probably from New York or Philadelphia or Somewhere Back East where everybody talked funny and where they all thought their milk came from supermarkets. He shook her hand for a second, remembering not to clamp down the way he would with another farmer. Probably best to treat this hand like an udder...

Not a good comparison. He backed away and wondered why he hadn't just stayed home or gone to the barn to do some work, the way he wasn't supposed to anymore.

"We didn't hear you come in, Grandpa." Mallory was still looking at him as if he'd done something sneaky, which he hadn't.

"Yeah, well, I seen the car, heard the music, you know."

You bet. That explained everything.

"Well," the teacher answered, "I was just telling Mallory and her mother what a beautiful instrument she has to practice on. It's really quite a fine upright."

"Belonged to my grandmother." He nodded, and that would have been enough of an explanation if she hadn't pressed for more.

"Have you played it, then?"

"Who, me?" He almost laughed. "Naw. Just fooling around. Most the other kids ever did was 'Chopsticks' before Oma chased 'em off. Guess Opa, my grandpa, had it brought from back East, early nineteen hundreds."

"Well, it's still quite a valuable instrument today." She ran a finger along one of the intricately carved twin Victorian columns. "The case looks almost new. Just needs a little bit of work."

Gerrit supposed that was true. Only a few missing ivory key caps
betrayed the age of the family heirloom, but they had been missing since
he had chipped them off when he was six, which was part of the reason
his grandmother always shooed the kids away—and he wasn't about to tell
that story. He supposed a couple of strings or hammers needed attention
after all these years, but that didn't seem to dampen the rich, full tone of
the old piano, especially when Joan Horton played it.

"Fella offered me four grand for it once." He shook his head.
"Thought he was nuts at the time. Turns out it's worth twice that, maybe
more. I told him I was saving it for my granddaughter, though."

The teacher smiled once more and rested her hand on Mallory's
shoulder. "Talent must run in the family around here."

"Not from my side." Liz hadn't changed out of her blue work coveralls and bandana yet. "I just want Mal to have a chance."

"Well," continued the teacher, "you're lucky to have such a supportive
family, Mallory. I think…"

Gerrit didn't catch the rest of what she said. Instead, his eyebrows fur-
rowed instinctively at the word "lucky," but he didn't correct the newcomer as he would have his granddaughter. Wouldn't have been proper.
Mallory glanced up at him as if expecting to hear it at any time.

The mantel clock ticked out a quiet rhythm. Three thirty already?

"Yes, well." The teacher finished what she'd been saying and headed
for the front door as Liz rose to her feet. "Thank you for letting me drop
by with your practice books, Mallory, Mrs. Appeldoorn. I know it's a little
unusual for the piano teacher to be visiting students in their homes, but I
just wanted to meet all of Mrs. Klopstra's students in their home environ-
ments before we got started. I like to see where they'll be practicing."

"Thanks for playing." Mallory beamed up at her new teacher, who
responded with a blush and a glance at the other two adults.

"I'm really very sorry about that, you must think I'm a…"

Her voice trailed off. *Show-off* would have been the word. But Gerrit would be the last to say it. It didn't fit this woman. And besides, Liz waved her off.

"Don't you apologize for anything, Mrs. Horton. And you stop by anytime you like. Please."

Mrs. Horton came back with a smile and a nod.

"Actually, my father used to be a pastor. When I was a little girl I used to accompany him on visitation. This sort of reminds me…"

"There you go." Liz sort of chuckled. "You're just out visiting the congregation."

Liz was young enough to have been the piano teacher's daughter, but by the way she talked, you might have thought they were high-school chums. That was just Liz though. After eleven years Gerrit was getting used to it.

But the piano teacher acted as if she wasn't so sure. She nodded again and pointed back at a small stack of music books she had left on top of the old piano.

"One other thing. I know Mallory used another book in her first year with Mrs. Klopstra, so we'll certainly continue with that course of study. But now that she's into her second year, I do have a few other ideas I'd like to try, things that worked with some of my college kids."

"You have college kids?" Liz wanted to know. Wasn't so long ago she'd been one of those herself.

"Oh, no, my two children are past that stage. In fact, my daughter, Alison, just had a baby seven weeks ago. No, I meant my students at Gaylord School of Music."

Oh, man. Gerrit scratched his chin. Mal's substitute piano teacher was a college professor. Good luck, kid. And *luck* was definitely the right word this time.

"Of course we'll see what works." The professor's voice kind of speeded up as she headed for the door. "It'll be simplified. I just want Mallory to have a chance to look over any new material for a couple of weeks before we meet. I'll call you with the date and time of our first lesson. And of course, family members are always welcome. Do you…oh!"

With a startled yelp she nearly stepped on Missy's sleeping hulk, then caught her breath before glancing back at Gerrit and Liz.

"Do you have any questions?"

"Just one thing." Gerrit grinned at the piano teacher as she tiptoed gingerly over Missy. "You never owned a dog before, eh?"

"How did you know?"

"Oh, I dunno." Gerrit shrugged. "You just don't look too comfort-able, that's all."

"We had a cat when I was little. Amadeus."

"Pardon?"

"Amadeus. That was the name of my cat."

"No kidding. Awful weird name. But we have plenty of those around here too."

"Cats? How many?"

"A dozen, I guess, maybe more. Haven't counted for a while. They're pretty much wild out there in the barn."

Her eyes grew large, as if she had never heard of barn cats.

"I put just enough food in their bowls to keep 'em hanging around," he went on. "Only not so much that they're not hungry to hunt."

"I see."

"You know," he added. "For mice?"

She nodded. Maybe Amadeus had never gone in for that sort of thing.

"By the way," he blurted. "That music. What were you playing?"

She paused before heading out the door. "*Scheherazade*. It's supposed to be a duet by Rimsky-Korsakov. I just played one part of it."

Chapter 4

Like the measles, love is most dangerous
when it comes late in life.
—LORD BYRON

*J*oan hurried down the neighborhood sidewalk, which was dappled with late August sunshine through the overhanging canopy of century-old elms. On this side of town the Thimble Bridge Road crossed Sockeye Creek twice before it snaked past the sprawling county fairgrounds where Alison had told her they would meet for the afternoon. A minivan pulled up beside her, and a woman leaned out the window.

"Can you tell me where there's parking?"

The puzzled expression on Joan's face must have signaled her confusion.

"For the fair?" added the woman. A couple of young children bounced in the backseat, obviously ready to bail if the car slowed any more than it already had. One of them reminded Joan of her new little piano student, Mallory Appeldoorn, not by the way she was using the backseat as a trampoline, but just by the look and shape of her face. Of course, to Joan's way of seeing, all these tow-headed Dutch kids seemed to look alike.

"Oh, the fair." It wasn't as if Joan hadn't heard or read about it. This week's *Van Dalen Sentinel* had carried a twelve-page insert full of fair articles and ads. Photos of kids and their cows. Two-for-one Dutch dinners at the Windmill Grill. And a big discount on a new John Deere Model 9520, complete with air conditioning and a CD player.

"Come on, Dad," chirped a young voice from inside the van. "The demolition derby'll be over by now. You promised!"

"I'm sorry," Joan tried to explain. "I just moved here. I don't really know where everything is yet."

True. But by this time a gaudy red and blue Ferris wheel jutted over nearby rooftops, along with a whirling Seismo-Rocko that twirled pairs of screaming kids into the air on long bungee cords. Twenty years ago that might have seemed fun. Now Joan only shivered at the thought of hanging on to life by a rubber band.

"That's all right." The woman's husband must have sighted a place; he pointed up ahead as they pulled away. "I think we found what we were looking for."

The sounds hit them about that time too: a wild symphony of machinery, thumping music, blaring bullhorns, howling carnival riders, and revving tractors.

Joan watched the van race to the corner and pull into a grassy side lot guarded by a teenager with a construction flag and a fistful of bills. The girl's "Fair Parking $3 US, $5 Canadian" sign must have told the family what they wanted to know.

"One adult, please." A minute later Joan pushed a bill at the ticket taker, collected her change, stepped through the turnstile, and almost skipped into the fairgrounds. Brightly painted sea green and white commercial barns stood straight ahead, 4-H barns to the left, and everything else to the right. Meet me under the big cow at one o'clock. Alison would be there with Joan's two-month-old granddaughter, Erin, with plenty of time to spare before Mallory Appeldoorn was supposed to show her cow at two.

Everyone else in Van Dalen had to be there too, not to mention the rest of the county and a good number of curious Canadians who had come south over the border to explore. The parking lot full of cars with colorful white, blue, and yellow BC plates testified to their presence. And she took back what she had thought before about no crowds in Van Dalen.

Reminds me of Central Park the time Pavarotti gave a free concert.

So she made her way through the mass of people, past lines of booths. Past ski boats and Sno Cones, the Republican party and Rhino truck-bed liners. Past the Bobcat backhoes and Built-Rite backyard barns and the quick-draw artist sketching distorted heads and bulging noses. If it wasn't here at the fair, she guessed, she probably didn't need it anyway. Cooper Ridge Feeds had their best horse-tack display up front. But that was just the entry promenade. And wasn't it past lunchtime?

Her stomach told her so, and she almost wished she had fixed herself a sandwich before leaving home. Almost, but not quite. She dipped her finger in a steaming portable spa and inhaled the heavenly scent of fair food, from slow-roasted barbeque beef sandwiches at the Young Life booth to Bavarian bratwurst at the Mount Baker Barbershop Singers' grill. Famous Fair Scones and stuffed spuds, elephant ears and curly fries. Philly cheesesteak sandwiches and funnel cakes, caramel corn and special-recipe baked beans, fresh-picked supersweet corn and homemade boysenberry-apple pies. New York City had nothing like this. Especially not the *poffertjes!*

A pair of blue-eyed high-schoolers looked up from a small stove where they fried the traditional Dutch doughnut holes. Both were dressed in costumes of stubby-brimmed wool hats, checkered scarves, bloomer pants, and wooden shoes. Joan couldn't help stopping.

"Care to sample a poffertje?" As one of the teens held out a pastry-loaded plate, the bakery smell drifted up to tickle her nose. *Well, perhaps just one.*

"I was wondering how you pronounced that." Joan smiled and couldn't refuse the sample, which had spent most of its brief life swimming in cooking oil or rolling in confectioner's sugar. Either way, she was doomed.

"Fat-free." The teen winked, and she thanked him for his honesty before buying just a couple more. But Joan wondered how many more calories she put on just by smelling everything else she walked by. She almost didn't make it past the large white County Dairy Women booth, topped by a ten-foot ice-cream cone and…there it was—a double-size plastic Hereford cow. The milking-demonstration booth next door provided bovine entertainment behind glass while families stood in line for cones, shakes, ice-cream bars, and old-fashioned moo-wiches—a large scoop of vanilla ice cream sandwiched between oversize chocolate chip cookies. Just across the plaza the PTA booth featured strawberry-raspberry shortcakes ("Tasty Local Berries!"), which proved equally difficult to ignore.

"There you are!" Alison pulled up with her stroller featuring Joan's wide-eyed, perfect two-month-old granddaughter. "Have any trouble finding it?"

Joan shook her head no. "Only getting through the crowds. I had no idea this was such a popular place."

She bent down to check on little Erin and marveled again at the beautiful bright eyes (only a little red from crying), the chubby cheeks, the ten perfect little fingers that curled around her own. The world had not seen a cuter granddaughter.

"What do you think of all this, Pumpkin? Too much noise for you?"

"Maybe too much for Mom." Alison checked the diaper bag as they headed for the needlework barn, then pushed through the 4-H display barn and past the glass cases bulging with Dutch chocolate cakes and rhubarb pies. She explained to Joan how they'd been up four times the night before, nonstop since 4:00 a.m., no morning nap, no afternoon nap—maybe Erin was getting sick. A woman from the Republican Party booth reached out her hand toward the baby but changed her mind at the sound of poor Erin's cry.

"Perhaps this wasn't such a good idea." Joan stroked her granddaughter's cheek.

"Not your fault, Mom. Any other day it would be terrific. I just don't think we're going to last through the whole cow-judging scene. But you should go. Shane gets daily free passes. I can see the rest of the fair another day."

Erin favored her with a momentary gurgle that might have resembled a smile. Then she switched gears into a scream that could be heard even over the ten-piece Peruvian folk band with mandolins and pan flutes. This little granddaughter definitely owned a healthy set of lungs.

"And besides," continued Alison, "I think it's great you're connecting with your students. Go."

Well, all right then. A reader board next to the milking demonstration booth announced times for the 4-H showings, and from what they could tell, the Jerseys were still coming up within the hour. After telling Alison good-bye, Joan planted a kiss on Erin's cheek, smiled at the just-changed sweet baby smell, and headed for the barns.

"Dad!" Warney held up his hand, but Gerrit heard it coming. "You know you're not supposed to help her. What are you trying to do, disqualify the whole group?"

" 'Course not." He wasn't about to do anything to hurt Mallory's chances of winning top honors for her 4-H Club's cow-barn display. Shoot. He knew full well the 4-H kids were supposed to do all the work themselves. It's just that when he saw something in a barn that needed doing, well, he naturally picked up the pitchfork and scooped it right up.

Just like back on Appeldoorn Farm.

And just like back on Appeldoorn Farm, nothing he did was ever right. At least not lately, and for sure as far as Warney was concerned. He put the tool down behind a manure barrel and leaned up against a corner of the stall to catch his breath. Warney gave him that look—the one that re-minded Gerrit of Miriam when she was annoyed—as he sipped on a cola.

But really, the kids had done a fine job of decorating their animal stalls. Real cute.

"My name is Mabel," read a hand-lettered cardboard poster. They'd nailed it to a crossbeam just above the eight-by-eight-foot stall where Mabel had been given a comfortable home for the duration of the week-long fair. Mallory had carefully illustrated her work with jumping calves, bumblebees, and snapshots of her and the animal. "I am a Jersey cow. I am two years old. This is the first time I have ever been to the fair. Back home at Appeldoorn Farm, I used to get into trouble by sneaking out of my pen. My owner's name is Mallory Ann Appeldoorn, and she is nine and a half years old."

Gerrit had to grin at his granddaughter's imagination, though it was true about Mabel getting into trouble. Only she neglected to mention the fact that Mabel the cow also liked to knock people down when they weren't looking.

"Yeah, I'm ready for you, little monster." He scratched her between the ears, and the brown-faced cow stared up at him with her large, black-rimmed eyes, as if to say, "Who, me?" Go ahead, act innocent. Gerrit waved at a fly and turned on his heel only to stand nearly face to face with his granddaughter's piano teacher.

"Look who I found outside, Grandpa!" Mallory held her teacher's hand and bobbed with excitement. "She's come to see us show Mabel."

"Mr. Appeldoorn." Once again she held out her hand like a New York lawyer. "It's good to see you again."

"You bet." Gerrit let go of her grip as soon as he politely could. In a flash of guilt he remembered Miriam and the way she would take his hand when they walked down the stairs after church. Or the times they had walked together on the gravel beach at Alder Bay, holding hands, watching the sun set into Puget Sound. He might forget his own name someday, but he could not forget the way Miriam's hand had always felt so soft and strong at the same time.

Just like the piano teacher's.

"Did you hear me, Dad?" Warney's mouth turned down in a frown when he looked at his father, as if to ask if anyone was home. Though he had obviously not inherited his father's large frame, he was still hard to ignore, mainly because he reminded Gerrit so much of Miriam. More than any of the other three kids, Warney had his mom's face, right down to the sprinkling of freckles on his cheekbones.

"Say, what?" Gerrit shook his head and returned to earth. Where had he been?

"I said, are you coming with us to the judging? Mal shows in forty minutes."

"Of course, sure. That's why we're here."

"Just don't go out there again and argue the judge's calls, huh?"

"Hey, come on. I was only trying to help him out the other day. They are so—"

"Dad, nobody needs that kind of help."

Okay, fine. As long as Mallory wasn't robbed. Gerrit held up his hands in resignation as they paraded across the barn to find a seat in the bleachers with the other families. While Mallory checked in with her 4-H leader, Liz joined them and chatted with the piano teacher, Mrs. Horton.

On the way they stopped to stare at Big Ben, the gleaming black Chianina Holstein bull, who stood as tall as the center for the Van Dalen High School basketball team (six foot three) and weighed about as much as the combined starting lineup of the football team (3,345 pounds). Even Gerrit had to admit that was a lot of bull. But when Big Ben snorted and a ceiling mist sprayer came on at the same time, Joan jumped backward as if she had been attacked.

"You've never seen dairy judging before?" Liz smiled at their guest.

"I suppose it shows. But you're right. No, this is the first time."

"Keep an eye on the judge to see which cows he's looking at most closely. Those are usually the animals that are going to get the blue ribbons."

Gerrit wasn't so sure about his daughter-in-law's theory, but as they found a place in the open bleacher seats (he got stuck on the end, next to the teacher), he did keep an eye on the judge strutting around the circus-size sawdust ring. Five young kids—most of them older and taller than Mallory—brought their animals in, single file, for their moment of truth. First came the Holsteins, black-and-white spotted cows that lately reminded him of his cursed computer.

"Are these like your cows?" Mrs. Horton asked him, and he shook his head. Not a bad question, though.

"We run Jerseys. They may not be Dutch, but they're smaller and smarter, and their milk's richer."

All the while he kept his eye on the showing. The kids led their animals around in a circle three or four times, tugging the bridles and straightening up their animals as they went. Before long the judge grabbed a microphone and began explaining his decision, so everyone's attention turned to him.

"This is a very sharp, very stylish cow," said the judge, pointing to the fifth-place animal. The remainder received their share of compliments as well.

"This one has the second-best udder in its class."

And to another, "Superior udder capacity and maturity."

Or, "She's got a great ligament."

"Not too sure about that," mumbled Gerrit. Comment by comment, the judge was proving his incompetence.

But with that the judge pointed up his choices for first and second before handing over the mike to the Nooksack County Dairy Princess. Gerrit sputtered and bit his tongue.

"What's he talking about?" Gerrit leaned backward and hissed. "He's got his first and second mixed up bad. Just look at the udder on that one—"

"Dad!" Warney leaned across from where he was sitting and raised a finger to his lips to hush his father. But Gerrit only shook his head and sighed while the dairy princess, Heather Huizenga, nuzzled the microphone.

"I want to thank you all for, like, coming out today and for, like, cheering us on."

And so they did, as the first three groupings of Holsteins were led out.

"How can you tell the difference between all those animals?" Mrs. Horton wanted to know. "They all look the same to me."

"The same? Nah." Gerrit smiled at the thought. "Every one of 'em's different, like a snowflake. Most farmers can tell their cows from a mile away. 'Course, my Jerseys are a little tougher to tell apart, 'cause they're all fawn colored, but I know 'em still."

He pointed out the difference between cows one and two, why the judge got it wrong, how much milk they produced, and what he used to do on the farm before selling to Warney.

But shoot, he didn't mean to go on and on. And for sure he wasn't about to moan and groan about his health or what a lousy cook he was, fixing his own meals since Miriam died of cancer sixteen years back. He was sure she probably didn't want to hear it anyway, did she?

No, that was quite all right. And they did have at least one thing in common, she admitted, turning the modest solitaire diamond and wedding band around her finger. Gerrit still wore his too. But besides the fact that they had both lost spouses, Gerrit doubted they had much else in common, if anything. She gladly answered his questions about her family, though, about Randy and Alison and the new baby, about teaching piano composition and performance back in New York, about her travels.

"So do they call you Professor Horton?" he finally asked.

"Not this year. I'm on a May-to-May sabbatical. And *Joan* would be fine."

Joan. She smiled as the first group of six Jerseys were led into the sawdust show ring. Already? According to the program, Mallory and Mabel were number three, just moments away.

"There she is!" Joan didn't need to point.

Gerrit straightened up so as not to miss anything.

"If this judge is as blind with the Jerseys as he was with the Holsteins," he mumbled, "we're in deep doo...er, trouble."

"I take it you don't have much of an opinion on these kinds of things."

"I'm entirely neutral."

"I see."

The way her dark Greek eyes danced when she laughed didn't exactly remind him of Miriam, but still it made him catch his breath and swallow wrong. So it wasn't his fault when he doubled over and started coughing.

"Are you all right?" Joan patted him on the back, but he couldn't answer. He couldn't breathe, either. He felt his cheeks turn crimson while his windpipe squeezed tight.

"Do the Heimlich maneuver," suggested someone sitting in the row behind them. Perfect. When he twisted around he could see the good Samaritan pulling out a cell phone. Gerrit shook his head as hard as he could and held up his hands. No Heimlich. No 911. Instead, he rolled off the bleachers and found a spot behind a pile of hay bales where he could choke to death in privacy.

"You're certain you're all right?" Joan rested a hand on his shoulder when he finally returned. He could think of a dozen better ways to get someone's attention, and no, he wasn't all right. At least no one had noticed his stupid coughing fit from down on the judging floor. This was Mallory's moment, not his. So he tried to catch his breath and fight off the viselike grip on his chest, even as he gave his granddaughter a strained smile and a thumbs-up when she paraded by.

"Just swallowed wrong, that's all."

They might believe him or not. But Gerrit knew he was the world's worst liar.

Chapter 5

All music is folk music. I ain't never heard no horse sing a song.

—LOUIS ARMSTRONG

*A*nd now you're going to hear…"

Gerrit turned up the volume on his little clock radio for his favorite suppertime program.

"…the rrrrest of the story."

Preach it, brother. Gerrit clunked around his kitchen while he listened, putting away pots and pans that had been drying on the counter, spreading peanut butter on soda crackers for dinner, straightening things up, listening.

And yes, he felt fine now, two weeks after his little coughing fit at the fair. Nothing to worry the doctor (or anyone else) about. Thanks for asking though. The cowhide computer hadn't been able to bother him either, seeing as how he'd left it unplugged for safety. It was the perfect doorstop.

He chewed carefully as the radio guy told how classical music had helped lower crime rates in a downtown when it had been piped in through loudspeakers mounted on light poles.

Good for them.

But more than that, people seemed happier and more productive in those places where classical music was a regular part of the background. Imagine that.

Gerrit looked into the living room at his two-foot stack of Hank Williams and Johnny Cash LPs, and he wondered how happy and productive everybody would be if they had to listen to "Your Cheatin' Heart" all day and all night.

"So what about this one?" He walked over and pulled out a Johnny Cash album from the middle of the stack. The description on the cardboard album jacket reminded him of a song he hadn't heard in years, so he figured he might as well turn off the radio and give it a listen while he was cleaning up.

Only thing was, it wasn't Mr. Cash's familiar deep bass that greeted him when needle met vinyl.

"Huh?" He couldn't recall ever having heard this classical piano piece. But instead of stripping it off the turntable, he listened just a little longer. The handwritten "MDA" on the record's rotating label told him all he needed to know.

"Miriam's," he guessed, and this LP must have been returned to the wrong album jacket. Maybe that said something about his housekeeping skills, and maybe it didn't. But he had to admit the piano stuff wasn't too bad. It reminded him of the piano teacher, swaying like a willow as she played his grandmother's piano, a breeze of notes dancing from beneath her fingers. He smiled at the thought, then realized what he was doing.

"Hang on, there." Gerrit's ears burned hot with a sudden sense of betrayal to the memory of the faded eight-by-ten that still held center stage on his bookshelf. He fidgeted and looked at his shoes. If he could wash that nagging feeling down with another glass of cold milk from the fridge, he would. But something else washed over him, and in an odd sort of way he was tempted to let it.

The music. Miriam's music. The piano teacher's music. Not "I'm So Lonesome I Could Cry," but good, and it surprised him. So he slid into his La-Z-Boy and soaked it up for the next half-hour. Once again, he told himself, old Paul Harvey was right.

Was he? The thought sent Gerrit bolt upright, just before the needle neared the end of its run and skipped into the center groove.

If it's good enough for the big city, he told himself, *it's good enough for the milking barn.*

Before he could talk himself out of it, he scooped up the record player, yanked out the cord, and trundled off to the barn with an armful of hi-fi.

⁀

"With your good credit, Alan, financing is a done deal." Randy Horton did his best to keep reeling in the line. "What would you think if I could get you that interest rate we were talking about?"

That should grab his interest. Literally. But the twenty-something guy next to him in the driver's seat only frowned and fiddled with the rearview mirror control. At least the AC was working, though it was kind of spitting out dust bunnies. Well, so what. All you had to do was roll down the window on a nice, cloudy, drizzly September day like today.

"Adam." Twenty-something's girlfriend in the backseat leaned forward between them.

"Huh?"

"Adam," she repeated. "His name is Adam, not Alan."

Ohh. Randy closed his eyes and tried to fight off the migraine that had already started to make his temples throb in time with the intermittent wiper blades that sort of worked. At this point he wasn't sure what was worse—driving around Hempstead with this no-sale couple or returning to Lou's West End Choice Pre-Owned Autos, where Lou the Horrible would be waiting. Maybe they could keep driving this wreck until they either broke down or ran out of gas or reached the eastern tip of Long Island—whichever came first. Speaking of gas, Randy snuck a glance at the gauge to make sure. His face must have turned white.

"You all right, man?" Adam the driver looked across at him as if he realized the salesman was about to get sick. If he only knew.

"Just a little headache." Randy swallowed hard. "No worries."

Despite the throbbing of his temples, he forced his brain not to shut down in panic, but to remember what his sales manager had said about recovering after a fumble. Something intelligent. Anything.

Think.

"Uh, the gas…" He finally managed a grin. Laugh. Let them know how honest you can be. "I think we're going to need to pull into this next station up here. Take a right on Peninsula Boulevard."

Wasn't there a Shell station right around the corner? There'd better be, by the look of the needle slipping down behind E. In the meantime, he still had a job to do.

"So what do you do, Al…I mean Adam?"

Good. A safe question, by the book. Reel them in the way Lou said to do. Ignore the killer headache. Breathe. Survive.

"Music student." Adam tugged at a longish beard and checked the little car's rearview before changing lanes.

"No kidding," Randy blurted out. "My mom teaches…"

But he knew before he spoke that he did not want to finish that sentence, so he let the errant words hang and shrivel while the familiar red spots began to sparkle and dance in his field of vision. He leaned back against the door, sideways.

"Hey, you really don't look so good." The girlfriend leaned forward for a better look. "I think we'd better turn around, Adam."

But Adam was pulling into the gas station by that time, which was probably a good thing. As they rolled to a stop, Randy reached for his wallet where he kept the company Visa but found only an empty back pocket.

"Oh no!" he groaned, checking the other pocket. He remembered now where he had left it, on the dresser back in his mom's house, when he was changing pants this morning, before he had to charge outside to catch the bus. The only thing left to do was ask the customer if he could borrow five dollars, just until they got back to the dealership. Maybe they would laugh about it later, after the ink had dried on the contract. After he had asked them, "So what would it take for you to drive off in this rig today?"

Or maybe not. He never got a chance to find out.

"What's *that?*" screeched the girlfriend. She pointed at a black cloud rising from under the hood. A couple of other people at the station noticed it too and came running. Someone started yelling. Adam dropped the gas hose and sprinted the other way, while an older man jumped out of a big blue pickup with a fire extinguisher in hand.

"It's all right!" Randy tried to wave everyone off while the girlfriend reached over the driver's seat and popped the hood release. "Just a cracked hose. Nothing serious."

White powder filled the air as their firefighter hero emptied his extinguisher into the engine compartment.

"No, wait!" But Randy couldn't look anymore. So he just covered his face and turned away. All he could see through the red spots was Lou's pink face and that chubby, nicotine-stained finger wagging at him one last time.

Maybe it was all for the best, Randy told himself two hours later as he rode home on the bus.

No sales, no job, no headaches. Maybe he could go back to his lame job at the local market.

He let his mind wander as he stared at passing strip malls, imagining he was instead crossing over on the Narrows Bridge or maybe the Brooklyn Bridge. Yeah, the Brooklyn Bridge. And for one dark moment he wondered who would miss him if the bus happened to take a wrong turn over the edge. What would the last moments of free fall be like? Like an episode of *Xtreme Home Videos* or just total terror?

Maybe not, he told himself as the bus driver hit the brakes to keep from slamming into traffic ahead. An idiot in a delivery truck behind them laid on his horn. Somehow the angry gestures and the mouthed curses reminded Randy of himself, the way he'd yelled at other cars with his windows rolled up when he still had his license, and the way he'd lived his life since the accident.

But he had promised himself not to think about Dad again, not now, not ever. Still the bus drove on, weaving through traffic, steering just clear of another accident. An accident? That would be too messy. If he ever was going to check out, it would be on his own terms—not in a twisted, ugly bus wreck or on the WRAM-TV 22 news for everybody in New York to gawk at.

No. Next stop, Port Hamilton, back to nothing. The Boston Pops had a Gershwin concert on that night, channel 12, unless the cable company had already cut him off. It was either that or *Jeopardy!*

As Randy neared his street, he almost laughed at the craziness of his so-called life. Tears blurred his vision even more, and he couldn't remember the last time he had cried. Probably not since the days when he used to go to church with his parents, the little stone church where everybody cried all the time, and they were always going up to the altar for something. Back before his dad died, a long time ago.

A very long time ago.

"You should've seen the way the kid at the Radio Shack looked at me." Gerrit stood ready the next day in the corner of the milking parlor when his midafternoon milker, Miguel Cervantes, stepped in. "That kid didn't even know what a turntable was, and he tries to sell me some kind of MP thing."

"Señor Gerrit?" The compact but well-muscled young Mexican looked at him with a question. Okay, so it had been months since the last time Gerrit had helped prep the afternoon shift. Ever since the farm had officially changed hands from father to son three years ago.

But that didn't matter now.

"I've got an idea, amigo. No more ranchero music. Drives me batty, anyway."

"Drives me batty!" There was something Miguel had heard before, and he grinned in recognition. Of course, he might have grinned the same way if Gerrit had begun reciting the latest milk prices or the Five Points of Dutch Calvinism.

"Yeah, *loco* in the *cabeza*." Gerrit tried once more to explain. "From now on we're upgrading the musical menu."

"Men? You?" Miguel shook his head. Cows he understood. And Gerrit was the first to admit that Miguel was one of the best milkers he'd ever worked with in ten years of hiring Hispanic guest workers. But he could not say that many words had passed between them.

"Right. Music-oh new-oh." Gerrit pointed to the battered portable boom box on the shelf from which Miguel played his favorites, then up at the new compact speaker he'd hung from the ceiling.

"See that? It's for the cows. The *vacas*. They're going to hear this music"—he pointed to his ears—"and they're going to make more milk. MASS milk-oh. You get it?"

Miguel stared at him blankly. The oversize ventilation fan above their heads droned on, pulling damp air from the parlor.

"Look, I'll show you. Just bring in the girls, and I'll fire up the music. You'll see."

By the way they stomped and huffed in the barnyard outside, the girls knew it was time for milking. A number had begun jostling each other for the best position nearest the door. So when the Miguel let them in, they waltzed right up and took their positions, four on each side, angled slightly away from the central concrete pit where Miguel did his work. After securing each cow in her own stall, he swabbed their udders with green disinfectant before wiping them off once more. Next, he gently pulled a tiny stream of milk from each teat, just the way Gerrit had once showed him, before attaching each of the slender rubber cups connected by tubes to the pulsating overhead Bou-Matic. This throbbing vacuum drew milk through clear tubes, *whoosh-gush,* out and up, through the cooler, and finally out to the gleaming two-thousand-gallon refrigerated stainless-steel holding tank.

Gerrit only watched for a moment, but he knew how Warney would scold him if he tried to help Miguel again. Truth be told, he wasn't sure he could keep up with Miguel's quick, fluid movements as the hired hand disconnected and swabbed the first crew, whistled them out, and brought in another eight cows to start the twelve-minute process all over again. So instead of getting in the way, Gerrit retreated to the tank room and powered up the spare record player, a secondhand unit he'd picked up at a garage sale in town, the kind with a turntable on top and a built-in tape player. No offense to the kid at the Radio Shack, but they didn't make 'em like this anymore.

"Maestro." Gerrit turned up the volume and strolled back out to the parlor to watch how the girls reacted. "How's that?"

But when he saw the closed-eye grimace on Miguel's face, he nearly called 911, like the guy sitting behind him at the fair when he'd started choking.

"Something wrong?" asked Gerrit.

Miguel dropped his hands from his ears before turning back to the next cow.

"Lo siento," he mumbled. "Sorry, Mr. Gerrit."

"You just wait." Gerrit pointed to the loudspeaker. "I got four more records piled on the spindle. That should keep you going for a couple of hours. The girls will love you for it."

Maybe Miguel didn't get it. But he continued his work, plugging and unplugging milking cups, prepping the animals, leading them in and out. By the second movement of Beethoven's Sixth Symphony, Gerrit decided he'd done all he could and headed back outside.

Mission accomplished. As he rinsed his boots, he decided not to tell Warney about the music. He'd wait until his son noticed how much milk production had gone up.

Wait till he sees.

"Grandpa!" Mallory came running out of the big house, Missy on her heels.

"Oh, there you are." Gerrit checked his watch. It was 3:45, fifteen minutes past the time Gerrit was supposed to take over baby-sitting his granddaughter. "I didn't hear the bus drop you off."

Missy sidled up for an ear scratching. Her tongue had long ago fallen out of its groove.

"That was a girl from the doctor's office," Mallory told him. "On the phone."

"Shoot. They say what time I was supposed to be there?"

"Fifteen minutes ago, I think. She said the doctor said, 'You tell that grandfather of yours to get himself down here right away.'"

Mallory did a pretty fair impression of John R. Eubanks, MD, who obviously wasn't going to be a happy camper by the time Gerrit made it to town. But what about Mallory? He looked around the gravel yard, bordered on one side by the house and on the other by the parlor and the fenced loafing yard, where the cows still waited. Warney was cleaning the barns. Liz was finishing up an afternoon shift at the plant.

"Look, you're going to have to ride into town with me. Hop in the truck."

"But Mom said you were going to take me in for my first piano lesson at four."

"That was today?"

Great planning. They both trotted toward Gerrit's ancient pickup. He paused for just a moment to fish his keys out of the pocket of his coveralls, just in time to hear music pouring from the milking parlor.

Ranchero music.

Chapter 6

If you don't know where you are going,
you might wind up someplace else.
—YOGI BERRA

Warney spun the wheel of the ancient, underpowered but still perfectly fine (according to Dad) kelly green 1955 John Deere Model 50 tractor and slid around the corner behind the loafing shed. No one could ever accuse him of shirking hard work. Farm boys grow up with hard work, with chores, with cleaning out the stalls.

He did a good job too, even if his father never recognized the fact. In fact, Warney had developed a pretty good routine, if he did say so himself, ever since Dr. Eubanks had told his father to slow down. Whose idea had it been, anyway, to sell the whole operation to Warney and Liz?

"Yours, dear. Remember?" Liz's reminder echoed in his head. Thanks a lot. That had been a stroke of brilliance she had only reluctantly agreed to. Turns out she had been the smart one. But if Dad had known how reluctant she'd been about taking over the farm, well, that would have only made things worse between them. Warney'd already married "outside the faith," as Dad liked to say.

"So we'll try it for twelve months," she'd told him. And Warney still remembered the warning expression on her face.

That was three years ago. But with no one else to take on the job, it had seemed like the only thing to do—God's will, even. God's will for the youngest son. And if anyone was supposed to be an expert at discerning God's intractable will, it would be Dad. Certainly not Warney, the little guy with the freckles that everybody told him looked just like his mom's.

And now, pushing a mound of fresh manure through the barn during the afternoon milking time, he wondered at his wife's three-year-old question:

"Is it really God's will for you to earn your MBA? Magna cum laude, only to come back here to this? Are you sure, dear?"

Was he sure, dear?

"Well, I'll tell you one thing." Now Warney didn't mind making his points to an audience of cows, who tended not to be skilled at debate. "Gene sure wasn't going to help clean up after you girls."

No, Warney's older brother was too busy flying up and down the East Coast and having babies with his wife, Nancy. At least he'd had the guts to move as far away from Van Dalen as possible, almost before the green graduation caps had dropped to the Van Dalen High gym floor. West Palm Beach, Florida, was about as far away as it got.

"Bruce?" Warney asked the cows, as if they cared. "What about Bruce, you ask?"

Bruce, the second oldest, had about the same idea as Gene: Get out of town, pronto. If he was lucky—and so far he had been—maybe he wouldn't pull icebreaker duty by the time his wife, Julianne, had their first baby. They had waited long enough to have kids. Maybe with a grandchild for Gerrit, they would visit more often than just on Christmas or Thanksgiving.

Visiting wasn't easy for anybody, though, and it was getting harder each year. Warney hardly knew his younger sister, Patti, who had two toddlers in tow. Her husband, Eric, had accepted an assistant pastor position in Montana after seminary in Dallas and a pastorate in Phoenix. So God had called her away from the farm almost as fast as her brothers, in search of her Mrs. degree at Calvin College.

"Sorry, Lord," he whispered, and he meant it. "You can take them wherever you want. It's up to you."

Dad had made sure he'd learned Lesson Number One, the one about the sovereignty of God. It's just that God seemed to have called Gene, Bruce, and Patti to places far away, leaving little Warney to hold the bag, the same way he always had, growing up.

"But hey," he told his cows, "do you hear me complaining?"

At least they all had one thing in common: Despite growing up here, none of the siblings seemed to see God's hand in the farm the way Dad had. Not in the manure, and not in the flies. Not in the 2:00 a.m. calvings, not in the twice daily, seven days a week, round-the-clock milkings. God, they had all agreed, was not a farmer.

Warney turned the corner a little too sharply, catching a corner of the barn with the front end of his tractor. He'd mounted a giant truck tire on the front end, hollow side facing forward. Cut in half, it served as a flexible C-shaped scooper and worked better on concrete floors than the typical steel bucket that came as standard equipment on many tractors. The homemade scoop did, however, have a tendency to catch its two rubber ends on cow stalls and such.

"Whoopsie." He jerked the shift knob, backed away, tried the corner again. A calf on the other side of the nearby fence glanced up at him from the safety of her little plastic igloo. Sort of like a doghouse for newborns. And of course it reminded him…

Who had been the one left holding the BB gun after Bruce had accidentally shot the calf in the eye?

Little Warney, age four.

Who had been the one left holding the matches after his two older brothers had accidentally burned down the old pump house by the creek?

Little Warney, age six.

And who had been the one left behind to shovel cow poop while all the rest of them traveled the world?

Little Warney, age thirty-three.

"Does anyone see a pattern here?" Warney asked the herd, but they

ignored him as they jostled for position and their turn to enter the milking parlor for their appointment with Miguel. Each sported a full udder
that nearly dragged the muddy concrete and a high-visibility red plastic
ID tag in her ear.

Number 112 bodychecked the cow in front of her while a couple of
the newer additions to the herd skittered out of the way. It was always easy
to make out the boss cow because the Appeldoorn herd, like every other
herd, had its own pecking order. And at times like these, driving in circles
around the open-sided barn behind a moving manure pile, Warney imagined himself somewhere near the bottom of that order. Why else did
people still call him Warney and not Warner? He couldn't shake it: the
flies, the chores, the nickname…and the debts clung to his family like the
barn smell to his clothes.

Never mind that he had brought it all on himself. And Liz had a way
of bringing it all back to ground zero.

"No one forced you to earn all those Future Farmer awards in high
school, did they?" she'd asked him once.

"No, but you should have seen Dad. He was happy. He really thought
I was following in his bootsteps."

"So what was the problem?" she had tried to understand. "Where did
it go wrong?"

Well, he hadn't gone wrong by earning his degree at Wazzu, Washington State University. Actually, that had probably been the best thing
he'd ever done with his life.

"The best thing?"

Well, considering he'd met his future wife there.

"And don't you forget it."

He grinned when he remembered the way Liz would cross her arms,
her half-serious look, her unending challenges.

"So what about your dreams then? What about being in the legisla-
ture or making a difference? What happened?"

The old question yanked him back to the present.

"I'll tell you what happened." He pulled the tractor up in front of the grate that opened into their treatment system. "Little Warney Appeldoorn got left behind in the manure."

Literally. From here it would be stored and blended for use as fertilizer, pumped across the fields when the wind was blowing from the south, away from town. Even so, he'd talked to his share of upset homeowners, some of them over the phone, most of them less than sympathetic.

"Can't you people stop that horrible STENCH?"

No, as a matter of fact they could not. Manure tends to come like this.

"I had to run inside with a handkerchief over my face when that dreadful odor nearly knocked me out! What are you farmers spraying out there, MANURE?"

You have no idea, ma'am.

Or, "I'm going to call the sheriff if you don't stop that spraying RIGHT AWAY!"

Just moved to the area, sir?

At least it was consistent. Nearly every whiner was a new arrival to Van Dalen, attracted by the neat little neighborhoods, captivated by the authentic-looking Dutch buildings and the full-scale windmill downtown. It was a cute place to live, all right, the kind of place you'd read about in the Sunday travel section of the Seattle papers. The schools were some of the region's best. A pretty Dutch Reformed church sat on nearly every corner downtown, each one built with that trim Dutch brick facade or nice white stucco, and usually a red-tile roof. And the high-school basketball team with its lanky Dutch boys nearly always went to state. Three years ago they'd even placed second in their division, giving a much more powerful team from North Seattle quite a scare.

Ah, but the newspaper travel articles usually didn't mention the... aroma. So there would always come a time, one of those perfect mid-summer evenings, when the new townies would be out in their fenced backyards, lighting up their barbecues, and the wind would shift just right. His high-school buddy Will Vermeulen over at the county sheriff's office said he could tell which way the wind was blowing whenever the dispatch board lit up with 911 calls.

Warney chuckled, but when he tried to back up, the big wheels only sank deeper into a soft spot, a trench he hadn't noticed before. Backward, forward, backward. That's what he got for daydreaming and talking to cows the way his dad did. His four-wheel-drive rig wouldn't have this problem, but it didn't fit into the barnyard here. He rocked the tractor again, in and out of gear, in hopes of working himself free. And as Dad would say...

"Shoot!" He pounded the steering wheel and idled down. If he could only handle a tractor through ankle-deep manure half as well as he could handle a scientific calculator, he wouldn't always be in so much trouble.

Dad had no clue that the fourth generation to run Appeldoorn Farm would likely be the last. No, for all Dad knew, Warney was still the bright-eyed Future Farmer of America, still trying his best to please his father with a steady hand on the tiller and plenty of cash reserves in the bank.

Funny thing was, Warney actually did care. About his family and their future. About Mallory and how she did in school and the church Awana program, how she did in her new piano lessons. And he cared about keeping Liz happy, though that had seemed impossible ever since she'd been convinced to help run the farm.

In the process, everything he touched seemed to turn out just like the tractor: stuck in manure. Interest payments on two new tractors he'd bought on credit, plus a new spreader and a sump pump for the manure lagoon. Vet bills. Thirty-two cows with mastitis, probably more. Refinancing hadn't helped; everything on the farm was at least fifty years old and needed replacing. The well was drying out, and on and on.

"Know where I can get a better interest rate on an equipment loan?"

he asked 112, who just looked up at him from the other side of the fence with her big brown eyes and mooed, long and low. Beyond the parlor, he noticed Dad and Mallory bumping down the driveway in his father's ancient Ford pickup.

"All right, Madame President," he told the cow. "You'll be milked in a minute, and I'm getting your dinner as soon as I can. Don't get huffy."

He bailed out from the tractor seat and sloshed his way over to where they stored feed in three large concrete bins, each the size of a small house and open in front. He sniffed as the faint beerlike aroma arose from the bin on the left, where a year's corn crop lay shredded and fermented and shrouded by black tarps weighted down by old tires.

His father had taught him long ago how to blend grass silage and baled hay; who needed a fancy college degree for that? Just fire up the small front-loader tractor (another Deere), scrape up a couple of scoops from under the tarps and dump the mix into a high-sided trailer, then drag everything under a small silo and dial in the nutrient mix. He set the trailer's ten-foot augers in motion and added a little water. Dinner would be blended and ready...

"In a jiffy!" he yelled at the cows, still milling around.

Only a screeching sound told him it wouldn't be quite that simple. Nothing ever was. With a grunt he hauled himself up and over the high side of the Dumpster-size trailer to see what was going on. In his hurry he'd probably scooped up a tire along with the feed in the front loader, and absently dumped it into the mix. Happened all the time.

Looking back, he realized how stupid he had been not to turn off the augers before trying to fix the jam. After all, if those two huge swirling screws could blend thousands of pounds of feed, surely they would have no trouble...

"Dumb tire," he mumbled to himself, and he reached down to fish it out. It had pretzeled itself badly, but he got a good grip and began to tug.

Afterward he didn't quite remember what happened next, it happened so fast. The tire must have been yanked under. And maybe his timing was just a little off: holding on for dear life with his left hand, letting go a little too late with his right. Even above the racket of the mixer, he heard his shoulder pop.

Chapter 7

It's easy to play any musical instrument: all you have to do is touch the right key at the right time and the instrument will play itself.
—J. S. BACH

J oan checked her watch once more and surveyed her studio. Her Yamaha baby grand stood in the corner, spotless, gleaming black, and ready. She'd arranged for a good voicing adjustment and had it tuned twice. It didn't matter if she was only going to be here for a year, she could not leave it behind in New York—no matter how much it had cost to ship.

And no, it wasn't quite a Steinway (only Steinways were), but who could fit a nine-foot concert grand into a compact living room like hers? The movers would have had to remove the entire wall rather than just the front door off its hinges. Joan had to admit she liked the chipper sound of the Japanese piano too, and especially enjoyed the springy, lively feel of the keyboard. She'd also paid quite a bit less for the Yamaha than for a concert-quality Steinway.

Joan had situated her student-upright Baldwin next to a short shelf of music books, closer to the door. Number two was a nice enough instrument on its own merits, claiming a fair measure of sentimental value. It reminded her of the rows of practice rooms back at Gaylord, where earnest young college students had once perfected their assignments on its keys. Joan stroked the oak finish and nodded. It would help her demonstrate some of the more difficult pieces. With such a piano they could also practice duets more easily than on just one keyboard.

A shy knock came at the front door.

"You don't need to knock, Mallory." As Joan opened the door, she greeted her first student with a cheery smile. "Just come on in."

But where was her mother? Joan looked up and down the street before closing the door.

"My grandpa dropped me off a few minutes ago," explained Mallory. "He had a doctor's appointment. Mom's going to pick me up."

"And you've been sitting out there, waiting? You should have come in." Joan stood in front of her Yamaha and remembered Gerrit's coughing attack at the fair. A doctor's appointment? She would find out more later. Now she had a lesson, a new apprentice. With a quiet prayer she straightened her skirt and took a deep breath, as if introducing this magic for the first time.

Not magic in the sense of a parlor trick or a stage show, a woman in glittering tights sawn in two. But ever since Joan was a little girl, she had known this was something powerful, especially when she realized how tiny black spots peppered across paper could be transformed into beautiful sounds from a wonderful instrument. And who knew? The sounds, she told Mallory, could lie dormant for hundreds of years only to spring back to life beneath her fingertips, timeless. If that wasn't magic, nothing was.

"Do you understand what I'm trying to say, Mallory?"

"I think so." Mallory nodded with a distant expression in her blue eyes that suggested otherwise. "Only how can sounds be *dormant?* I thought you either heard them or you didn't."

Oh, dear, Joan felt her palms growing damp. *I'm already losing her.*

"Well, you're a farm girl. Think about it: Trees go dormant for the winter, but when the right season comes along, the spring, they wake up again. Right?"

"I guess so."

"It's the same with great music. On paper it's dormant. It just takes the right musician, with the right emotion, to bring it to life again."

And what did it take to awaken dormant emotions? Joan suddenly felt as if she were juggling several she'd forgotten since her first recital, her first day teaching, her first date with Jim back in grad school.

"Okay." Mallory perched on the polished piano bench while Joan gathered her notes and her courage. Where to begin? The girl's blue-jeaned legs dangled free as she waited for the lesson to begin.

"First I'd like to see what you've learned this past year with Mrs. Klopstra. So let's review how we're going to sit here at the piano. With our backs straight and our hands so…"

And so they sat together, the afternoon sunlight filtering through Joan's lace curtains. They fingered the piano, talked about music, tried a few simple pieces. And though she could tell Mallory was sweet and intelligent, Joan could already sense the tension. A stiff uncertainty hung over the piano where they sat as Mallory looked around the room. Was there a question, dear?

"Sort of." Mallory picked up a score from behind the practice book. A look of panic had crossed her face. "I mean, I was wondering. Grandpa said you were going to be a hard teacher. You're not going to try to make me play that kind of music, are you?"

Joan finally noticed what Mallory was looking at, and she couldn't help chuckling.

"Well, I think we'll wait a bit before we tackle Rachmaninoff's Piano Concerto Number 3 in D Minor. It's the most difficult concerto ever written. But perhaps your grandfather should come give it a try himself sometime."

Mallory's eyes widened at the suggestion before she grinned.

"Of course I'm just kidding, dear. That was for one of my best college students, back at Gaylord. Let's you and me start a little more slowly. Show me how much you know from this book."

She slid another volume into place in front of them, a crisp new copy of *Alfred's Piano Lesson Book 1A*, the one her friend Penny Lange from

New York had told her about. And Penny should know; she'd been teaching beginners for the past twenty years. Nothing to it, she'd told Joan in her last e-mail. If you can teach the most talented young pianists in the world, Penny said, you can teach first- or second-year students in a farm town.

Joan still wasn't quite so sure. She folded back the first page and prayed once more, and for a moment she remembered the feeling of holding her first child for the first time, wondering what to do with such a helpless little bundle.

Please help me reach her.

⁓

"Lord!"

Warney's yell was no curse and every bit a cry for help. One moment he had nearly become part of the afternoon mix, the next moment he was lying on his back next to the trailer, gasping.

"I can't believe I just did that." If he had been anyone else—Mallory, for instance—he could feel the fire and brimstone of a safety lecture coming on.

What were you thinking?

You could have been killed.

Did you want to end up like that silage, ground into bite-size bovine bits?

He wasn't, he could have, and no. So he sat up, looked around to make sure no one saw him, and promptly fell back on his face the moment he tried to push himself up with his right hand.

"Ow!" He cried as a lightning bolt of hot white pain made his side go limp in shock. As he got to his feet, he knew it was much more than a bump or a bruise.

He'd broken his arm before, trying to hold on to the halter of a frisky calf when he was twelve. And an ankle, jumping out of the tree fort he and his brothers had built the year before. The collarbone didn't count; that happened in the sixth grade at school, and it hardly slowed him down, though it had hurt a bit. But he didn't remember ever feeling this kind of naked, high-voltage pain.

So he clutched his arm against his chest as he tried to finish his afternoon chores. But every step brought tears to his eyes, every jolt of the tractor nearly made him pass out, and it was all he could do not to yelp in pain. Ten minutes later he hauled himself into his truck and drove into town to the North Nooksack County Clinic.

"It's your lucky day, Warney," the girl behind the appointment counter chirped at him. She'd graduated from VDHS same year as him, and her dad ran the Case Tractor dealership in town. Nice girl. Kinda chatty. And a genuine blonde, beyond just her hair color. Everyone still called her Birdy, since her maiden name had been Tracey Birdsall.

"Lucky wasn't exactly what I would have called it, and don't ever let my dad hear you say that word." He didn't dare move his head or his neck or anything remotely connected to his shoulder, which hurt even when he just breathed.

"Sorry. I just meant that Dr. Eubanks has an opening, so we can slip you into the schedule as soon as he's done with the next patient."

"Swell."

"Is it swelling?" She squinted to look at his shoulder, which he wasn't about to display for anybody but Dr. Eubanks.

"Maybe it just needs an ice pack." Warney knew it would need much more than that, but a familiar voice from behind the door to the examining rooms caught his attention.

Dad?

"I just don't know, doc." Gerrit's normally booming voice sounded muffled behind the door, but clear enough to make out. "When it's my time to go, it's my time to go. You know the Lord has it all planned out."

"I'm not disagreeing with you, Gerrit." That was Dr. Eubanks, probably only a few years older than Warney's father. And despite not coming from a Dutch family, he was a deacon at First Dutch Reformed as well. "But that still doesn't mean you don't need to take care of yourself. As I've been saying, light exercise, no stress."

Gerrit grumbled something Warney couldn't make out as a hand turned the doorknob from the other side.

"I'm telling you, Gerrit, there's no way around it anymore. I could do more tests or refer you to another cardiologist, but he's going to tell you the same thing he did before, when we first found out about your angina. We may be talking triple bypass if we don't get this condition under control with medication and lifestyle adjustments. I'm going to call the hospital and find out what their schedule is like. We'll get back to you."

Triple bypass? Birdy picked up a ringing phone and looked away, but of course she would have heard too. The door opened into the lobby before Warney could avoid it. Where could he have hidden anyway?

"What are you doing here?" Gerrit stood planted in the doorway, a question mark on his face. "What'd you do this time?"

Warney put aside the ridiculous feeling that he was eleven years old and had just jumped out of the tree again. Instead he swallowed the pain and pointed to his shoulder.

"Just pulled my arm the wrong way. No big deal. Thought I'd have the doc take a peek at it, just to be sure. Maybe it needs an ice pack or something."

Just to show that it didn't hurt, he held up his right arm...and nearly passed out. Dr. Eubanks stepped in with his clipboard in hand and led him back through the door, past a frowning Gerrit.

"What was it this time, Bruce?" asked the doctor. "Cow kick you, again?"

Bruce. He called me Bruce. Never mind that Doc Eubanks had delivered him and that he had cared for their family for the past thirty years. He still could not get the names of the Appeldoorn boys straight.

"Uh, maybe you don't want to know, Doc." Warney would at least wait until his father was out of earshot.

Goodness, had this child really sat through a full year of instruction already? Joan was certain they would need to reteach many of the fundamentals students were supposed to have learned the first year. So they covered how to make the sounds soft and loud, how to curl the fingers the right way. She even used the teaching suggestion in the Alfred book, and the memory came flooding back to her. For the first time in many years she recalled her first piano teacher in Iowa, Frau Siegenthaller—Gerta Siegenthaller—always in a prim black skirt and with gnarled, liver-spotted hands that could still flit across the keyboard of her ancient baby grand.

"This way?" Mallory showed surprising strength in her fingers.

"Not quite, Mallory. Don't attack the keys. Massage them. Here, try again."

It was Frau Siegenthaller who had introduced the young American girl to the magic of Beethoven and Bach, Mozart and Chopin. To curtsies and exacting rhythm, to counting and clapping and quarter notes, to theory and proper form. Frau Siegenthaller had opened the door wide enough for Joan to slip through into a world of music, a world where she had grown up and found a home despite her family's many moves, once every couple of years, from Iowa and Arkansas to Alberta.

And, oh yes, she remembered the hands, only Joan hoped hers didn't look quite as aged. How old had she herself been at the time, seven or eight? Not much younger than Mallory here.

"One more time, Mallory."

Mallory complied with a sigh.

"Zo. Imagine a bubble in your handt you hold," Frau Siegenthaller would say, time after time, in her delightfully soft Swiss German accent. "A bubble, ja? And you hold it just zo. And you must be very careful dis bubble…"

"…doesn't break." Joan repeated the advice to her own student half a century later.

"A bubble, a bubble." Mallory wrinkled her eyebrows in concentration and looked as if she would will her hands into submission. But no matter how hard she tried, the pretend bubble always seemed to break or her fingers refused to move one at a time. Her shoulders slumped after several tries at playing "Dublin Town," a simple but lively tune.

"I can't do it!" Mallory jabbed the keys in frustration.

Joan rested a hand on the little girl's shoulder. "Mallory! You don't need to get so upset about it. Let's just go back a few pages and try something different."

Mallory nodded silently and attempted a simpler tune with a simpler rhythm, this one about a skyscraper. Joan swallowed hard and tried not to wince at each sour note. Was she expecting too much? Pushing too hard? By that time Mallory's mother had slipped inside, five minutes before the end of the lesson. As they rose from the bench, Joan consulted her Palm Pilot to see who was next on the schedule. Cassie Van den Bregge, in four minutes.

"That sounded very nice by the way, Mallory." Mother smiled at daughter. "I wish I could play like that."

Joan added her thanks for the good effort, while Mallory bit her lip and collected her things. Yes, she would review pages 7 through 10 for next week, just as Joan had written out for her in the new little steno book. She would practice at least thirty minutes each day. Then she escaped out the front door while her mother hung back.

"We had to go back over a lot of basics," Joan explained, "so I'm afraid it may not be terribly exciting just yet. If you could just encourage her, Mrs. Appeldoorn."

"Please. It's Liz." Mallory's mom looked back with a strained smile as she stepped outside. "And yes, I will try. It's just that…"

She lowered her voice and leaned closer.

"It's just that that girl would rather do about anything but practice piano. She ends up spending half her time out in the barn with her animals and her Grandpa Gerrit. I'm afraid I haven't been very strict with her the past year."

"Well." Joan tried to reassure her with a smile of her own. "We'll have to capture her interest then. I'm sure she'll do fine."

Perhaps she would. But this piano teacher had an uneasy feeling the first lesson with her first student might as well have been her last.

Chapter 8

Love is a friendship set to music.

—E. JOSEPH COSSMAN

"Triple bypass." Gerrit crossed his arms and paced his tiny living-room floor. "Dumbest thing I've ever heard."

And it was the dumbest thing that had ever kept him awake every night all last week, ever since Dr. Eubanks had tried to scare him with all that talk about operations. Hooey.

He resisted the urge to talk it over with Miriam's photo or put on another record; he just kept pacing and stewing. Maybe that would do him good, a little more walking. Five paces one way, turn around, five paces back. He'd seen a Steve McQueen movie like this once. McQueen is captured by the bad guys and thrown into solitary confinement at a prison camp before he digs a tunnel and makes a run for it. Then he steals a motorcycle, which Dr. Eubanks would never approve of, but who cared about that anyway?

"Maybe a tunnel wouldn't be such a bad idea." He peeked out through the shade to see if Miguel had shown up yet for the afternoon milking, but he didn't see the familiar bronze Mercury, a big boat of a car only slightly longer than the old hay barn was wide.

"Where is that guy anyway?" Gerrit stepped out on the little front porch in his stocking feet. He didn't need to look at his watch to know the ladies were getting restless. And it wasn't like Miguel to be more than a couple of minutes late.

"Hey, Warney!" He hollered toward the house as he pulled on his boots, the same way he'd done hundreds of times before, before the doctor turned into a prison guard and put him into solitary confinement, just like Steve McQueen, only he supposed McQueen had one over on him on account of his looks. "Where's that milker of yours?"

The house remained quiet and empty, and only when Gerrit stopped to listen more carefully did he hear the distant sputter of a tractor. That'd be Warney, cleaning out stalls at half-speed. And the kicker was that the kid wouldn't say exactly how he dislocated his shoulder, only that it was "something stupid" and could they change the subject please. Well, Gerrit supposed it was none of his business anyway. He walked across the gravel drive and poked his head into the milking parlor.

"Hey, hallo?"

No one answered, but the girls were sure making a racket on the other side of the door.

"I don't blame you." And for a moment he thought of doing the milking himself. How was it that something as easy as milking a cow would be bad for his heart? Five minutes later he was welcoming the girls inside to the strains of a little Claude Debussy, the *Suite Bergamasque*.

"Entray, see voo play." He bowed to the first cow in the door and tried not to think of what Warney would say when he learned what was going on.

He didn't have to wait long to find out. Not three sets of cows had come and gone before the outside door flew open.

"Don't break the other shoulder." Gerrit turned slowly.

"What are you doing here, Dad?" puffed Warney, his face flushed from running. Actually he got around pretty well with his right arm in a sling, strapped close to his chest. "The doctor said—"

"We both know what the doctor said, don't we?"—Though he wasn't so sure Warney knew the whole story.

"That's between you and Doc Eubanks." Warney took no bait. "All I know is you need to take it easy on account of your heart. I can't let you do this."

"Why don't you let me decide what I can and cannot do?" Gerrit sighed. "This is just a little milking, for goodness' sake. You don't need to have a hissy fit about a little milking."

"Hissy fit? Dad, if you're wrestling the animals around, you're lifting, you're moving, you're on your feet. It's too strenuous."

Gerrit unhooked another cow and sent her on her way with a slap on her back.

"Fine. Just thought I'd help, since your milker didn't show."

"Miguel just got word his mother was sick, back in Mexico. Took his family and left to go back home this morning."

"Called you?"

"I found out."

"Hmm." Gerrit frowned. "Least he could have done was call you. He should've done that."

"Listen, you don't need to worry about that sort of thing anymore. Okay?" He moved in to take over the work. "I've got it covered until I can find somebody permanent."

"Who?" His dad didn't budge.

"Larry said he would stop by."

"He's got his own herd."

Right. Their neighbor Larry Kroodsma hardly had time to milk his own cows, much less theirs, too. Finally Warney cleared his throat.

"Okay, Dad, so if I were to let you help Larry today, just *if,* you would need to take it real easy. I mean *real* easy."

"From one gimp to another, eh?" Gerrit chuckled again. "You don't exactly look as if you're going to be getting much work done yourself with that mystery shoulder."

"It's no mystery." His voice rose an octave. "Just a little dislocation."

"Uh-huh." Gerrit nodded, waiting, wisking disinfectant onto another set of udders. Finally he looked up at his son.

"So you going to let me do this or not?"

"Only if Larry helps you. He should be here any time. But I have an important meeting I have to go to in a few minutes."

Gerrit sighed, too loud. "It's your farm, Warney."

"See? That's what I mean. You get that look on your face, like I'm doing it all wrong."

"Never said that."

"No?" By this time his cheeks had ripened up like strawberries in June. "Well, you get the message across pretty well."

"Warney, come on."

"No, it's true. No matter how hard I try, I still can't do anything you approve of. In fact, three whole years after you sold us the place, you still make me feel like I'm just a hired hand."

"That's nuts." Gerrit slammed his bucket to the floor, sloshing green disinfectant all over his boots.

"You got that right, Dad. Every time I've made a decision, you let me know it was a mistake."

"Name me one time."

"Like the time I bought the four-wheel-drive John Deere."

A slight pause.

"Okay, name me another."

Warney threw up his hands. Point made. But…

"Warney, you're blowing this way out of proportion. I just never used credit the way you do. And I'm seeing a lot of shiny new equipment around here, wondering where the money's coming from."

"Just because I don't keep a piece of machinery until it rusts through. Like the Pyle."

He meant the Ford pickup Gerrit had bought new from Vinnie

DeKoster's dad in 1965. Actually, Gomer had been the first and only vehicle Gerrit had bought straight off the showroom floor, and that had been in a burst of extravagance during a good year. Miriam had playfully named it after Gomer Pyle, the less-than-intelligent but always faithful TV sitcom soldier.

"You're talking about a truck that doesn't have a spot of rust," Gerrit told his son, "except maybe that little bit around the fenders, which doesn't hurt a thing."

"Whatever, Dad. But the interest rates lately have been getting better. You have no idea."

"Interest rates." He spat the word like a bug had flown between his teeth.

"Well, I may not be the farmer you were, or the farmer Grandpa was, but at least I have a…"

Warney's teakettle had suddenly been taken off the burner.

"Say it, Warney. At least you have a what?"

Gerrit tried to read his son's expression. But Warney leaned against a stainless-steel railing and fiddled with a vacuum hose.

"A life, Dad. At least I have a life."

"You tell me what that's supposed to mean."

Warney didn't answer this time. So Gerrit faced his son head-on, as if they had rehearsed the lines many times before.

"Say it!"

"It's not supposed to mean anything. I was just thinking maybe you needed a hobby or something. Get that computer set up. That's why I was trying to help you with that. Get out of the milking parlor. Go out on a da—"

Again Warney bit his tongue, but the meaning was clear.

"Did you say *date?*"

Warney cleared his throat and looked at his boots. "I didn't mean anything by it. Just that Mom's been gone a long time."

"Maybe so, but let's get one thing straight." He held up a finger to nail down his words. "And then I don't ever want to have this conversation again. First, I appreciate your concern. Don't get me wrong. But I am not looking for any dates, and I don't need anybody to fix me up. Ever. Been married once to one wonderful woman, end of story. That clear?"

"Totally."

"Oh, and one other thing. The computer? Thanks for the offer, but you can put it on your top ten list of useless things with an electric plug. I'm thinking of giving it to Ben Kootstra as an anchor for his little fishing boat."

"Dad, I had 'em install extra RAM on it."

"Will that make it sink faster?"

This time Warney just shook his head. Wasn't Larry going to get here pretty soon? Gerrit's classical music played on, keeping time with the drone of the fan and the rhythmic slurping of the milking pumps.

"What is that noise anyway?" Warney stared up at the loudspeaker.

"Not noise. It's Debussy."

"You think that's better than Johnny Cash now?"

Gerrit shrugged and finally allowed a small grin.

"Wow." Warney ran his fingers through his hair and turned around to see the door swing open again, this time much more tentatively.

"Knock knock?" Mallory's piano teacher stuck her head inside.

"Mrs. Horton!" Gerrit stood up straighter and wiped his hands on his jeans.

"How come you guys are fighting?" asked Mallory, pushing in behind her teacher. "I don't like it when you argue."

"We're not ar—" her father began, then changed his mind. "Well. We were just discussing. And I was just leaving."

"I'm sorry to hear about your shoulder." The teacher kept an eye to the damp cement floor as she tiptoed inside. This was definitely no place for open-toed sandals. "Mallory told me about your accident on our way here."

"On your way…" Warney held up his hand. "Oh no. Did I forget to pick her up?"

"Quite all right, Mr. Appeldoorn." Joan smiled. "My next student called in sick today."

"I am so sorry." Warney looked it, but no one else seemed to mind.

"I told her she had to see the milking." Mallory grinned and held her teacher's hand. "She said she's never seen a real cow being milked on a real farm."

Was this the same girl who had run from her first piano lesson? Her mother had already told Gerrit about the disaster. And one thing about his granddaughter: One minute she could be bawling her eyes out, the next she could be giggling and laughing. She was a lot like her mom that way.

"If this is a bad time…" Joan looked around the parlor after Warney left. She must have heard the ruckus.

"No, not at all." Gerrit continued his work as the teacher looked on. "I'm just prepping a couple more of the girls here."

He showed her how the cows came in and took their own stations, how they were cleaned and prepared, how the milking cups were applied.

"Do they hurt?" Joan winced as Gerrit snapped on another set of four.

"Hurt? No, no. You'd hear it if it hurt. I think the little calves hurt more than these things ever could. You know, one of them can really latch onto the tea…er, I mean, udder…you know."

Joan brought a hand to her face and giggled. "I thought farmers were used to talking about such things. They're just cows, you know."

"Just cows in the company of ladies." Gerrit brushed off the teasing as he would a fly. "So why don't you give it a try?"

He motioned to the nearest cow, the next one in line.

"Me?" She backed away.

"Go ahead, Mrs. Horton." Mallory was a good cheerleader.

"Nothing to it." Gerrit led her forward. "I take a little squirt before we start 'em on the machine. Helps clean it out."

With that he showed her how to hold the cow's teat and how to squeeze.

"Ohh. Like this?" She tried twice before getting anything. Then it was his turn to chuckle.

"Like you said," he told her, "they're just cows. Just udders."

"You seem to have a lot more patience with them than I ever would."

He shrugged. "You get used to them, their personalities. Each one is different, these Jerseys. They respond to attention a lot more than Holsteins. I'd be lying if I said I didn't miss it."

She didn't press him to explain more, just nodded. But she gasped as she looked up at the big Darigold electric clock on the wall. Five after six. Gerrit was afraid to tell her that years ago he'd set it fifteen minutes ahead, back when he'd had a milker who was always late, and that no one had ever bothered to set it back.

"Is that really the time? Oh, dear, I told Alison I'd baby-sit in ten minutes."

"Wear your rubber boots next time," he told her. "Warney says I need help."

When she laughed, Gerrit caught himself smiling again at this odd city woman. And though he could straighten his face, he could not keep his heart from fluttering. Maybe Warney was right. The work was physical.

"Oh, one more thing, Gerrit." She turned at the door and inclined her head. "I like your music."

But for the first time since she arrived, she wasn't watching where she stepped. Maybe she was going to be late after all.

Chapter 9

If you judge people, you have no time to love them.
—MOTHER TERESA

*B*eeep.

Randy Horton poked at his answering machine one more time, trying to get to the bottom of a long list of ten or twelve calls, thirteen… Who cared anyway? He brushed an orphaned sock from the top of the machine to join assorted piles of dirty laundry and an empty pizza box on the floor next to his bed. His mother would have a heart attack if she ever saw this, which she obviously wouldn't, so why clean it up? It would just get messy again anyway.

"Mr. Horton," came the now familiar male voice, "Virgil Kennedy with NorthEast One Visa again. I really need to speak with you soon, sir, so we can work out a payment plan, and—"

Randy jabbed the erase button with the verve of a punch-drunk fencing master.

"Touché." He smiled, but it didn't feel as good as it used to.

The second call was a telemarketer from a Bermuda time-share vacation scam, the third a hang-up. But the fourth, fifth, and sixth… He listened to the pleas over and over, letting his mother's words wash past him one more time. She felt closer that way, which really wasn't so bad as long as she couldn't see what her house looked like.

Naturally the first call, the oldest one, sounded the most cheerful: "Hi, Randy. Mom here. I was just thinking of you, wanted to see how your job was going. Is it still working out at the market?"

Oh, boy. They hadn't talked in a while. But the next call came four days later, still cheerful: "Hi, it's me again. Don't want to bother you, and maybe you're busy, but I just wanted to chat. Call me when you have a chance."

And the next, three days after that: "Randy, I just talked to Mr. Atkins at the market, and he said you haven't worked there for weeks. I had no idea. They told me you had come by for your check, though, so I know you're alive. But honey, are you all right? What's going on? Please call me right away."

Then the next three or four calls came once a day, shorter, more to the point. "Call me." "Please call me." "Randy, where are you?" Though his mother's voice seemed to sooth his nerves, he could not answer, could not reach out of the cloud that hung over his head and pulled him back to sleep, even sleep with the midday sunlight pressing through the shades. Someone knocked on the door, probably the paperboy again, trying to collect for another month. But just like everything else, the knocking sound soon faded away, except for the *COPS* rerun blaring on the little television on his dresser—which seemed appropriate: a show about a woman going berserk when a repossessor came to tow away her beautiful car. Good thing his dented old Toyota Corolla stashed in the little garage wasn't worth anything, or he'd be tempted to sell it. Maybe it would make a difference if it started. Maybe he would take another look at it tomorrow.

If there was a tomorrow. Right now all he could think of was falling asleep again.

Sleep, sleep. Beautiful sleep. Better than the drinks the gal at the bar had talked him into buying her, among other things. Unlike beer, sleep was free, and he was proud to say that he was getting quite good at it. Yeah, Mom, I'm getting plenty of sleep, so don't worry about me. Who else spent twelve to fourteen hours a day in bed, sometimes more? He had discovered the uncomplicated escape, with hardly any side effects. Natural. Not like the…

The phone rang in his ear once more, waking him with a snort from his drowsy cocoon. With a roar he swung at the enemy, ripping off his thin covers and connecting with the base of a white ceramic bedside lamp. The lamp flew across the room and shattered on the far wall with a wicked flash and sizzle.

"Youch!" The short circuit would have been enough to wake him if the pain in his hand hadn't. Either way he jerked upright, cradling his injury and waiting for the phone to stop.

Man, that hurts.

"Hey, it's Randy," came his own recorded voice, sounding strangely normal. "You know what to do."

His mother's voice followed a few moments later, louder and breathless, as if she was calling 911 and not her wayward son.

"Randy, I know you're there." She paused. "The neighbor said he saw you."

Another pause.

"Randy, please pick up the phone."

He winced from the throbbing in his hand and tried to catch his breath. Didn't matter. Nothing mattered. But Mr. King must have seen him when he slipped outside for the mail yesterday. *Can't believe it.* He hadn't thought anyone would be watching at midnight.

"Randy, honey? Please. Please pick up the phone. We have to talk. Please."

He reached out his hand and nearly picked up the receiver, but it hurt too much. Everything hurt. His head hurt. His back hurt. His heart hurt. And he couldn't talk about it, not now. He had slipped too far past the point where he could just lie and tell her he was doing fine, the way he always had before.

Maybe he would be able to call her back after a good nap.

"Randy? For goodness' sake this is your mother, not some telemarketer. I'm going to wait right here until you pick up the phone. Did you hear me? I'm not giving up."

"I'm really sorry, Mom." He reached out with his good hand and hit the off button, but his words only echoed hollowly in his bare bedroom. "Maybe I'll try to call you soon. Really. I promise."

Sure, he had made that promise dozens of times in the past two weeks. But this time he meant it. And with that he found an opened bottle of prescription sleeping tablets next to his bed and downed one more for good measure, this time without water. For a glass of water he would have to get up out of bed. And the more he drank, the more he would have to get up to go to the bathroom. He laid back down, curled into a ball, and fell asleep again.

⁓

Joan tried not to let her mind wander, did her best not to worry her daughter and son-in-law. This was not the time, not at a quiet dinner around Alison's table. Still Joan could not forget the sound of the telephone *click*, the sound of Randy hanging up on her again after his usual "You know what to do" message. The memory still stung, still rang in her ears.

She simply didn't know what to do, just as she hadn't known what to do with Jim. Perhaps she should have stayed in New York awhile longer, until he was on his feet again. But he'd told her he was going to be okay. Promised her. Here in Van Dalen at least she could be a grandmother.

But if there was any motherly consolation, it was in at least knowing that her prodigal was still alive. And at least her neighbor had promised to pass along her message, next time he caught up to him. Perhaps he could eventually put her in touch with Randy before something awful happened, before Randy ran out of food.

Of course he would be all right. He had always been such a tender-hearted boy, perhaps a bit moody (much like his father), but always a sweet kid. She once thought she understood why Jim's death had hit him so hard. Now, though, she wasn't so sure. Maybe he just needed to meet a nice girl…

"So what do you think?" asked Alison. A shy smile flickered on her lips.

"What? Oh, I'm sorry, dear. What was that?"

"The salad, Mom." Alison's shoulders slumped as she pointed at the bowl set before them on the lace tablecloth. "Do you think the dressing is too sweet?"

"Oh." Joan fumbled for a spoon, then a fork. "I think so, I mean, no, of course it isn't."

She couldn't recall how much she'd eaten, but she was sure that if Alison had made it, then it had to taste wonderful, especially with sunflower seeds, chopped broccoli, and just the right amount of red onion. Perfect, of course. Wouldn't change a thing, and you are such a good cook, so much better than your mother, and was the baby down for the night?

"She's sleeping fine, Mom." Alison took another sip of coffee and studied her mother's expression. "But what about you? You're not even here."

"Don't give her such a hard time, Alison." Joan's son-in-law, Shane, passed the grilled chicken around again. "Your mom has a lot on her mind. New house, new town, new students, being a new grandma…"

"It's not just that." Joan dabbed at the corner of her eye with a cloth napkin. They waited for her to explain, until finally Joan sighed and faced her daughter straight on.

"It's your brother," she admitted. "I think he was under a lot of stress with his job."

Alison frowned as if the subject annoyed her.

"Which job are you talking about? Circuit City? The Port Hamilton Market? And now you say he quit?"

"He's been trying to find somewhere to fit in."

"Yeah, but five jobs in two years? Maybe he's trying too hard."

Joan bit her lip fiercely, trying to stem a flood of tears. She'd worn an excellent mask up to now. Alison placed a hand on hers.

"I'm sorry. I didn't mean to sound too cold, Mom. He's my brother, and I love him, but I've never understood why he doesn't just get his life together."

"It's just not that easy for some people."

"I know that, but don't you think Randy could at least find time in his schedule to talk to his family? He's either never home, or he's just not answering the phone."

"How many times have you tried?" Joan knew the feeling.

"At least three times in the past month. And I know he's there because he's changed the answering message. Before it was your voice; now it's his. But if he doesn't answer the phone pretty soon, I'm thinking of sending Shane out there to check on him."

"Whoa. I'm a county agent, not an FBI agent." Shane held up his hands in surrender. "But come to think of it, I do have a cattle prod."

"A cattle—" Joan gasped.

"Just kidding." He grinned. "Speaking of rounding people up, though, anybody special you want us to invite to the baby dedication next week? We're thinking of having a little reception afterward."

"No." Joan finally took another piece of chicken as she thought about it. "No one else that I can think of."

Except perhaps...

Sometimes Joan startled herself with the random images that popped into her mind. Certainly they had no bearing on her actual desires or fears or anything else. And besides, she hardly knew him, had only met him a couple of times, so why in the world should such an odd thing cross her mind?

Gerrit Appeldoorn?

~

"How come it doesn't turn off when it's supposed to, Grandpa?" Mallory gripped her piano practice books and looked back at her grandfather. He patted Gomer's metal dashboard.

Old Gomer the Truck had earned its keep, no arguments there. It's just that sometimes...

"Sometimes good old Gomer just doesn't know when to stop working." The explanation seemed to fit while the engine finally wheezed to an unsteady stop.

"Sort of like my Grandpa." She said it with a pixie smile and slipped off the well-worn black vinyl bench seat, patched in only a few places with duct tape, mostly from the place Mallory's baby seat had been strapped down. And of course he had to smile. Sometimes his nine-year-old granddaughter reminded him of someone twice her age.

"Want me to go in with you this time?" He wasn't going to tell her that he might run down to Karol's Koffee Kup for a few minutes to see if anyone had stopped in for a midafternoon break. Only the old guys would be there at this time of day, but oh well.

"Only if you want to."

Well, sure he did. Joan had told her before not to knock, just to come in and take a seat at the piano. Apparently that was the way piano teachers liked to do things. A small flowered love seat had been set up for parents and such, and maybe the occasional grandfather. And as Mallory got herself settled on the piano bench, Gerrit glanced at the books on Joan's bookshelf, because he figured that checking out someone's reading was the quickest way to tell what a person was all about.

Teaching Piano: A Comprehensive Guide and Reference Book for the Instructor, by Denes Agay. No surprise there. He pulled it off the shelf and noticed the inscription on the first inside page: "With love from Jim, Christmas..."

Jim. Her husband? He slipped the book back and scanned a few more.

Gaylord: A History. Something about a music school back East.

Principles of Debate, or How to Win Any Argument. Okay.

Hymns of Charles Wesley. Hmm, the great Arminian.

Streams in the Desert by L. B. Cowman. Nice name. Wonder if he ever ran a dairy.

"Feel free to read anything you like there."

This woman had eyes in the back of her head, somewhere beneath that thick black hair. She must have been a good mother.

"Oh, I was just…"

Snooping. But not really. It wasn't like he was checking out her medicine cabinet. She swiveled back to look at him.

"Really, it's no problem. That book you have there was put together by a remarkable woman, a former missionary, after her husband died. What kinds of books do you like to read, Mr. Appeldoorn?"

"Gerrit." He reshelved Cowman. "Everybody calls me Gerrit, except telemarketers, who call me Mr. Appledoo or Mr. Uppeldork, and I just hang up on 'em."

She laughed softly and it sounded real nice. And when she peered over the rims of her half-moon reading glasses, she looked just a little like a teacher Gerrit had once had. Grade school, if he remembered correctly.

Miss Tilstra. Second grade. His first crush.

"All right, Gerrit. What kinds of books do you like to read?"

And what if he didn't? But it was an innocent question, he supposed.

"Louis L'Amour. Tom Clancy. Al Gansky. Westerns and thrillers, mostly."

"Nothing serious? I have a copy of Calvin's *Institutes* up there, if you're interested in a little light reading while Mallory and I practice."

Now it was his turn to raise his eyebrows.

"You've read Calvin?"

"Required reading at Mid-Atlantic Nazarene College." She pointed with her eyes at a diploma hanging on the wall above her window. "That's where I did my undergrad work, before going to Gaylord. Good Arminian school."

A hint of a smile visited the corner of her mouth.

"We had to learn what other people believed," she continued.

"So you could defend the faith, huh?"

Gerrit remembered the *How to Win Any Argument* book on her shelf, and he was pretty sure he didn't want to get into one with this woman. Especially since that disarming smile of hers punched a hole straight through his gas tank. So he just watched quietly as the teacher and her reluctant pupil practiced scales, good posture, and numbered fingers (the little pinkies were fives, the thumbs were ones). He hung on every word as she reviewed time signatures, staffs and clefs, trebles and basses. Look what they could do with eighty-eight keys, three pedals, ten fingers, and two feet. But for now, not to worry about the pedals or the feet.

"We'll have plenty of time for that later," Joan told Mallory, pulling out a different book. "Now I want you to look at these songs, and I want you to listen to these quarter notes. You're going to play it very soon."

As Mallory obeyed, Gerrit couldn't help but stare. He'd never seen or heard anything like it, this snake charming. Joan went on to show how to play basic versions of "Merrily We Roll Along" and "Oh, Susannah." As she did, Gerrit held on to his hands to keep his own fingers from moving. And he had to look away, for fear he'd be charmed as well. Actually, he wondered if he might not have been better off at the Koffee Kup, where he could reread last week's *Sentinel,* down a hot cup of day-old coffee, and not worry about having his heart flustered.

Part of it was painful, though, as well, listening to his granddaughter struggle so. Even with the simplest of tunes, Mallory tended to miss most of the notes. She sighed and brushed the hair out of her face while Joan brought out the weekly assignment notebook.

"All right, dear. That was a good effort for this week. Let me show you what I want you to practice…"

By that time the next student had arrived, a gangly little girl with pigtails, Jake Van den Bregge's girl. After getting her assignment, Mallory stopped on her way out, pointing to an eight-by-ten portrait on the mantel, one that had lost its glass somewhere along the line.

"Are these your sons?"

"Only the one on the left." Something crossed Joan's face, like a shadow from a faraway cloud, but only for a moment. "He's staying in my home on Long Island, sort of housesitting. The one wearing the funny baseball cap is my husband."

"Really?" Mallory was about to get her first lesson in tact. "I didn't know you were married. Where is he?"

"He died shortly after that picture was taken. Six years ago."

"Wow. Kind of like my grandma. What happ—"

"That's enough, Mal." Gerrit interrupted her. "We don't need to be quite so nosy."

Mallory looked up at her grandfather as if he were speaking Swahili, and Joan didn't offer any more explanations as they stepped outside. Gerrit did feel a surge of relief that she didn't offer to shake hands again, though. Well, yeah, and maybe a little regret, too—not that he would admit it to anyone.

Chapter 10

Nothing separates the generations more than music.
By the time a child is eight or nine, he has developed a
passion for his own music that is even stronger than
his passions for procrastination and weird clothes.
—BILL COSBY

*M*allory checked out the window to see if Grandpa was anywhere close by. All clear. So from her piano bench, she folded her hands, bowed her head, and shut her eyes tight.

"Sorry to bother you, Lord. But I was thinking if I'm really predestinated to be a piano player, then maybe could we just get it over with, skip all the practice stuff. What do you think?"

Well, it made perfect sense to her. Still she shook a little as she unfolded her hands and let them hover over the keyboard, prepared for her miracle. Even her friend Gina Hortegas from 4-H who went to the church across town that was not Reformed believed in miracles. Mallory gulped, and goose bumps began to tingle her spine, just a little. That would be the Holy Ghost tingle Gina had told her about.

Gina said the Holy Ghost visited her church about once every two weeks, and that He was speaking through a man named Brother James at a three-day revival there. An older lady, who used to have goiters, got healed by Brother James, so she figured if God could take something gross and disgusting from an old lady, maybe He could give her, Mallory, a new set of smarter fingers if she asked Him nicely.

"All right," she whispered. "This is it, God. Please?"

With her eyes still closed, she lowered her hands to the keyboard and began to let her fingers move up and down, chord after chord. God, not Mrs. Horton, was going to teach her.

"Mallory?" Her grandfather's voice interrupted the magic miracle fingers. "What is that horrible noise?"

Mallory swallowed so hard it made her cough.

"Didn't mean to startle you." Her grandfather looked in from the kitchen with a pair of pliers in his hand. "I was just going to fix that storm door your mom was complaining about. You just keep practicing. But..."

He looked at her with his head cocked to the side, sort of the way Missy would do.

"Was that the kind of sound Mrs. Horton taught you to make?"

Mallory let all of her seventy-two pounds slump on the worn oak piano bench.

"No, Grandpa, but..."

She paused, wondering how to ask. He wouldn't want to hear about Gina and the Holy Ghost tingle.

"Grandpa, do you believe in miracles?"

"Miracles, eh?" He looked as if he were taking the question apart with his pliers. "Well, uh, sure. Like the calf born yesterday. That's one of God's best miracles, don't you think?"

"I guess."

He seemed pleased with his answer, but if God did those kinds of things every day, then that wasn't really a miracle, was it? At least not the way Gina talked about miracles. Miracles like Moses's parting the Red Sea or Jonah's living in the belly of the big fish or Jesus's healing the guy who was lowered through the roof. Those were real miracles, and she still hadn't ever seen one. Maybe Gina had, but not her.

Worse yet, she had a feeling by now that God wasn't ever going to do a miracle on her fingers, no matter how hard she pounded the piano and no matter what Gina said.

Truth was, she sounded awful. So she turned back to her music with a sigh, and tried to focus on the little black dots that somehow turned into "Row, Row, Row Your Boat" or "Merrily We Roll Along" when Mrs. Horton looked at them. Come to think of it, maybe that was the only real miracle she'd ever seen.

So forget Gina's miracles. God did not want her to play the piano. She tried not to let her tears drop on the keyboard as she jabbed at a key with her index finger, not finger number five like it said in Mrs. Horton's book. She wondered how much longer she had to practice.

Gerrit didn't need his watch to tell him it was milking time any more than the cows needed a reminder to gather outside the gate to the milking parlor twice a day. So after he fixed the storm door in the big house, he slipped on his rubber boots the way he had for the past half-century and ambled across the gravel courtyard toward the barns.

"Takes a licking and keeps on ticking," he told himself with a dry chuckle, but come on, he wasn't even sixty years old yet. He could do this. But the smile evaporated soon enough when he caught sight of Warney's storm cloud headed his way on an intercept course. A diversion? Make the kid smile, and maybe all the recent friction between them would go away.

"Hey, Warney Boy. You look like you're headed for a funeral. You're going to be a little more chipper at mine, aren't you?"

"Dad." Warney held up his hand like a traffic cop as he planted himself in his father's path. "I'm sorry. I should have told you before this."

"We can talk while we're doing the milking, if that's what you want. The girls are waiting, you know."

As if on cue several of the cows broke out into plaintive moos.

"That's just it." Warney's left eye started twitching nervously. "You can't keep doing this, and I can't keep asking Larry. So I finally got a re-placement milker, and he's starting today. He's in there now."

Oh. Already? He'd heard nothing about a replacement milker. But then he'd heard nothing about anything. And he still didn't quite get it.

"You didn't even have time to advertise in the *Sentinel*. Where did he come from?"

"Miguel's second cousin. Miguel told him about the job."

"And you didn't ask me?"

Whoops. Gerrit knew how that sounded the moment it slipped out of his mouth. Warney didn't have to remind him who owned the farm now.

"All right, all right," Gerrit backtracked. "So I can train him, if that's what you want."

"No thanks, Dad. You're not getting any better. And Liz and I don't want you dying in there while you're wrestling cows through the parlor."

Gerrit groaned. Not *that* argument again.

"So what'd you do," he said, "put me on the prayer chain at that church of hers?"

"Church of *hers?* It's my church too, Dad. How do I get you to under-stand that?"

"Well, now that's funny, 'cause First Church still lists Warner K. Appeldoorn on its membership rolls."

"Even after eleven years, and all the times I've asked to be taken off. You're the one who keeps slipping my name in. It's embarrassing, Dad."

"Not half as embarrassing as me having to explain what happened to my son after he married outside—"

"Dad, will you cut it out with that 'outside the faith' junk? You always talk about Liz's and my church as if it's some kind of cult."

"Well?"

"Since when has Free Methodist been a cult?"

"Since about 1619."

"I am not going to get into the whole Synod of Dorks argument with you again."

"Synod of *Dordt*, and besides that the Belgic Confessions, and the Five—"

"The Five Points of Dutch Calvinism, I know, I know. But I'm sorry, Dad. I just don't think we're ever going to agree on this."

"You agreed when you joined our church. You agreed before you met Liz."

Where had he and Miriam gone wrong with this kid? They'd brought him through the Young Calvinist Youth program, the Cadets, catechism classes, youth group, everything. They'd prayed at the dinner table, helped him memorize verses for Sunday school.

But then he started dating Liz Matthews...

"Forget it." Warney sighed. "You're just getting yourself all steamed up, and that's what the doctor says you're not supposed to do."

"You've just gotta remember, Warney, that the only way anything is going to happen to me is if it's God's time."

"Well, that sounds like a good Calvinist thing to say. I'm gonna die when I'm gonna die. But you know what? I don't think it has anything to do with what your church really teaches. I think you're just scared of the operation."

The zinger hit home, and Gerrit narrowed his eyes at the impact.

"Well, I can't just sit in the cottage all day staring at a blank computer screen or listening to records."

"Your e-mail still isn't working? Tonight, tonight after dinner I'll stop by and help you get that straightened out. Oh, except the water rights committee is—"

"Is meeting, I know. You go do your thing, Warney. Don't worry about me."

"Are you going back to the doctor pretty soon?"

"Make you a deal. You let me worry about me, and I'll let you worry about your farm. All right?"

Gerrit held out his hand.

"Hmm." Warney still didn't look too sure but took the offer anyway. "Only if you promise not to keep playing that Mozart stuff in the parlor. I don't want you scaring off our new milker."

"Don't see what that has to do with anything." But Warney would not let go until his father finally nodded. "All right, all right. No more Mozart. Just a little Bach."

"What?"

Gerrit didn't stick around to give an answer; he just turned on his heel and left. All that arguing gave him heartburn. And no, the occasional chest pain didn't bother him much. Not enough to keep him from working, and certainly not enough to keep him from his latest project, the one he had been thinking about for the past couple of days.

As he shuffled back to his little house, he decided he would have to make doubly sure no one saw him from the barns. Give Warney a few minutes to leave for town. At least Mallory had disappeared; maybe she was feeding her goats. And Liz was at work, as usual.

So ten minutes later the big house was clear, and surely no one would mind him practicing a bit on his Oma's piano. Actually, "practicing" wasn't the right word for it. He would just try to repeat what Mallory's teacher had introduced at the lesson this week. After all, if he was going to be able to help his granddaughter with her music, he should familiarize himself with what was going on.

It all came back to him when he sat at the keyboard, as if he were sitting in the teacher's small front room once again. The numbered fingers, the soft and loud tones, the quarter notes.

"Almost like milking a Jersey," he told himself. This had to be easier than following the directions on that blasted computer. Could it really be as frustrating as Mallory seemed to think?

He squinted at the music, experimented with several exercises. The notes made sense, and the right- and left-hand stuff made sense too. And when he closed his eyes, he could hear the teacher clapping her hands in rhythm.

"Mer-ri-ly-we-roll-a-loong, o'er-the-deep-blue-sea-two-three-four."

So far, so good. Left hand, right hand. He had always known what it was like to have his rough, work-worn hands "remember" a job on the farm. But was this how pianists felt?

He turned the page to tackle another familiar tune, something about Big Ben, and the next "Jolly Old Saint Nicholas," then "Old MacDonald." Forte meant louder, piano meant softer. Count and rest and count. And each time he heard the teacher's soft voice:

"Don't forget to curve your fingertips."

"The weight on your hand should be like the weight of a feather."

"Don't look at the keys. Look at the music. Feel the inner beat. Feel the music."

He felt the inner beat, felt the music, and it came from a part of him that had once only listened from the couch. He imagined himself sitting next to the piano teacher, playing a duet. Her beautiful hands flew across the keyboard, barely brushing by his, and the music sounded pretty good.

Until he looked down at his watch and realized he hadn't moved from the bench in the past hour.

What? Worse yet, he heard the back storm door creak open and slam. And the voice of his daughter-in-law floated through the house.

"Oh, Mallory! That is so, so beautiful. I had no idea you were..."

She stopped dead at the coved entry to the living room, eyes wide. Gerrit wished he could have scrambled a little quicker.

"...doing so well."

For a moment more she stared, and she was certainly not surprised to see her father-in-law in the house; he often came in to do repairs, eat dinner with the family, or simply use the rest room. The doors had never been locked for as long as anyone remembered, and Gerrit wasn't even sure if the locks worked in the first place. Liz held a hand to the back of her short-cut dark hair as she looked from the piano and back to him, obviously still unsure of what her eyes were telling her.

"Gerrit?"

"Just making sure it was working for Mallory." He dropped the keyboard cover in place with a gentle clunk and got to his feet. "Trying to figure out what that fancy New York teacher of hers was giving her so much grief about. That's all."

That's right. Nothing more.

Liz dropped her green and white windbreaker on the back of the sofa and stepped aside to let her father-in-law escape. Her shift at the plant must have let out a little early, which was fine, except what was she doing working there in the first place? Miriam never had to work outside the farm, never had to take on shift work when the kids were young. But Gerrit wasn't about to mention it to Warney again. Once had been more than enough. He wasted no time pulling his boots on while she held the storm door open.

"Dad?"

He looked up, and the surprise must have showed on his face. For the past eleven years, it had always been Gerrit. Just Gerrit.

"You talking to me?"

"Yeah. I was just thinking. Nobody's saying you can't learn to play the piano too, you know. I mean, if that's what you want to do."

How was he supposed to answer her? Salmon out of water flapped their gills the same way. She went on.

"I know what Dr. Eubanks is saying. But piano playing has to be okay."

When had Warney told her what the doctor said?

"Uh, yeah. I don't think so."

Yeah, the guys down at Karol's Koffee Kup would be sure to get a good chuckle out of it if they ever heard.

"Oh." Her voice fell to a whisper. "Well, anyway, your playing sounded really nice to me. You sure you've never done this sort of thing before?"

Who wanted to hear about a little boy plunking on Oma's old piano?

"Like I said, I was just seeing what Mal was up against. But all the same..."

He held up a finger as he tugged his second boot into place.

"I'd kind of appreciate it if...maybe you could kind of keep this to yourself, you know? I mean, next thing you know, the guys at the Kup will be thinking I'm some kind of Liberace."

"Liberace?" She smiled when he mentioned the flamboyant '60s performer. "I have a hard time imagining you in a pink sequined suit, doing Beethoven to fireworks."

"The original fruitcake." He chuckled. How about that, she recognized the name. "Wasn't he on the *Ed Sullivan Show*?"

"Before my time, Gerrit. Although... I don't know... With Halloween coming up in a couple of weeks, this might be an idea. Sequins are you!"

"Hmmph." But Gerrit heaved a sigh of relief as he turned away from the back door, sure that Liz would not spill any beans.

Next time, however, he would have to be more careful about when he practiced and for how long.

Much more careful.

Chapter 11

Anyone who has never made a mistake has
never tried anything new.
—ALBERT EINSTEIN

*D*o I really have to play the piano in front of people, Grandpa?"

"Mal, Mal, Mal," Gerrit sighed as he came up behind his grand-daughter while she practiced, and rested his hands on her shoulders. "You tell me."

"I say no, because what if it sounds ugly and they all laugh?"

"First of all, it does not sound ugly. You're just learning. And second, by the time the Christmas recital gets here in a couple months, you'll be an old pro. Nobody's gonna laugh."

"They will too."

Gerrit scratched his chin and wondered what to say next.

"Okay," he finally said. "Look at it this way. You like raising your animals, right?"

"Sure."

"And you liked showing your cow at the fair, didn't you?"

By the sound of her groan, Gerrit guessed she must have uncovered his analogy.

"But showing animals and playing piano aren't the same thing."

"Why not? They're both in front of an audience."

"But I don't have to practice on Mabel. And my hands don't hurt with Mabel. And people like to look at Mabel, but not me!"

Gerrit paused and smiled. "Maybe you're going to be a good lawyer someday, girl."

"Maybe I'll be a lawyer who raises dairy cows and pygmy goats. And a mom."

"Okay." He laughed. "A lawyer mom who raises dairy cattle and kids and plays the piano. But still, you just wait till December. I know you're going to sound great."

She hit another sour note in Beethoven's "Ode to Joy," started over, and repeated her mistake. Well, she did have weeks to practice. And come to think of it, maybe that was a good thing.

"This is stupid." When she slammed her palms down, Gerrit circled around to her side, knelt, and took her hands in his own.

"It is not stupid, and I don't want you using that word."

"But you do. I heard you. You said 'stupid economy' and 'stupid farm supports.'"

Gerrit wondered when she had been listening in on his grumblings. But that wasn't the point.

"Never mind that, just listen. You also heard your teacher telling you that sharing your music is part of playing. So you just have to take her word for it. At least give it a chance."

"I *have* been giving it a chance, Grandpa."

"For a month, you mean?" Gerrit shook his head. "One month is nothing. When I put a seed down in the field, what does it look like a month later?"

"Depends on what it is."

"Exactly." Gerrit dotted an imaginary *i* in midair. "What if it's a seed for a little puny plant? How long does that take to sprout and grow?"

"A month, maybe."

"Right again. But nice big plants, like corn? How long does corn take?"

"A little longer?"

Gerrit laughed out loud. "Ah, you're a good student, my Mallory

Ann. That's just what I'm trying to say to you. You're a big plant, a great plant. You have to give it some more time. More than just a few weeks."

"But I hate it. I'm no good. Not like Mrs. Horton. All I want to do is quit."

"Not yet. Don't you think Mrs. Horton had to practice a long time before she got to be so good?"

"Uh-uh. I think she was playing Beethoven before she was potty trained."

Again Gerrit had to stifle a laugh. Where did this child get her imagination?

"Did she tell you that?"

Mallory shrugged.

"Well, then, you just take my word for it. She did have to practice. Long and hard."

"How do you know she didn't just get it from an alien mind transplant?"

"Now you're getting too silly. You can ask her yourself at your lesson tomorrow."

"I don't know if I'm *going* to my lesson tomorrow. I'm going to be sick. I'll have the chicken pox, and I wouldn't want her to get sick too. It's going to be…outrageous."

"I think you mean *contagious*."

"That's it. Highly outrageous contagious." She giggled.

"Listen, Mal." This time the grandfather looked straight into his granddaughter's blue eyes. "I know this is tough. But I'm going to be there for you, understand? We're going to be in this together."

Mallory looked over at her grandfather and opened her mouth to argue once more. But this time nothing came out. Maybe she had run out of excuses.

"Haven't I ever told you that Appeldoorns never quit?"

"Only about a hundred million times, Grandpa."

"And are you an Appeldoorn?"

"I was a gypsy baby who was abandoned in the barn and raised by the cows until I was two years old when Mom found me, and—"

"You and that crazy bone of yours are going to get yourselves into big trouble someday." Gerrit mussed her hair as he got to his feet. "It's time for you to get back to your practicing. Looks like you have one there about a dog that you need to practice too, right?"

Mallory nodded her head and returned to her music. But old Mr. Beethoven would still have had a tough time recognizing his song.

"All right, dear." Joan tried to relax as the lesson began the following day. After all, she had no reason to feel butterflies in her stomach, did she? After all, he wasn't paying attention. Mallory's grandfather had retreated to the corner of the room and seemed to have his nose buried in last week's *Sentinel*, though goodness knows there wasn't much to read in that little paper besides school-board minutes, obituaries, and police reports about livestock loose on the highway. They were a long way from the *New York Times*.

"Have you been practicing this past week?"

"Yes ma'am. My grandpa helped me."

"Oh really?"

Mallory nodded weakly, the same way she always did, and for a moment Joan wondered how she could light a fire under this sweet girl. Most of her other students were already warming up to the challenge after a few weeks of uncertainty. Mallory, it seemed, was only retreating deeper and deeper into her frustration.

"All right. Then let's review what you've already learned."

Joan pointed at a series of notes in "My Clever Pup," that week's practice piece, and did her best to coax a response. The bar line separated each four count, correct. The little piece was written in four-four time signature, that's right, which meant that eighth notes received…

Mallory labored her way through the simple piece, counting furiously, stopping twice, scolding herself, and finally finishing with a heavy sigh.

"There now," said her teacher. "That wasn't so bad, was it?"

"No ma'am."

Joan paused. "Mallory, I know you're trying hard. I appreciate that. And you're very brave to keep coming back and giving it your best."

"My parents make me. So does Grandpa." It was only under her breath, but the message was clear.

"Yes, of course they do. They want you to learn. But I can only promise you that it will get easier the more you try and the more you practice. Perhaps never easy. Nothing good is easy. But easier. And more fun."

Joan strained for a way to ease the stiff give-and-take that only increased each week.

"So this song is about my clever pup. You have a dog too, don't you, Mallory? I remember him from when I visited your farm."

"Well, yes." Mallory relaxed for a moment. Good. A connection. "We've had Missy since she was a couple years old. Her momma was a golden, and we don't know what her dad was. Grandpa said he was an overachiever, but I don't think that's a dog breed."

Joan stifled a grin. "So how about if you just think of Missy when you play this piece one more time? And do you remember what this little f means, right here at the beginning?"

Mallory frowned and stiffened once again before glancing back at her grandfather. From over the top of the newspaper he mouthed the word at her, which she didn't quite get. What was that?

"Forte," he repeated, just a little above a whisper.

"Oh yeah. Forte."

"Well, now." Joan glanced back at their audience. "Does your grand-father have a musical background?"

"He plays lots of old records in his house. They're kind of like big, black CDs. I've heard him sing along to the old country twang stuff."

"Hmm." Joan pretended to scratch her nose to conceal a smile.

"I keep a close watch on this heart of mine." Mallory lowered her voice in a fairly reasonable Johnny Cash imitation for a ten-year-old girl. "Because you're mine, I walk the line."

Because it was the first time all day that Joan had seen her reluctant pupil smile, she couldn't help but laugh along.

"Now, wait a minute!" Gerrit put down his paper, but he was grin-ning as well, a pleasant smile that seemed to light up his rugged face and bright Dutch eyes. Funny how golden retrievers and Johnny Cash had managed to change the atmosphere so quickly.

"You say he sings that a lot?" Joan couldn't help but join in the teasing.

But Mallory shook her head no. "He used to, but not anymore. Now he only plays piano music on the record player, over and over, and he waves his hands a lot, like he's conducting the orchestra, and..."

And that was as far as she would go; he looked at her like a baseball coach signaling from the sidelines. And his signal was clear: That's enough, girl. Joan pushed aside the odd twinge of disappointment, as if someone had read the first couple chapters of an intriguing novel to her only to abruptly close the book and replace it on the shelf.

Would she be allowed to read another chapter? She caught herself smiling once more, this time at the mental image of a tall Gerrit Appel-doorn in his little cottage as he conducted an imaginary orchestra. Sort of like John Wayne meets the Boston Pops.

"I didn't know people still had those big, black CDs," she said.

"Just a scratchy old soundtrack record from a sappy old movie," he finally admitted, settling back in the love seat and picking up the paper once again. "Miriam's record; has a bunch of skips. She made me go out and see the movie with her. Starred the gal who played that frontier doctor on television. One of the James Bond girls? British accent."

"Dr. Quinn?" asked Mallory.

"That's her," he continued. "She was back in time, and this fella from the present day sees a painting of her and wants to go back too. You know, the guy who used to play Superman. He had a riding accident?"

"That would be Christopher Reeve," Joan replied. She did happen to know the answer to *that* trivia question. "And I believe the music from the movie you're talking about was called 'Rhapsody on a Theme of Paganini, opus 43.'"

"Pag-uh-ninny. You bet. I knew that."

"Er, actually the composer is Rachmaninoff. He wrote the music in 1934. The movie score picked it up in 1980."

By this time it looked as if Gerrit had settled into the sports page. But the thought occurred to Joan that if this man could be persuaded to encourage his granddaughter a bit more, perhaps he could be a key to helping her past this difficult stage. And if he liked Rachmaninoff, well then... She stepped over to her compact stereo and riffled through the adjoining teak CD case.

"Mendelssohn, Mozart, Offenbach... Here it is. Rachmaninoff."

She pulled the CD and extended it to Gerrit.

"You're certainly welcome to borrow it if you like. No skips on a CD. The soloist is Idil Beret. Polish. I met him once. He's quite brilliant."

"I'm sure he is." He avoided her eyes as he folded the paper, set it aside, and rose to his feet. "But I don't own a CD player."

"Oh, of course," Joan stammered. The possibility hadn't crossed her mind any more than the possibility of someone's not owning a telephone or a refrigerator.

"Record player still works just fine; never had any reason to replace it. You remember record players, don't you?"

By that time Joan was quite ready to kick herself for her insensitivity. *Shall we see how many more farmers we can humiliate before the day is done?* Without another word, Joan slipped the CD back into its place, in alphabetical order between Prokofiev and Rimsky-Korsakov.

"I'll be out in the truck, Mal." Gerrit Appeldoorn wasn't going to wait in the house any longer.

⌒

"This isn't the way home, Grandpa, is it?"

Mallory looked out the window at the Hollandia Center, a Dutch-themed shopping center that had recently been built on the outskirts of Van Dalen, complete with tiled roofs and bell towers. If it was the way home, Grandpa was suddenly very lost.

"Not quite." Gerrit pulled into an open parking space and brought the wheezing Gomer to a halt. A couple bringing groceries out to their car from the new Deelstra Market stared at the sputtering, rocking beast.

What, like they've never seen a pickup truck before?

"We're going to Radio Shack," he told her, slamming the door behind him. "And you're going to help me pick out the best CD player in the store."

Chapter 12

We don't stop playing because we grow old;
We grow old because we stop playing.
—GEORGE BERNARD SHAW

*L*ike I said, I usually don't come out this far north." Michael Nightingale of M. Nightingale Piano Tuning, Refinishing, and Reconditioning, Incorporated, pulled his head back out of the insides of the old piano with a grin and dusted his hands on a clean rag. "But when you told me you had a 130-year-old Steinway, I knew I just had to see it. Wonderful instrument. Wonderful, wonderful."

"Yeah, that's what Lawrence Welk used to say, wasn't it."

"Who?"

"Sorry." Gerrit guessed at the piano man's age and did a little mental math. "Must have been before your time. So what do you think about fixing it up?"

"Well…" M. Nightingale scratched his nose with the stub of a pencil and started down a clipboard checklist. "They sure don't build them like this anymore. Look at this rosewood carving detail, cabriole legs…unbelievable. Probably late 1860s, early 1870s. You say it's never had any work done to it?"

Gerrit shook his head. "Obviously I can't say for sure. Opa said he got it from back East."

"Opa?" The tuner wrinkled his nose. Obviously he wasn't Dutch.

"My grandfather. Anyway, I don't think it's ever even been moved from that spot since he brought it in the house."

"Which makes it even more remarkable. Still, it could use some work."

"How much work?"

"Well, first we would take it to our shop. I would remove all the old wire and block, remove and rebronze the plate, inspect and refinish the soundboard, install and reset the plate and bearing, install a new pinblock, repin and restring with new pins and wire, and finish off with two tunings."

Gerrit's eyes were beginning to glaze as Michael Nightingale punched some figures into his handheld calculator.

"How much for all that?"

"Two thousand, seven hundred four dollars and twenty-seven cents."

Gerrit took a deep breath. *That much?*

"And then there's the new hammers, shanks, and flanges."

"Which is?"

A few more taps on the calculator brought the total to—

"That adds another two thousand, two hundred."

"Which brings us to four thousand, nine hundred four."

"And twenty-seven cents."

"Right. Anything else?"

"Only the ivories. The entire keyboard is in remarkably good condition. But four ivories should be replaced, which I'll throw in at forty-five dollars apiece."

"Another hundred and eighty."

Michael Nightingale punched a few more numbers and looked up expectantly. "Shall I schedule a time for us to get started?"

But Gerrit waved him off.

"I only have one problem. See, my granddaughter is needing to practice on this thing nearly every day. So it has to stay right here, and it has to stay usable. Playable, I mean."

"I see." Michael Nightingale's face fell. "That's going to seriously limit what I can accomplish."

"And another thing. This is a secret, so you've got to be able to do the work here when nobody's home. I live over there in that white cottage if you need to get ahold of me."

By this time Michael Nightingale was folding up his small tool kit and heading for the door.

"So let me see if I understand correctly. You don't own this piano, and you don't live in this house. You want all this work done here, secretly, during certain hours of the day, and no others. Correct?"

"Bingo." Gerrit nodded. "This is my son's house now. But the tune-up here is for my granddaughter, so nobody else needs to know until it's a done deal. What can you do for a thousand bucks?"

Gerrit thought he heard the piano tuner groan. But that was his best offer, take it or leave it. Better than a poke in the eye with a sharp stick.

"I'll see what I can do," the tuner finally replied, and he went down his list, crossing off item after item. "Yeah, I can replace a couple of the weakest strings, and I think we can re-felt the worst of the hammers. After that a good tuning, and we'll see where we're at."

"That'll bring it up to snuff enough for Mallory's teacher to hear the difference?"

"Oh, it'll be much better than it is. Not quite what I would have recommended, but much better than nothing. Her teacher will love you for it."

Gerrit felt his cheeks flame as he walked the tuner to the door. Liz kept her heat turned up too high.

"One thing, then," Gerrit replied. "This has to be between you and me. No bills or mail to this address. I'll pay you direct, and we'll all stay out of trouble. Deal?"

"I understand."

Good. This could work just fine. Outside, he took a deep breath of cool October air as they walked to the man's little Japanese truck. Gerrit reached into the pocket of his flannel shirt and brought out a couple of Dubbel Zouts, lozenges marked with the distinctive "DZ."

"Care for one?"

"What is it?" asked the piano man. He accepted the offering but turned it over in his hand before wrinkling his nose and giving it a good whiff. For a moment Gerrit thought of giving a fair warning, but only for a brief moment. This way was much more fun.

"Just a piece of Dutch licorice. You know, around Halloween we have far too much of that stuff around the house. Help us get rid of it so the kids don't get sick. It's good, see?"

To demonstrate how harmless the stuff was, Gerrit popped a couple into his mouth, smiled, and chewed away. Drug dealers performed the same act, didn't they? Mr. Nightingale shrugged and followed Gerrit's example.

To Gerrit, the best part of the prank was that delicious three-second interval before the victim quite knew what had been done to him, before he knew what had assaulted his unsuspecting mouth with such ferocity. Before the sharp bite of that odd Dutch treat sunk its fangs into poor Mr. Nightingale's taste buds. In the past fifty years he had never seen anyone whose eyes didn't bulge nearly out of his skull at the first taste, just like Mr. Nightingale's. And ever since Gerrit had first tricked Jonathan Dorsey in the second grade into trying some Dubbel Zout, he had never met anyone who didn't spit the candy out the same way they would expel a hot coal from their mouth. The rejected candy sailed over a shoulder-high rhododendron bush and landed somewhere in the bark underneath to serve out its life as a soil conditioner. (Which is probably what Mr. Nightingale thought it was in the first place.)

Of course, Jonathan wasn't Dutch. Neither was Michael Nightingale.

"You don't like it?" Gerrit asked with a straight face—an expression he had perfected over the years. As in, *how could you not?* As expected, it took a minute for the man to regain his composure, to catch his breath.

"What *is* that stuff, really? Tastes like a chunk of rock salt."

"Just Dutch licorice." Gerrit popped one more into his mouth, just for good measure. "Kind of clears out the sinuses, don't you think?"

The piano tuner shook his head as he tried to clear his mouth of the lingering Dubbel Zout, but he wasted no further time at Appeldoorn Farm.

Despite Michael Nightingale's encounter with ethnic candy, he did return the next week as promised. And Gerrit's plan to keep the piano work quiet turned out to be pretty good—until the piano tuner's fourth visit. Gerrit looked up from his frying pan when he heard the knock at his back door.

"It's open!"

He wondered who would have been so formal as to knock. Usually a head poked in the door and a "hallo" worked just fine.

"Yeow!" A splatter of grease from the potato sausage caught him on the back of the hand, and he brought it to his mouth for first aid. Who in the world was at the door?

"I said to come on in." But this time he needn't have shouted; Warney stood just inside the door, leaning against the doorjamb, waiting.

"Want me to put another Gelderse wurst on, kid?" He held up a package of Dutch-labeled sausages. "I've got plenty of *rode kool* and raw-fried potatoes, too. Just like your mother used to make, except this is store-boughten and canned. What do they call this, 'German-style sweet-and-sour red cabbage?' Close, but no cigar. Still, you take what you can—"

"Dad." Warney wasn't there for dinner, and he wasn't smiling either.

"What, you're not hungry for some authentic imitation Dutch food?"

"We already ate, Dad. And I hope you're not frying that stuff in lard."

"You wouldn't want me to use that spray-on chemical stuff? What if it causes cancer? But I suppose you didn't come here to criticize my cooking."

"No, I didn't." He held up a business card like a lawyer presenting a crucial piece of evidence. "You want to tell me what this is all about?"

"From this distance, looks like a business card." He swirled the red cabbage around in the frying pan, sending an aromatic cloud of steam into the room. "Why don't you solve the mystery and just tell me?"

"M. Nightingale Piano Tuning, Refinishing, and Reconditioning. Does that ring a bell?"

"Vaguely."

"Oh, come on, Dad. Mallory told us this guy has been coming to the house while Liz and I are gone, doing a lot of work on the old piano, and that you told her it was a secret, that she wasn't supposed to say anything to us."

"And I told him not to leave his card or anything. Can you believe it?"

"I found it on the floor where he probably dropped it. But what I believe is that you shouldn't have been doing this, Dad."

His voice quivered slightly, as if he was doing his best not to lose his temper. But over the silly old piano? And whose money was it anyway? Gerrit dished out his cabbage, potato, and sausage concoction onto a plate, adding a generous dollop of mayonnaise for the spuds.

"You sure you won't have any?"

"Dad, listen, you're the one who always lectures me about spending too much, and now look at this. I can't believe you did this under our noses. First of all, you didn't ask us, and second, you bring Mallory into it."

"Warney, I had no idea you would get so bent out of shape about this kind of trivia. I was just testing your theory about secrets."

"My theory?"

"That we Appeldoorns aren't good at 'em. You were right."

"Be serious." Warney sighed. "How much are you paying to have this work done on my piano?"

By that time Gerrit had bowed his head to pray silently over his dinner, while Warney was obliged to wait. Finally the elder Appeldoorn looked up after a lengthy discussion with the Lord.

"You say something?"

"I asked how much you were paying to have the piano reconditioned."

"Well, I think I'm entitled to a little privacy about that, eh?"

"Not when it's my piano."

"Warney, Warney. I don't think it's really about the thousand dollars, is it?"

"A *thousand?* You're dumping a thousand dollars into that old piano?"

"Mal's teacher said it was worth fixing. It's an antique. A classic. A Steinway. Part of music history."

"But a thousand. That's still way more than…"

"Than what?"

"Forget it." Warney had said more than he'd intended to say, and his voice trailed off in embarrassment—though the fire in his eyes never dimmed.

"Well, you'll be happy to know I talked the piano guy down from more than four thousand dollars. So I think we're getting a pretty good deal."

"That's wonderful." Warney shifted from one foot to the other.

"Actually, the bill came to eleven-hundred twenty-something, including tax. I took it out of my IRA account, if you're curious. And it's all for that little girl of yours. Merry Christmas or Happy Thanksgiving. Take your pick."

"All right." Warney closed his eyes, maybe searching for his own way out of the corner they had talked themselves into. "But do you think Mallory really appreciates it, Dad? I thought Liz and you were dragging her kicking and screaming to those piano lessons."

"She's not giving up, if that's what you're thinking." Gerrit squared his jaw and speared his sausage as if it were still alive. "I've been talking to her about that. Appeldoorns don't give up."

"Right. At least that's what you always told me."

"Did you listen?"

Warney moved his jaw a couple of times, and by then it was clear their argument had lost its steam. Just like Gerrit's cooling dinner plate.

"Listen, I do appreciate it," Warney managed. "I was just thinking it wasn't quite appropriate, is all."

"Appropriate." Gerrit rolled the word around on the end of his tongue.

"And that if you were going to spend any more of your retirement money in my household, maybe we could have talked about it first, that's all."

Gerrit felt a surprising twinge of regret, and the possibility that maybe his son was right flickered before him. For once, did Warney have a point? Sure, he could have talked it over with his son before he'd done it. But the work was done, and so it was meant to be. There was no use regretting. He clinked the plate as he scooped up another lukewarm bite and said nothing. He should have nuked the food once more for good measure.

"Sorry to bother you at dinnertime." Warney pulled up the collar of his windbreaker and turned back to the door. "Enjoy the wurst."

No pun intended, but the words fit. By this time Gerrit's dinner was nearly cold, and he considered feeding it to Missy, who must have followed Warney over and ambled inside before the door slammed.

"Looking for some more dinner?" Gerrit asked her.

Thump-thump. At least her tail still worked, and maybe her nose, but not her eyes. She looked straight ahead through the misty white fog of cataracts.

"Yeah, maybe you want some of this German *rode kool* from a jar," he told her. "Tastes like cardboard chips soaked in vinegar."

Almost as bitter as the argument with Warney. And no, it was nothing like Miriam used to make, nothing at all. She used to add plenty of brown sugar to the cooked cabbage, along with chopped red onions and raisins for flavor. He should have bought himself another Budget Gourmet rather than trying to get fancy with his own cooking. He worked the red cabbage around in his mouth as he stared at the half-eaten food on his plate, suddenly wishing he could take back the ingredients to the Deelstra Market for a refund.

And along with it, how about if he could take back some of the words he had dished out to his son over the past few months?

"Here, girl."

He lowered his plate to the floor.

Chapter 13

Waiter: Into how many pieces do you want your pizza cut?
Yogi Berra: "Four. I don't think I can eat eight."

Gerrit fingered the note as he stood ready to head out into the November gloom.

Mal's coming home on the 3:30 bus; she can have graham crackers and milk for a snack before you take her into town for her 4:00 piano lesson, and could you please make sure she wears her new red rain parka, not the old one with holes?

He actually appreciated Liz's carefully worded to-do lists and notes, always written in the same perfect handwriting, the typewriter-tiny lettering that he had to squint to read.

They were just so busy all the time, Warney running around town doing his ag committee stuff, and Liz working overtime at the Darigold plant, coming home later and later, looking more and more like a wrung-out dishrag when she finally did get off work. One of these days he might go down to the plant himself, if Burt Haarsma was still the supervisor, and give him a piece of his mind.

"Nothing wrong with a little hard work," he muttered as he pulled open the door. "But a mother ought to be there for her kids—"

The wind snatched the words right out of his mouth and the note from his hand. He could only watch as the paper took flight and tumbled into the soggy leaves that swirled in tiny tornados in the front yard, then skittered on and disappeared into the woods on the other side of the Vanderkrans Road. And as another gust shook his little house, he could only hang on to the tiny porch railing for balance.

"Seems like Dorothy made it to Oz this way," he told himself as he two-handed the doorknob to wrestle it shut. Something inside caught the draft and crashed to the floor as he did, maybe something glass. He would have to take care of that later. A glance at his watch told him it was nearly 3:40, and this baby-sitter was late for duty.

Shoot. He was supposed to have been waiting for Mallory when she arrived home. And the bus from Van Dalen Elementary rarely arrived late, even on those chilly winter afternoons when it had to navigate snowdrifts or driving rain. Betty Van der Werf, the driver, made sure of that, the way she had for the past twenty-some years. So Betty would surely have dropped Mallory off exactly ten minutes ago, at the end of the gravel drive where last year Gerrit had built a little red barn–styled bus shelter for her.

"Mal!" Gerrit shouted up the stairwell inside the big house. "Get yourself a snack and we'll leave for your lesson in about ten."

Mallory didn't answer. Maybe the door to her room was closed.

"Mallory?" A little louder this time. "Did you hear me?"

Still no answer, so Gerrit tromped up the stairs to see what his granddaughter was up to. But the upstairs hallway light wasn't on, her books weren't tossed on the bed as usual, and all the doors swung open to empty rooms.

"Mallory?" he called again, but the words just echoed through the house. Had she already been inside? Hard to tell really. He'd been in and out of the house several times that day, and the tracked-in soggy leaf collection on the kitchen linoleum could have been his or Mallory's. Missy was still hunkered down in her igloo outside, not bothering to step out into the blustery day. Smart old dog.

"Mal's probably out in the barn feeding Lilbit."

But a quick glance into the dark barn showed no evidence of Mallory, only the usual group of twenty or so dry cows shuffling around, waiting for their afternoon feeding.

"Mallory?"

He glanced around at the barn, just to be sure. Sure, there were still plenty of places she could be. But Mallory knew her schedule. Gerrit trotted back to the house to make a phone call to the school.

"You're sure she got on the bus... No, no problem. She's gotta be here somewhere, then... Yeah, that's what I thought... Uh-huh. Just wanted to check, thanks."

Gerrit slammed down the receiver and looked around the kitchen once more, as if Mallory would magically appear at the kitchen counter for her graham crackers and milk. This was all his fault for being late. The note had said she would be home on the regular bus, hadn't it? Home at 3:30 just like always. Take her to her 4:00 piano lesson. He checked his watch one more time. Two minutes to four.

"Where are you, girl?"

He ran out to the barn, this time forgetting his windbreaker back in the kitchen. There's no way she would have just wandered down the road to the Kroodsmas to watch their llamas. Not in this snotty weather. She would have asked first anyway. She knew better. And she knew about her Tuesday lesson.

He wondered how long it would take Sheriff de Blom to get out to the farm if he dialed 911. He'd never done that before, but there was always a first time. He watched the news like everybody else, and kidnappings only happened in Seattle and Vancouver. Not in Van Dalen, and not on this farm. This was crazy, and he wasn't going to even think about calling 911. Not yet.

But where was she? The only place she would have wandered was here to the barn, maybe to feed the barn cats, which...

Which were nowhere to be found either.

So he paused in the middle of the barn to listen to the sounds he had grown up hearing. The cows softly mooing and shuffling. A couple of new calves, safe and warm in their own little stalls, making little whimpering sounds from under a heat lamp. The metal roof, panels of which were picked up and let down with a clang by the southwester. And the faint mew of barn cats, somewhere up in the hay loft, where he used to make forts when he was a boy. Maybe...

Only this time he didn't call Mallory's name, just climbed the wide ladder that led up to the stored bales. He could still manage, except that by the time he reached the top he was pulling a bit for air, and his chest did feel a little tight. Keep it slow.

The loft was even dimmer than usual, with only a gray hint of sunshine filtering in from between the cracks in the siding. He followed the mewing sound over a bale, then down a small gap between two piles, just wide enough for him to squeeze through sideways before he had to stoop. The gap opened into a little sort-of hay room, filled with a dozen cats... and his granddaughter Mallory. She looked up at him with surprise written on her face.

"Are you all right, Grandpa?"

He smoothed back wild wisps of windblown hair and tried to catch his breath quietly.

"I'm...fine. I was just starting to get worried about you."

"How did you know I was up here?"

"These cats." He looked down at the small tabby at his feet, jostling with five or six of its brothers and sisters around an aluminum pie plate filled with milk. "You were missing, they were missing. I know you like to feed 'em. So I figured you all might be missing in the same place."

He waited for her to say something else. She looked rather comfy in the spot she had carved out for herself in the hay.

"You know I used to make forts up here when I was your age." He lowered himself down to join her, and she looked away. "Mostly to get away from my brothers, when they teased me. Once I even brought up a candle, don't know what I was thinking. Could've burned the whole place down. My daddy paddled me real good. Never did that again. In fact, never came up here to hide after that."

"How old were you?"

"About your age."

"And you used to hide from things too?"

He nodded. "Speaking of hiding, do you know what time it is?"

She looked at her feet.

"I'm not going."

"Oh you're not, eh? What happened to keeping your word?"

"It's not my word. It's Mom's word. She's the one who told Mrs. Horton I would take these stupid lessons."

"There you go with that word again."

"That's what they are."

"You don't think Mrs. Horton is stupid, do you?"

Mallory paused and looked up, wiping tears from her cheeks.

"No. She's really nice."

"And did you stop to think that you're letting her down by not coming?"

"She has lots of other kids taking lessons from her now."

"That doesn't mean you can skip out on her. Remember what I said about quitting."

"But I'm—"

"Ah-ah-ah." Gerrit held up his hand to interrupt her. "We've been through all this before. You have to practice for the Christmas recital coming up. And now by the time we make it to Mrs. Horton's house, your lesson will be nearly over."

"So doesn't that mean we should just skip it today? Maybe I'm not feeling so good."

"No, you're not going to skip anything. You're feeling just fine." He took her hand and led her toward the ladder, taking care not to step on any of the cats. "So you're going to march right up to Mrs. Horton, apologize for what happened, and tell her it's not going to happen again."

Gerrit wanted to take his handkerchief and dry the tears that streamed down Mallory's face, but it was too late.

"You just wait, Mal. In a couple of weeks you're going to be playing like a champ at the Christmas recital, everybody's going to be clappin' and cheerin', and you'll be wondering what you ever worried about."

Not looking very convinced, Mallory climbed down the ladder without another word.

Chapter 14

*Love is like playing the piano. First you must learn
to play by the rules, then you must forget the rules
and play from your heart.*

—UNKNOWN

M r. Appeldoorn." Joan Horton smiled broadly as the families
stepped into the foyer of Van Dalen's First Dutch Reformed
Church. "So glad you could all make it. Is it snowing out there yet?"

Warney shook his head but stamped his Sunday shoes on the tile
entry. "Not yet, but I wouldn't be surprised. All we need is a little wet to
go with this nor'easter. We'll get some white stuff overnight."

As if to reinforce her husband's weather forecast, Liz hugged her
shoulders more tightly and drew her ankle-length dark green coat a little
closer. Obviously, the church furnace had not been adjusted soon enough
for tonight's special event, and the thought crossed Joan's mind: Had the
janitor received word of their recital in time?

Don't worry, she reminded herself as she glanced over at the refresh-
ment table, where several mothers, still in their heavy coats, were setting
up a couple of gleaming coffee urns. The brew would be strong enough to
stand up a spoon, no doubt, and Joan had learned early on that they didn't
believe in decaf around here. No ma'am, they'd sooner serve hibiscus
herbal tea than contaminate the coffeepots. They'd also planted a small
forest of miniature holly Christmas trees in between plates piled high with
speculaas, Dutch spice cookies.

These good people had experienced much worse cold snaps, Joan was certain. So had she for that matter. But this had to be the chilliest day she'd experienced since moving to Van Dalen. She turned in time to see Gerrit pulling the front double doors closed behind his family. He nodded at her.

"You're all here," she squeaked, then cleared her throat.

"Wouldn't miss it for anything, would we, Mal?" He patted his grand-daughter on the shoulder, the kind of tender gesture Joan had come to admire. Although at first she'd expected him to track cow manure onto the living room rug or spit tobacco juice on the floor, the boots had turned out to be clean tennis shoes, and the tobacco juice was simply some kind of vile Dutch licorice. At their lessons he'd politely offered her some, which she'd politely accepted but then quickly and discreetly found a place for in the heart-leaf philodendron's potting soil.

No wonder the poor plant had passed away shortly after that.

Tonight she hoped the dear man had left his licorice at home, though he did seem to be chewing something.

As for Mallory, she wore the same deer-in-the-headlights expression she'd demonstrated regularly in the weeks leading up to their recital. Joan had even offered her parents an out, telling them that if Mallory felt too intimidated at the prospect of performing at the Christmas recital, they could reschedule her for the spring. But no, no. She would be ready, they said. Joan caught the girl's attention with both hands on her shoulders.

"How are you doing, dear? Your poor little fingers look absolutely blue. Are you ready?"

Mallory nodded nervously and huffed on her hands as another family entered behind them, then another. First Dutch Reformed would proba-bly fill up tonight—the quaint brick church normally had seating for three hundred, perhaps a few more under slightly cozier conditions.

"She practiced this one long and hard," her father assured them. "Mal's going to break a leg."

At that, Liz squeezed his arm and gave him a mama-bear glare.

"What?" he replied. "Isn't that what you're supposed to say at recitals?"

"That's not funny," she whispered, just loud enough for the rest of them to hear.

"But she has the song down cold."

"Shh. You're just making her more nervous."

Of course, if there was a way to appear more nervous than Mallory Appeldoorn already did, Joan wasn't aware of it. They tried to include the girl in their small talk, but that soon proved to be impractical as more and more families joined them in the foyer.

"Here, Mallory." Joan reached into her purse and leaned down to Mal's level. "Would you like a mint?"

Mallory accepted one with a smile as even more people pressed in.

"Joan, honey." A small woman with tall hair gestured to her from the other side of the room. That would be Linda Boer, president of the Van Dalen Area Music Educators Association. "I want you to meet someone. Mayor Van der Klock."

Joan knew Linda was teaching the mayor's two young sons, and she naturally appreciated the friendly introduction. But the way Mallory slipped off toward the bathroom with an ashen look on her face made her feel even more badly for the poor girl.

Lord, please help her get through this, she prayed, as she had several times already.

⁓

Mallory knew she didn't need to be so scared. Jesus was taking care of her. Jesus was in charge. And that's what she repeated to herself all the way to the girls' rest room. Plus she did her best to keep a serious game face, which is what Dad said the Seattle Seahawks players did when they were getting ready to play football. They put on their game faces in the locker room, and then when they ran out on the field and everybody saw them on television, they looked like they knew what they were doing.

So Mallory looked in the mirror too and pretended she was in the locker room, putting on her big shoulder pads and her Seahawks helmet. Seriously, that might not have been a bad idea. Except that she would probably have a hard time seeing out through the faceguard. And right now she needed to see as much as she could.

Gina was going to be here with her parents to watch too, but it was okay, because Gina knew that God hadn't given her miracle hands after all. Actually, neither of them could figure out what Mallory had been pre-destinated for. Gina thought she might be predestinated to be a mission-ary in Africa after a missionary from Africa came to her church. (The one that was not Reformed.) Mallory wasn't sure about that, since she hadn't been there. She still thought she had definitely *not* been predestinated to play the piano, but here she was.

And Gina hadn't given up on the Holy Ghost tingle stuff.

"Give me the signal when you feel the tingle," she'd told Mallory yesterday after school.

"What's the signal?" Mallory still didn't quite know what the tingle was either.

"How about you pull on your ear? Then I'll pull on my ear, too. That'll be our signal."

"Cool." She could do that much. "But what if I'm still using both my hands to play the piano? How can I give you the signal then?"

They hadn't come up with any big ideas about that, except that Gina thought God would find a way. And that was okay with Mallory. She wasn't expecting any tingles anyway. So she stood in front of the mirror a minute longer, practicing her curtsy, bobbing up and down a couple of times while trying not to lose her balance.

She almost did, though, when two eighth-grade girls stepped into the room, laughing and giggling. Good thing they looked right through her, as if she blended into the mirror. Enough practice curtsies for now.

"Are you really going to do show-PAN?" one of them asked the other.

The taller one brushed her hair back out of her eyes and shrugged. "Mrs. Leegsma said I was ready."

The way they talked told anybody who wanted to know that it was no big deal. Mallory shrank into the wallpaper next to the changing table and watched them put on makeup one of the girls had obviously smuggled into her little black opera purse, the same kind her Barbie doll had, only a little bigger. None of their mothers would allow them to wear it, not yet.

"You should have seen Natasha's little sister at this recital last year," said the first one, the one with the purse and the lipstick.

"Oooh, I heard. Was she the one who cried in front of everybody when she was trying to play?"

No-no-no-no. Mallory couldn't listen anymore. Forget about the game face. She took her chance to escape when the two girls almost fell to the floor giggling. And again they didn't even look at her, which gave her a weird feeling that maybe God had come to her rescue after all. Maybe Gina was right. So when she spotted her friend in the fourth row on the right side of the nearly full church, she decided to test her theory.

She waved.

But Gina smiled and waved back.

Maybe I'm only visible to people who know me, she told herself. *Maybe I'm invisible to everybody else, like the eighth-grade girls in the bathroom. Strangers.*

"Excuse me," whispered Mallory. And somebody's mom she didn't know stepped to the side of the aisle to let Mallory get by.

So much for that idea. God was still going to have to rescue her from this disaster. He was just going to have to find a different way to do it.

"Well, *there* you are." Her grandfather scooted over from his spot on the aisle in the second row. She would get the aisle seat so she could get out quicker. "We were about to send out the police for you."

"Gerrit." Mallory's mom poked her grandfather the same way she poked her dad. "She's just a little nervous, that's all. It's natural. She'll be fine. You said so yourself."

Mallory had heard that before. But she didn't say anything, just sat on her left hand to keep it warm and buried her nose in the program to see when she was up. Fifth, after Erica Laanstra, Adam Verhoorn, Chantrelle Wilson, and Lilly Eenkema. All of them had taken piano for a million years. As far as Mallory could tell, she and a boy named Richard were the only second-year students on the whole all-city Christmas recital program. She tried to picture her hands in her mind, playing the Beethoven Ninth Symphony part that she had practiced so many times with Mrs. Horton and in front of Grandpa. "Once more," they'd told her, over and over, and she had done her best because she wanted them to be happy with her and smile and clap the way she knew they would if only she could be a good piano player. She still didn't think she was predestined to be a piano player, and she still hated every minute, but maybe God still had a miracle for her tonight.

≈⌐

"Thank you, everyone, for coming, and welcome to the twenty-seventh annual Van Dalen Music Educators Association Combined Christmas Recital."

Gerrit clapped along with everyone else and was suddenly glad Warney and Liz hadn't asked Linda Boer to teach Mallory the piano. Now that he thought about it, maybe they had, but Linda's schedule had been full. Of course, her schedule had always been full, ever since they had gone to school together. Linda had been class president, cheerleader, valedictorian, all that. And president of the piano teachers group for as long as anyone could remember. Oh, well.

"This has already been a special year for us," she went on, straining on her tiptoes to reach the podium microphone. "And in a moment you'll hear the results of much hard work on the part of your children. But we've also been honored to welcome a wonderfully talented new teacher to our midst."

When Gerrit glanced over at where Joan sat, he thought she winced. Linda went on, as she often did.

"A former professor of musicology at the world-famous Gaylord School of Music in New York, Professor Joan Horton. Let's all give her a warm Van Dalen welcome."

Which Gerrit had no trouble doing. This time he was sure Joan was blushing, however, as she raised her hand shoulder high and nodded at the little crowd. Following that, without further ado, Linda Boer droned on about the association and how proud they were of three members who had completed special certification training in Seattle this past year, and about their wonderful annual Labor Day kickoff potluck, and about Mary's incredible homemade *oliebollen* that they really shouldn't have eaten so many of, and finally...

By that time Warney was bouncing his foot impatiently, and Gerrit didn't blame him. He leaned over and whispered in Mallory's ear. "How much will you give me if I stand up and start singing?" he asked her with a wink.

And for the first time all day he caught sight of a smile playing on her lips, until she remembered where she was and buried her nose once again in the program. By now she'd probably memorized it, at least as well as she'd memorized her Beethoven piece. It wasn't a Christmas song like so many others on the program, but that was what she and her teacher had chosen, and that was fine.

Suddenly, everyone was clapping again, probably as much due to the fact that Linda had stopped yakking as anything else. But if his granddaughter's stomach was anywhere near as knotted as his own, she had to be hurting. He noticed she had her game face on. Maybe that would help.

Another round of applause, this time for Erica Laanstra. One down. Adam Verhoorn played next, a short piece about sleigh bells. Fine. He made it, and so did Chantrelle Wilson and Lilly Eenkema, though he had to say that, after Lilly, Mallory was bound to sound good. So he gave her a wink, but his granddaughter's expression didn't crack as she left to find her place next to the big, black baby-grand piano before turning around to face the congregation. Or the audience. Whatever.

"I shall play the 'Ode to Joy,' by Ludwig Beethoven...van Beethoven." She stuttered for just a moment before retreating to the relative safety of the piano bench. So far, so good. He'd heard her because they were sitting in the second row. But people behind them didn't need to hear. They could read their programs, couldn't they?

Gerrit forced himself to breathe. He didn't dare look over at Warney and Liz, but he didn't hear any breathing over there either. Somebody coughed—shouldn't they have stayed home if they were sick? A toddler started to fuss, and that was somebody else who should have stayed home. Did they bring their toddler to the movies, too? He was about to turn around and give them a stare to remember when Mallory finished fidgeting and began to play.

First measure, good, and the second through to the fourth. Repeat. He looked down at his program, which he had twisted into a pretzel. But the girl had memorized it well.

Hadn't she?

He winced when she hit a wrong note and paused. She backed up for a running start and missed the note again.

"Come on," he whispered silently. "You can do it."

But she couldn't. Not after two tries, not after three tries. And after all her practicing. He could feel his own hands take over, but they were powerless in his lap. As every eye in the church must have noticed, Mallory's lower lip had begun to quiver as her hands floated above the keyboard.

Okay, so she was stuck. Frozen, as surely as if she had parked herself on the bench outside for the past hour.

Without knowing what he was doing or why, Gerrit slipped out of his own seat to find a place next to Mal on the piano bench. She only looked at him once, wide-eyed, and then again without thinking he moved his hands to cover hers.

"You remember how you practiced," he whispered. "Find the first chord."

Without a word she obeyed, and after he had helped her find her place, he nodded for her to begin again.

Joyful, joyful, we adore thee…

They played the parts together, following the same beat but separated by an octave.

God of Glory, Lord of love.

Gerrit remembered the words printed below the music they now followed. The music he had memorized with his hands but had never shown to anyone, not even Mallory. And now she led on, not missing a note, not missing a beat, not hesitating. Good. Good.

Hearts unfold like flowers before thee, opening to the sun above.

He closed his eyes, and it was as if God had taken hold of his hands, and if there was a more Calvinistic way of feeling a hymn, he'd never felt it.

Giver of immortal gladness, fill us with the light of day!

And that was it, and they ended together. It wasn't long, after all, this first recital piece. But by the way people stood and clapped, you'd have thought Mr. van Beethoven himself had performed the duet. So they had to stand together and bow, the way people did at piano recitals. Or actually, he bowed and Mallory curtsied—curtsied and tugged at her ear.

Chapter 15

Many waters cannot quench love,
neither can the floods drown it.
—SONG OF SOLOMON 8:7

*B*y the end of Mallory's Beethoven, Joan could tell she wasn't the only one in the audience dabbing her eyes with a tissue. Even after more than twenty years of concerts with students who graduated to become the world's finest musicians, she had never experienced anything quite like this. But for a moment she felt almost guilty, watching such tenderness between a girl and her grandpa. And the way they bowed together, with Mallory's awkward little curtsy that almost sent her tumbling onto her face. Joan smiled and cried at the same time, and it was okay.

The clapping gave her a chance to scan the back of the crowd as well, where Alison and Shane sat in the row with the sign that read "Reserved for Families with Children." Even from across the sanctuary she could see Alison bobbing slightly with little Erin Joan Nelson, undeniably the most perfect baby she had ever seen and as quiet as anyone in the audience. Alison caught her eye and smiled.

She turned back in time to see her wonderful pupil with her wonderful grandfather returning hand in hand to their seats, and she noticed something else: Gerrit Appeldoorn cleaned up quite nicely.

"No, no. You would have done the same thing." Gerrit raised his hand to deflect the praise. "Besides, you sit in on those lessons enough times, and the music just kind of rubs off on you, that's all."

Yeah, that's all. At least, that's all he wanted to say to Mrs. Leegsma at the moment. Styrofoam coffee cup in hand, he shuffled his way through the postrecital foyer crowd, nodding good morning to several people before he remembered this was not the fellowship hour after Sunday school. Same place, same folks, different time.

Joan Horton was holding court on the other side of the foyer, a bright light in the hubbub of farmers' wives in simple dresses and their farmer-husbands in their Mr. Rogers sweaters. Of course, he'd grown up with most of them, and so calling any Van Dalen neighbor "plain" was akin to the kettle calling the pot black, which wasn't very original but apt none-theless. His own gray sweater was thin at the elbows too, but there was no use throwing something out that still did a fair job of covering him up. No, they were good people, people who loved their Lord and who had made Gerrit plenty of Dutch *hutspot* and *boerenkool* stews for three full months after Miriam died. He would not forget that, though of course none of the charity food tasted half as good as what Miriam used to make. He knew better'n to say that out loud to anyone though. And he would not forget that these were the folks who showed up to help paint his barn and helped him move into the missionary cottage after Warney bought the farm and moved out from Dave Van der Bei's rental house, where he and Liz had started out.

They didn't do community barn raisings in Van Dalen or ride around in horse-and-buggy rigs like the people did in that Amish Harrison Ford movie (which he liked except for that one scene), but still they had their share of Norman Rockwell moments. Like when everybody packed into the Van Dalen Middle School auditorium for the all-community Christ-mas carol singing the first week of every December. Everyone busted their guts singing the good old hymns, though not so many newcomers knew the one Dutch song they saved for last. Or when the kids all met down at Koster Lake to swim on the day school let out in June. His dad had done it; so had he. Warney had even gone along with the tradition, though he wasn't much of a swimmer.

Traditions? Besides that, most people tended to leave their front doors unlocked, and the dairymen favored good, solid green John Deere tractors. Generally, it was easy to trust people like that. They were good people, even if they attended one of the other Reformed fellowships besides First Church. Those kids who couldn't find anyone in town to marry whom they weren't related to occasionally ventured back east to Calvin College or Dordt College, where they could still meet other kids from families with names like De Hoop or Van Rejn. That was a good thing. And they were all good tithing families at First Church, which helped when they'd wanted to add a modest CE wing with nice stained-glass windows a couple of years back. Nothing flashy, but paid for with dairy cash when milk prices had spiked for a couple months.

Despite all those good qualities, none of them stood out from the crowd the way this woman did, not one. And though he tried valiantly, he could not keep himself from staring any more than he could keep from nodding during the Reverend Jongsma's fine sermons. Shoot, what was it, anyway?

Not the way she dressed, though that of course was impeccable and East Coast, far as he could tell. He imagined she probably wore the same modest black dress to the Metropolitan Opera in New York City and blended in just as well there. The string of pearls was probably real too, but that didn't exactly cause her to stand out either. (Though he noticed Marilyn Leegsma was taking a pretty good look-see.)

So what was it? He decided that since he couldn't tell from such a distance, the only option would be to slip in a little closer. As he shuffled in her direction, he made sure he was armed and ready, just in case he got close enough to join her conversation.

Thanks for your encouragement to Mallory? No, Mal was a big girl and could certainly say that for herself. He stopped for a moment, one layer away in the elbow-to-elbow crowd, still debating what he would say to the piano teacher…but why in the world did he give a fig?

Before he could think it through, a young woman who looked a bit like Joan popped through the kitchen door, heading their direction. That would be Joan's daughter, Gerrit guessed, the one who was married to Shane Nelson, the new county agent. Gerrit had of course seen Nelson several times since he'd arrived in town, once at one of Warney's ag committee meetings, once at a water-rights hearing. Seemed like a decent sort of guy. Used two-dollar words for twenty-five-cent ideas, but that was what the guy was paid for. He probably couldn't help it.

Joan's daughter was probably a nice enough gal. Only in this case, she brought along with her a personal black storm cloud, just as real on her face as if it had been visible above her head, and every bit as severe as if her entire herd had run dry overnight. Didn't there used to be a comic-strip character like that? Somebody in Li'l Abner, if he remembered right. Storm cloud in tow, the daughter navigated past a half-dozen parents and whispered something in her mother's ear. Didn't wait to say, "Excuse me, please." Just leaned in, just like that, the way actors would do on television when someone interrupted the president to tell him the Russians had just launched a nuclear strike.

"Is there anything I can do?" Joan asked her daughter, but the young woman had already backed away and shook her head no.

"Call me." Joan was left standing with a half-cup of strong Dutch Douwe Egberts coffee, the Styrofoam marked with her lipstick. Her daughter waved before she pushed out the side door. And as the others drifted off, Gerrit found his chance.

"Trouble?" It wasn't the opening line he had practiced, but it would have to do. Joan turned back to him with a hint of a grateful smile.

"Oh, it's little Erin. She was sleeping so well through the concert, but then she started crying at the applause and now she won't stop."

"Hmm." Gerrit frowned in concern, but Joan shrugged and shook her head.

"My daughter, Alison, thinks she has a fever. I think maybe she's teething. It was time for them to take her home to bed anyway."

"Right. Teething. I think I remember that." He sipped his own coffee. "I mean, not me personally, just the kids. Warney especially, if I remember right. Had a good set of lungs when he was your little granddaughter's age. You could hear him all the way through the walls of the cry room over there."

They both laughed at that and then at the stories of raising kids and teaching fourth-grade Sunday school and driving kids to baseball practice and those kinds of things. Did they have that much in common? Maybe, maybe not. To tell the truth, though, her Randy sounded an awful lot like Warney, a couple years younger, sure, but a lot the same.

"He brought home birds with broken wings too?" She laughed again, and Gerrit couldn't remember a nicer sound. And she seemed to like hearing his stories about Warney, Gene, Bruce, and Patti when they were younger. She told him about Alison and Randy learning to water-ski at Great Sacka-something Lake, and he told her about the annual swim at Koster Lake. She listened and nodded, and it never occurred to Gerrit to talk to anybody else in the room until someone cleared her throat from behind where they were standing.

"Um, is it okay if I use the vacuum cleaner in here?" Agnes Oostdorp stood at the foyer entry with her commercial Hoover at the ready and her hair net firmly in place.

"Oh, dear, I'm sorry." Joan looked around too. "I didn't realize we were the last ones here."

"Holy smoke." Gerrit tossed his empty cup in the garbage.

"Yup." Agnes uncoiled her extension cord, tossing it to the carpet. "Warney said to tell you he'd bring his car around. I think they're waiting for you out front."

Then she fired up the vacuum as Gerrit and Joan headed for the front door.

Chapter 16

I don't know anything about music. In my line you don't have to.
—ELVIS PRESLEY

Anyone could tell the cows had been milked that day by looking at the line of pickups outside Karol's Koffee Kup at 7:00 a.m. Gerrit found his spot at the end of the line and left Gomer sputtering. The ice still hadn't cleared all the way from his windows, but this morning he could not bring himself to care.

"Hey, how's it going, Maestro?" the words greeted him even as the bell jingled on the front door. Ben Kootstra and Marty Middelkoop had the booth closest to the door. Ben did quite well on 120 acres over on Hoogsteen Road, while Marty helped operate his family's raspberry operation, one of the largest in the state. Gerrit slipped onto a counter stool and grunted an answer, something about never better.

Carol (she spelled her name with a K only on the sign) wisely didn't add to the other men's comments, just pulled down Gerrit's faded Seattle Mariners mug from the pegboard and filled it to the brim. No cream, no sugar, as hot as she could make it. He nodded to her silent question so she turned to prepare his two eggs, over hard, with toast and a single slice of bacon. Bacon only on Mondays, Wednesdays, and Fridays. He was cutting back on his cholesterol, not that it mattered a fig, but it seemed to make everybody happy that he appeared to be trying.

"I hear musicians are pretty temperamental." While the other fellows chuckled at Ben's quips, Gerrit wondered why he had come this morning, except that fixing his own eggs at home didn't sound like a good idea. Besides, he was out of eggs.

"Don't mind us." Marty wasn't giving up that easily. "We were just discussing milk prices and the latest Beethoven concerto."

"Yeah," added Ben, "we're going to miss you when you go on your ten-city concert tour, Gerrit."

More chuckles.

"Hey, you guys think it's a big joke." Ben was just warming up. "Me, I'm going to make a fortune. I've got a file full of grain delivery receipts with his signature. What do you think I can sell them for, about fifty bucks apiece? a hundred?"

When a dozen farmers joined in the joke, Gerrit knew he didn't have a chance. He finally forced a smile and picked up last July's *Ag Monthly*.

"You weren't even there last night, Ben," he fired back. "How do you know what happened?"

"You kidding? The wife was there. She came home in tears, said it was the sweetest thing she'd ever seen in her life, all on account of what you did. Very extremely sweet."

If he'd only known what would happen. Gerrit buried his face in the paper while Ben stood up and tapped his juice glass with a knife.

"Ben—" Gerrit started to object, but it was like standing in front of a rush of cows coming in to be milked. They had their minds made up that something was going to happen. So did Ben.

"No, that's okay, Gerrit. You don't need to be so modest." He raised his voice. "So did everybody hear what our own Gerrit Appeldoorn did last night?"

Ben didn't wait for the rest of the crowd to respond.

"Well, I'm sure it's going to be all over next week's *Sentinel*, but in case you weren't there, Maestro Appeldoorn blew the socks off everybody at the Van Dalen all-city piano recital with his rendition of Beethoven's Sixth Symphony."

"Ninth," Gerrit corrected him. It was the least he could do.

"Ninth Symphony, right." He looked back at Gerrit, who shifted his attention to an article about Russian grain exports. "Did I leave anything out, Sir Maestro?"

Gerrit burned his tongue on his coffee, so Ben continued.

"Oh yeah, it was a duet with his granddaughter Mallory. Let's all give him a hand."

Everyone applauded while Gerrit gave them the pleasure of tipping his cap. Oh, well. That would help them get all this good-natured ribbing out of their systems. Why had he ever decided to come into town this morning?

"Actually," said Ben, "I hear he's been taking lessons from that new piano teacher. Easier than asking her out on a date."

A couple of stray chuckles faded away as Gerrit closed his eyes and groaned. Not again.

"Ben, look. First of all…"

Gerrit crumpled the edges of his paper and tried without luck to keep his ears from flaming. Carol's eggs sizzled and popped on the grill. No one else said a word as Sheriff de Blom pushed open the door and looked around.

"Well, well," he said, his voice echoing through the room. "Did I just step into a funeral?"

"Not at all, Sheriff." Carol was quick to fill in the silence as she stepped forward with a coffee mug and a steaming glass carafe. "Come on in, have a seat. Glazed or chocolate today?"

⌣

Mallory almost couldn't keep from dancing as she scooped out another portion of Purina goat food for Lilbit, her cute little black-and-white pygmy goat. She added an extra dollop of feed to celebrate.

"So did you already know," she asked her goat, "or do we have to tell you?"

Mallory wasn't sure, so she climbed up on the edge of the wood railing to mount the little hand-lettered sign she'd made last night. A couple of thumbtacks, and—

"There you are."

Still chewing, Lilbit gazed up at her with its peculiar goat eyes. Would there be more to eat out of this deal?

"Well, since you can't read, I'll read it for you: 'I think I am expecting. My kids are due May 10.'"

So there. Mallory had made the sign last night at her 4-H meeting, after Mrs. Bolkenbaas had returned her goat with a smile and a thumbs-up. She told her Lilbit's weekend visit with Billy G, the Kroodsmas' goat, had been a busy one, and that five months from now they could probably expect kids.

But that wasn't her really good, good news. She'd been thinking about the really good, good news ever since the horrible-wonderful recital three days ago. Even Gina had agreed that this was a great idea. Maybe a God idea. Gina said they had those kinds of things in her church all the time, and why shouldn't Mallory have them in hers? Whether it was a God idea or not, Mallory knew she couldn't keep it to herself any longer.

"You in here, Mal?" Her grandfather stepped in with a shovel in hand, just like she knew he would. He wasn't really supposed to help her clean and care for her 4-H animals. But since Dad had told him he couldn't help with milking the cows on account of his health, what else was he supposed to do? He said he didn't want to watch any more episodes of *The Young and the Restless,* and she was pretty sure he was kidding. It was *Grandpa* who was restless, though not very young. The Geezers and the Restless. Anyway, how could she say no when he offered to help clean the goat pens every morning?

"I think your mom has oatmeal steaming up the kitchen. And one of the bowls has your name on it."

Mallory's tummy rumbled at the thought of breakfast, but this was her chance. She leaned on the little pitchfork she'd been using to clean stalls.

"Grandpa, do you think God answers prayer if we ask Him?"

Gerrit thought for a moment and squinted, even though there was really nothing to squint at. He just did that when he was thinking.

"Of course. Just not always the way we expect."

She nodded. Exactly.

"So if I tell you something, will you promise not to tell?"

"Well, sure, honey. I suppose. But what does that have to do with God answering prayer?"

"I prayed for special hands," she blurted out.

"Special hands?" He didn't get it, naturally.

"Hands like Mrs. Horton's. Hands that could play the piano. Gina told me that's what I should do."

"Well, I sure like Gina, don't get me wrong. But she goes to a different church."

"I know that. So does Mrs. Horton. But what I mean is, God didn't answer my prayer the way I expected. Just like you said. But He answered it, Grandpa."

"How's that?"

"I think He gave *you* the hands instead."

Grandpa didn't say anything this time, just kind of stood there, knee-deep in hay. So Mallory took a deep breath and went on to the Big Idea.

"So I have a deal for you, Grandpa. Don't say no until you think about it, okay?"

He nodded, but slowly, like a cow had kicked him in the head and he was deciding if he could see straight.

"I'll clean up the barn for the next ten years with no complaining if you'll trade places with me at piano lessons. Mrs. Horton wouldn't care. I'll tell her it's okay and everything."

"Oh, Mal." Finally he caught on, but he only smiled a little and shook his head. Not a good sign. He did that when he thought something was cute but ridiculous.

"I have it all figured out. You wouldn't have to pay her anything. You could just trade."

"And what would I have to trade?"

"You know, handyman stuff. You could recaulk the bathtub, fix a couple leaky faucets. She's always saying she needs help with that stuff, and the guy who rents her the house doesn't ever have time."

"Well, look, Mal, I would be happy to help someone who needs it, but—"

"But you said yourself that God doesn't always answer prayer the way we expect. I thought this would be a great deal for both of us. I'd get to spend more time with my animals, and you'd get to hang out with Mrs., er…"

By the color that crossed her grandfather's cheeks, something told Mallory she'd better not go there. But the damage was done, and he tossed the shovel to the side.

"I don't know where you get your crazy ideas, Mallory Ann." He turned to leave. "But that's one of your crazier ones. I'll tell your mother you'll be right in."

Mallory could have kicked herself.

"Oh, Lilbit!" She sighed and crossed her arms in disgust. "Maybe he would have said yes if I hadn't mentioned Mrs. Horton. I ruined it!"

Lilbit just wiggled her ears and flicked her tail at a stray fly.

*G*errit tapped his finger on the receiver as he waited for the message once more.

"Come on, come on."

"If this is an emergency, and you would like to leave a callback number for Dr. DeGroot, please press one…"

There. The vet's pager should be beeping again with Gerrit's number, and if it was one of those vibrator things, he ought to be getting a pretty good hip massage just about now. Unless of course he didn't have the pager turned on, or if he was off playing golf in Palm Springs with his buddies. Gerrit crossed his arms and bounced on his toes, waiting in vain for the phone to ring.

"Man, where's a vet when you need one? You'd think they understood that people might have an emergency once in a while. Talk about incompetent." He punched the number again, hung up on a pizza delivery service, and tried once more, this time a little more slowly.

"If you would like to leave a message for Dr. DeGroot, press two."

Gerrit punched two so hard his knuckle crackled.

"Listen, Charlie, I don't know where you are, but I sure could use some help here," he told the machine. "Turns out one of my heifers is having trouble delivering, and I think we're going to need to walk the calf out. Been more than six hours in stage-two delivery, and I see the little guy's front hooves peeking out every once in a while, but that's about it. It's"—he glanced at his watch—"five thirty, Friday. Would you get over here as soon as you can? I don't want to lose another one."

Or actually, Warney didn't want to lose another one. But Warney didn't know. Bad time for him and Liz to be out to dinner, some kind of Christmas banquet with one of Warney's buddies. You bet, kids, have a good time. No, you don't need to take the cell phone with you. Who needs to stay in touch all the time? I'll take care of the place, don't worry about a thing. Really. This heifer has been in labor for a few hours, but I'll just do a couple of crosswords and watch a rerun of *It's a Wonderful Life*. (For about the fifteenth time.) No reason to think the heifer won't be just fine.

And now this.

Bad time for Mallory to be sleeping overnight at her little girlfriend's house too, though he wouldn't have admitted it to anyone. Despite her age, she could have been a big help. But he could just imagine the call: "Hi, Mrs. Hortegas? Mallory's grandpa here. I'm going to have to come pick her up from your Christmas party sleepover. Yeah, she needs to help me deliver a calf."

Of course he couldn't do that. But why should he? He'd done this hundreds of times before. Who needed incompetent vets, anyway?

"Thanks a lot, Charlie." He slammed down the phone and headed for the door, but not before rummaging around under a pile of plastic buckets and feed catalogs stacked up in the corner of the living room. There. A quick slash of his pocket knife gave him a couple of nice, clean six-foot lengths of nylon cord. If he was going to do what he thought he was going to have to do, he would need them fairly soon.

He tossed the rope into a five-gallon former laundry-soap bucket before adding a generous dollop of yellow antibacterial dish soap from the squirt bottle under his sink. Next came the steaming hot water, which would probably cool by the time he made it to the barn, but, oh, well. He heard a knock at the front door just before the bubbles reached the top. Charlie, already? Maybe the guy wasn't so incompetent after all. But—

"Oh!" The last person he'd expected to see was Joan Horton.

"I'm sorry. " She shifted from foot to foot under the little porch roof, caught in the uncertain focus of the yellow bug light. This time she wasn't wearing her usual high heels or fancy blouse, though. Funny to see her in a pair of jeans, sneakers, and a faded New York Giants sweatshirt. "Looks like you're doing quite a load of dishes there."

Gerrit looked at the flecks of soapsuds on his hands, then realized she was looking over his shoulder through the front room all the way to the sink. The sink!

"Oh, yeah, right." He ran back to turn off the hot water, but by that time the suds had overflowed and created a small snowdrift on the floor.

"At least it will be clean," she called from the door. "But listen, I didn't want to interrupt you or anything. It's just that there was no one home at the big house, and I just realized today that Mallory forgot her books at her last lesson. Probably because you weren't there to remind her."

"Yeah, you bet." He kicked at the suds but made no attempt to clean them up. "I had a few things on my to-do list last week. And tonight I have a heifer needs help."

"Oh, of course. I won't keep you."

She stood at the front door with her piano books while Gerrit grabbed the bucket and sloshed toward the kitchen entry.

"Thanks for bringing 'em by," he hollered. " 'Preciate it."

"Actually, there is one other thing."

"Listen, can we talk about that, whatever it is, next week or something? I'm actually in a bit of a crisis here."

"I can see that."

He straddled the bucket as he walked out, bowlegged. "Do me a favor and pull the front door shut, would you? Just leave the books on the couch there, if you can find a clear spot. I'll make sure Mal gets 'em."

"Of course." She closed the door and followed him toward the barn, around the side of the cottage where she'd parked her Volvo. Tonight, though, he wasn't slowing down. He'd already lost enough time, messing with the bubble bath and trying to get a message to Dr. Dolittle. Only now it sounded as if she wasn't through asking questions. If that was true, her timing was a bit off.

"I was just curious about something, Gerrit. Mallory told me at her last lesson that you might be interested in taking piano instruction yourself. Is that true?"

What? He slowed to a crawl and looked over his shoulder. In the blue light from the buzzing overhead floodlight he could just make out the question in her dark eyes.

"She said that?"

"Also that you might be interested in trading handyman jobs for lessons."

As Gerrit tried to recall that conversation, she went on.

"Well, of course I wasn't sure if you had discussed it with her in detail or not. But then after what happened at the recital, I thought perhaps you had. So that's all. I just wanted to check with you personally."

"Sounds like something Mal might have cooked up."

He wasn't sure why he didn't just blow off the idea. Shoot, this had to be the craziest thing he'd ever heard. Even so...

"Perhaps," she admitted. "But I suppose now isn't the best time to discuss it."

"Yeah, okay." He simply agreed and started off for the barn once more, still gripping the steaming bucket with both hands. "But me, I'm just not very good at multi...whatever. You know, juggling more'n one thing at a time."

"Multitasking."

"That's it. I'm kind of a one-thing-at-a-time guy, so that's what I'm doing. Sorry 'bout that."

"I understand."

He wasn't so sure she did.

"Anyways, the vet's out, doesn't return his calls. Maybe if I knew how to e-mail him, eh? Either he skipped off to Hawaii for Christmas, or he's out on another call. And now we've got a dystocia to deal with."

"Pardon me if my Latin is a little rusty. You mean—"

"Dystocia. Tough calving."

As if on cue, a regular, high-pitched moo of the distressed mother-to-be drifted from the dark barn.

"That's her?" asked Joan, holding open the big door for him.

"Yup." When Gerrit hesitated, warm water slopped on his boots. Not that he minded. But Gerrit still wondered why she hadn't left yet. She'd delivered her music books.

"Thanks for stopping by," he began, "I appreciate your help, but—"

"That animal sounds as if she's in horrible pain. You're not thinking of doing this alone, are you?"

"Nobody else around." He pointed at the sad-looking old dog sniffing his feet. "And old Missy sure ain't much help. But I've delivered a few calves in my day."

"Let me help you." She looked as if she was searching for an excuse. "I...I watched my cat have kittens once, when I was a little girl."

Who was she kidding? Gerrit might have laughed out loud, but he didn't have time for this debate. And since he could use an extra hand, he shrugged and stepped inside the musty barn with the dog tottering along after him.

"Come on, then. But I guarantee this'll be nothing like your cat having kittens."

⌒

"Here comes the good part." Randy kept his eyes open for the classic movie's next scene, though he had watched it at least once every Christmas season of his adult life and could quote every character, every scene, every line. He could even add that little bit of Jimmy Stewart twang if the audience called for it. People used to laugh at his impressions, Jimmy Stewart and John Wayne, mostly actors like that.

There would be no audience this year, however, not here in his mother's cold, empty living room with only a dark, gaping hole where the fire should have been.

Good thing nobody had invited themselves over, though. He didn't want to have to pick last week's socks up off the floor or shave a week's stubble off his face. No time for that. Mary Bailey, played by Donna Reed, was calling the entire town of Bedford Falls to help. Her husband George, played by Jimmy Stewart, was in trouble, big trouble. And wouldn't you know it, even the cranky bank commissioner was going to help. Just watch.

From his place on the flowered couch, Randy stuffed another handful of chips into his mouth, wiped away a tear, and shook his head. This was out of control, he knew that much. Good thing no one else was here to see him bawling over a rerun of *It's a Wonderful Life*. A very good thing. He didn't need Pastor Tim to talk to him about being a melancholic or to remind him how much God loved him and that he had no reason to feel the way he did. He already knew all that, thank you. And if his faith were where it should have been, instead of buried, he wouldn't be so afraid of everything. He knew that, too.

The phone rang in the other room, and he let it ring. Probably Pastor Tim asking him over to another Bible study or Mom telling him he could still visit them for Christmas or a telemarketer trying to sell him another home-refinance loan. He would call them back, just not now. This was the good part.

But where did these tears come from? Ever since he'd lost his last two jobs, his real life had frozen over like the sidewalk outside. Frozen stiff, kind of like having nerve damage. Like holding a hand over a live flame, knowing it was burning but not feeling a thing. If this had been an actual life, he might have had actual feelings. But this was weird and getting weirder. Now only the pretend seemed really real. Only Bedford Falls in the movie seemed like a good place to live.

So there was George, running to the bridge in the snow where he'd once thought of jumping off into the icy waters. "Why, you're worth more dead than you are alive." (Old Mr. Potter's line when he heard about George's life insurance policy.)

Well, there was George, yelling for help, trying to get the attention of his goofball apprentice guardian angel, Clarence. Or Clarence's boss, for that matter. There he was at the bridge railing, desperate, that wild look on his face.

"I wanna live, God," said Randy, pointing at the television like a director cueing up lines. "Please, God, I wanna live."

"I wanna live, God," echoed Jimmy Stewart. "Please, God, I wanna live."

Randy glanced at the light snowfall outside and shivered at the chill. The movie snow stopped. He could say the line about wanting to live; he had it memorized like the rest of the movie.

He just wished he could mean it.

Chapter 18

One hundred percent of the shots you don't take don't go in.
—WAYNE GRETZKY

O kay, shine that light over here so I can see what I'm doing."
Joan did what she was told, but she could hardly look. This wasn't anything like the time Amadeus had her kittens. (Never mind that Amadeus had been a girl cat with a boy name.) But if one could be horrified and fascinated at the same time, Joan was. Gerrit was up to his elbows in the poor bellowing cow, doing his best to find out what was wrong.

"The little guy is trying to come out a little sideways," he grunted. "But it shouldn't be this tough."

Joan closed her eyes and shivered at the thought. *A little sideways?*

"Obviously a man speaking," she whispered and tried to stroke the glistening chocolate hide of this struggling young animal. The heifer's nostrils blew vapor like a steam engine, and her big eyes bulged in breaking waves of panic and pain. Occasionally she struggled against both the constraining halter that kept her standing in place and the unceremonious way her tail had been tied up out of the way. While it had been a long time and the circumstances a little different, the basics were still the same, and Joan could clearly sympathize.

"I know, dear," she cooed. "It's no fun. But this'll be over before you know it."

"What's that?" Gerrit reached deeper. "Hey, watch the light!"

Considering where he was at the moment, Joan wasn't sure why he needed a spotlight. But she had to admit shadows fell deeply in the hay-strewn corner stall. This part of the barn only featured a half-dozen lone bulbs hanging here and there from the high ceiling, dimmed and deco-rated by a generous seasoning of flyspecks. No one had thought much of the need for extra task lighting in this makeshift birthing center. A flash-light would have to do.

"Okay! I've got one leg," he counted, straining against the bulk of the young heifer. This was, of course, the heifer's first experience with such a thing, and she struggled mightily. "And…I think there's the nose. Good, now hand me that rope. Be sure to wash your hands in the disinfectant before you touch it."

"You're not going to pull it out by the nose?" Joan still had no clear idea what this farmer was up to. He chuckled.

"No ma'am. We'll put a couple of hitches around each ankle—actu-ally one below the ankle, the other above—and then just walk him out into the world. You'll see."

By this time Joan wasn't all that sure she *wanted* to see, but it was too late to back out, too late to do anything but follow his instructions. And it was probably a good thing. Gerrit would have had a tough time with this all by himself. Finally, he managed to loop one end of the rope around the calf's foreleg, then one around the other.

"You're sure this is going to work?" When Joan's head felt a little light, she grabbed the top of a rough half-wall, the side of the pen. Gerrit didn't notice. In fact, he was sweating like a pig concentrating on his task. Kind of like building a ship in a bottle, and then trying to get it back out.

"Need some more of that jelly." He pointed with his nose. "Here, squirt some around my elbows."

She squared up her shoulders and did what she was told. The poor cow—make that *heifer*—bellowed and bawled and thrashed more than ever.

"You'd think there was a better way to do things than this." Joan was thinking of the whole birth process, the pain, the fright this creature had to be experiencing.

"Believe me, if I knew of a better way, I'd be happy to try it."

By that time he had disentangled himself and held the end of one of the ropes for her.

"So here's what we're going to do." He took his own rope and stood by. "On my signal we're going to pull, but not both at once. First me, then you. Upward, like this." He showed her the angle he wanted.

"Once we see shoulders, we start pulling down, kind of like an arc, okay?"

She nodded and swallowed. She had just driven over to deliver Mallory's music practice book, hadn't she? And now she was about to—

"All right, PULL!" he yelled, and the seesaw began, first Gerrit, then her, and back. They leaned into their tug-of-war rhythm until the glistening tips of tiny hooves showed themselves, followed by the spindly forelegs, which Joan was sure would break at the pressure they must have been feeling. So this was "walking" the calf out, but she had little time to wonder.

Pull and rest, then pull again, but not too hard and not too lightly either.

All of that must have taken at least a half-hour, perhaps longer, but Joan had so focused on the rhythm of the contest that it might as well have been an hour or two or three. It didn't matter. When they rested, she could not take her eyes off Gerrit's. Under the circumstances he didn't avoid her gaze either, only took a breath and began pulling once more. His expression told her there was no time for rest, and she mirrored his efforts without a word.

Pull, wait, pull.

The New York Giants sweatshirt was ready for the ragbag anyway. No matter. She found a clean spot on her shoulder to wipe the sweat from her forehead. Wait and pull. Finally they had a nose, black and quivering.

"We're getting close now." It was the first thing he'd said in several minutes. With three more pulls, the tiny shoulders finally twisted forth.

"Watch it there, little fella." When Gerrit reached out to cradle the limp calf, Joan did the same. Their hands linked beneath the newborn, and their noses nearly touched. Once more Joan could not look away. The rest of the little calf slipped out with a final heave and a surprised bellow from the mother.

"You've had a rough time of it, eh?" He knelt over the glistening brown bundle of calf. Joan's heart dropped when it didn't move, didn't respond. The heifer turned to see, her tongue flicking.

"Is he…?" Joan's eyes filled with tears. All that work.

Gerrit didn't answer, just held up a hand for her to be quiet. He rested a hand on the little body's chest, just behind the front legs, still attached to their ropes.

"I can't feel a heartbeat," he whispered, and for a moment panic overtook his face. Joan bent toward the calf's face and nearly broke down. Everything looked so perfect—the nose and ears, even the little eyes, staring at her vacantly. Without thinking she reached out and gently touched the eye—and it blinked.

"Did you see that!" She couldn't keep her voice down, and yes, he had.

"All right." He returned instantly to his command mode. "Throw me that towel. I'm going to clear the airway. You rub the back. Let's get this little guy breathing."

Joan sprang to her task, rubbing the calf's back, patting it gently, massaging it the way she'd seen people give back massages in airports.

"Breathe, little guy. Breathe."

Meanwhile, Gerrit took a stem of straw and tickled the calf's nostril. He didn't need to explain what he was attempting when they were both greeted by an enormous gasp and a wonderful sneeze.

"That's it!" Joan laughed and had to give up her massage when the calf began wobbling toward its mother. From that point on, all they could do was release the halter and watch. The mother cow seemed to know exactly how to clean and feed her newborn.

"Do you ever get tired of this?" she wondered aloud. "Watching this kind of miracle?"

"Never." He shook his head. "I...I get to thinking that some of the best things the world's ever seen have happened in a stable."

"I guess they have." She smiled again, and this time her eyes were tinged with fatigue.

So they stood there for a few minutes longer as the new mother nursed her Christmas calf. Joan mentioned that her Randy had sent her a postcard saying he'd been looking for another part-time job, that Alison's baby was already sitting up and pulling down Christmas decorations. But what about Christmas in Van Dalen?

Well, as always, Bruce and his family were visiting for the week after Christmas, which was good. Gene and Nancy were celebrating with her parents in Tampa this year. Patti and Eric still weren't sure. With kids so spread out it was tough to build traditions. At least *Sinterklaas* had been on time. She'd seen it, right? Well, he always came riding into town on a white horse on the Eve of St. Nicholas (three weeks before Christmas Day), and one year Gerrit's own father had even played the part. Gerrit had been about five at the time. Oh, and this fellow was dressed as the bishop saint, not in red, and was certainly not to be confused with the American Santa Claus.

"That's a lovely tradition." Steam rose from the animal's back, just as it did from Joan's ruined sweatshirt. Missy thunked her tail at them from her spot in the hay. And for a fleeting, unreal moment, Joan could not think of a time since she had moved to Van Dalen when she had felt happier. Here in a cold barn.

"Yeah, well. Good things happen in December sometimes. Thanks for the help." He avoided her gaze this time as he picked up his bucket, as if they had not just spent the evening wrestling new life from such a reluctant womb. "Not bad for a city girl."

"City girl, huh? I told you I'd watched my cat have kittens. And I think perhaps I was sent here to help you, Mr. Appeldoorn."

"Hmm."

She'd said too much and knew it immediately. Because he turned serious as he nodded, just before he seemed to remember something.

"About those lessons?"

What had she been thinking? As if she were visiting the farm country, recruiting new pupils! She considered the question she had come to ask him, and then she knew how out of place it would sound. Not now, and especially not after all this.

"I'm sorry. I really shouldn't have brought it up." She washed her hands in the bucket and dried off with a stiff old towel that, judging from the aroma, had probably been well used as a goat blanket.

"Aw, don't apologize."

But she did. She looked down at her hands and arms. The goat blanket had rubbed her skin a bright ruddy red, like sandpaper. Certainly uncomfortable, but at this point it didn't matter anymore.

"It was probably just one of those things that Mallory…" She searched for the words to make that now horribly awkward idea go away. "I suppose you know how Mallory seems to get those ideas."

"Oh, I know."

"But I'm sure you're not interested, and I understand."

There. End of subject. That would give him an honorable way out.

"Let me think about it, okay?"

"Pardon?" She folded the towel and set it on a hay bale.

"I mean, is that all right, to think about something?" He seemed as if he honestly wanted to know.

"Of course it's all right," she stammered. "Very certainly. I mean, yes. No hurry."

"Good. I'll let you know then."

Behind them, the new mother cow mooed, low and content, and it might have been nice to linger there for just a few minutes more. But

Gerrit opened the door for her as they left the barn, and they stepped back into a fresh tingle of cold December mist just in time to see a pair of head-lights bouncing up the drive. That would be Liz and Warney, and Liz rolled down her window as they pulled up.

"Is that you, Joan?"

Joan stepped into the light.

"I, ah, just stopped by to drop off some books for Mallory." She brushed at her sweatshirt. "They're in the little house. And then—"

"And then she helped me deliver a calf," put in Gerrit. "She makes a pretty good vet's assistant."

"You're kidding." Liz stared, eyes wide, and flapped her lower jaw a couple of times. "I mean…no, really?"

Warney looked over with the same expression, as if E.T. had just walked out of their barn. Joan could only smile.

"I'd best be getting home." Joan turned back to her car. "Merry Christmas."

Once more the cow mooed.

Chapter 19

Forrest Gump: What's my destiny, Mama?
Mrs. Gump: You're gonna have to figure that out for
yourself. Life is like a box of chocolates,
Forrest. You never know what you're gonna get.
—from *Forrest Gump* (1994)

Okay, Miriam." Gerrit paced back and forth across the orange and brown rag rug in his living room. "You think it's a crazy idea, don't you?"

Dr. Laura, the radio talk-show queen, would probably tell him he needed to take responsibility for his decisions or that he needed professional counseling to bring closure to his sixteen-year-old grief. Probably both.

Closure? He hated that word, as if Miriam would be put in a box and closed away like last month's Christmas decorations. The way her body had been boxed away. No, not closure. Anything but closure. *Coping* was a little better, maybe because that seemed closer to what he actually went through each morning. He coped. He would cope again tomorrow. And he would still have to cope until the day he died.

Of course, he had dutifully proceeded through all the stages the grief books from the church library and the Van Dalen Boekhandel said he would go through. There had been shock and denial and anger and bargaining and all the rest. Some happened in the right order, the way the books said they would happen. Some didn't.

After sixteen years, though, he had learned to cope. Most people would say that sixteen years was a long time to mourn the loss of someone you loved the way he had loved Miriam. So he didn't break down crying in public anymore. He didn't try to bargain her back. He didn't even pound the walls and ask God, "Why?" When he thought about it, somehow it didn't seem respectful to keep repeating a question he knew did not come with an answer. And besides, he'd bruised his knuckles more than once doing that.

Oh, and he couldn't lose himself in hard labor anymore, thanks to Dr. Eubanks and Warney. That had been a good one. When it got too hard, escape to the barn and attack something with a pitchfork. Like hay! These days he had been reduced to pacing and chatting with the portrait they'd had taken two years before Miriam died, when the Watson Photography people had come up from Bellingham to do a church photo directory.

Gerrit supposed that if Reverend Jongsma were a fly on the wall, he would raise his eyebrows and wonder. After all, talking to his dead wife's portrait wasn't exactly in line with Reformed theology. But then again, Reverend Jongsma hadn't lost his wife. And more than anything, Gerrit wished there was a way to know: Would Miriam have anything against his taking piano lessons from a widow lady?

Closer to home he imagined the guys at the Kup razzing him even more. If they called him "Maestro" after Mallory's piano recital, what would they say if they found out what he was thinking now?

"Get a grip," he scolded himself. He was the one who had taught the "Decision Making and the Will of God" Sunday-school class, and he was the church elder who had recited portions of the Belgic Confession as part of his presentation. But that was while Miriam was still with him, so he had a good excuse for being confused now about God's will. Of course, he still remembered the opening lines of article 13: *"We believe that this good God, after he created all things, did not abandon them to chance or fortune but leads and governs them according to his holy will, in such a way that nothing happens in this world without his orderly arrangement."*

All true, without a doubt. And at the time it had seemed enough, as if the pronouncement of those old words (from 1561, no less) should have been enough for anyone wondering about divine providence. But though he still believed it with all his heart, since then he'd had to admit there were times when he wondered: Couldn't God give the elect a few more clues about His orderly arrangement? A few more hints? And it occurred to Gerrit as he carved a trail into his little rug that his dear deceased wife, from her perspective, now understood a whole lot more than he once professed to know about God's will.

"All right then." He stopped pacing and looked out the window. "But not *instead* of Mallory. *Because* of her. See, if I do this, maybe that'll help her to not give up. But it's going to have to be done quietly."

At least that would be scriptural, he thought. *As in, "We beseech you, brethren…that ye study to be quiet, and to do your own business, and to work with your own hands" First Thessalonians 4:10-11. Good.* He repeated the verse over and over to himself that afternoon, then as he met up with Mallory in front of where Gomer was parked. He drove quickly to town and knocked on Joan Horton's front door. He checked his watch once more just to be sure.

"She always told me to walk right in for my lesson," Mallory told him.

He shook his head. "Not my first time. Do you have all our practice books?"

"Grandpa, you already asked me that. I think we're early."

As long as no one else saw them. He looked up and down Delft Street just to be sure. But as far as anyone else could tell, he was just delivering his granddaughter to her usual lesson. No one would have a clue. The door opened to show Joan Horton's smiling face.

"Oh, you're early! Come in, come in. Did you walk from some-where?"

She couldn't see Gomer, parked safely around the corner behind a holly hedge. Better not to give the guys at the Kup more ammunition. And better to tell her right away.

"Uh, we're just over there." He pointed quickly. "And listen. I'll do this, but you should know a couple of things before we begin."

"Oh, of course." She looked at him uncertainly. "But…"

"First, Mallory has agreed to be here whenever I would take a lesson, so you don't need to worry about any…er, awkwardness. She can bring her homework or her music and study while we're playing."

"I see. That's thoughtful of her. But I've never had any concerns or problems in that area. And I've had quite a few lessons with college students, after all. Female and male."

"Good. So you get what I'm saying. Second, I'd be willing to work out a fair swap with you, the way you said. One hour of lessons for one hour of maintenance work around your house. Even trade. Plumbing, carpentry, painting…whatever you need."

"Oh." She pondered his offer for a second. "Well, goodness knows I do need work done around the house, and I would welcome your help. I'm not very enthusiastic about plumbing, for one thing."

"Okay. And third, I'm not going to play in public or for any recitals or anything like that. I've done my one and only recital already."

"So what about autographs?"

"Autographs?" He stared at her, trying to figure out her East Coast humor, but she didn't give a clue. "Well, I'm just coming here because I kind of like the music, and I want to learn how to play a couple of tunes. So this is just between you and me, and if I want anybody else to know I'm taking piano lessons, I'll let 'em know myself."

"Anything else?" She stepped back and held open the door. "Or would you like my lawyer to review the confidentiality clause of your contract?"

"A contract." He stepped inside. "Maybe that would have been a good idea in New York. Not here in Van Dalen."

"Gerrit." She laughed softly as they came inside. "I can never tell when you're pulling my leg."

"You're not so bad at leg-pulling yourself."

"So how is the calf doing then?"

"Well, he came into the world with a few more pounds than most any other calf I've seen. So I have no idea how we managed to yank him out of there. And he's always hungry, right, Mal?"

"I have to feed him a huge bottle three times a day." She settled into the corner chair with a copy of a *Clubhouse* magazine, the first of a sub-scription she'd just received from her folks for her tenth birthday. "And if I give him my finger instead, he just about sucks the skin off."

They all laughed.

"But I don't mind taking care of calves half as much as pra—"

Mallory must have remembered where she was and hid behind her magazine. Joan chuckled again, and this time she seemed more at ease in her own world behind the keyboards.

"You were going to say 'practice,' weren't you? Well, no one really cares for practice. It's what we can accomplish *with* that practice. So now, Mr. Appeldoorn, *Gerrit,* let's see what *we* can accomplish."

He pointed a finger to his chest, as if to ask, "Me?"

"That *is* why you came this afternoon, is it not? Now, please seat yourself on the piano bench over there, and we'll get started. Would you like to begin at the beginning, or do you already know all those fundamentals?"

Here goes. He sat down where Mallory usually sat while Mallory's teacher, *his* teacher, reached over his shoulder and opened up the *Alfred's Basic Piano* book to page 50.

"I think I understand how to play from the middle C position and these harmonic things," he told her, "but I was wondering if you could show me how to play from the key of G."

She smiled and shook her head. "You are full of surprises, aren't you? Here I thought you were just sitting in the back of the room, reading the paper or dozing, almost like Mallory is doing now."

"I wasn't dozing," he defended himself.

"See? I think you've been paying attention to Mallory's lessons a little more carefully than I suspected."

He shrugged. "They make sense to me."

Unfortunately, everything Joan Horton said made sense in a maddening, unorthodox way. Even if she went to a different church, and he probably didn't agree with her theology, he found himself telling her more.

"You're sure you've never played before?" she asked.

Gerrit studied the keyboard for a moment, dipping a fingertip into a well of memories that had lain silent and untouched for…how long? But when he stirred them, they all blended together—memories of Warney, Gene, Bruce, and Patti as young kids. Memories of growing up in the same house where he and Miriam had raised their family. Memories of his Dutch grandmother, who held on to traditions so fiercely and insisted on only speaking Dutch to her grandchildren. Memories of that summer. That memory finally floated to the surface bit by bit.

"One summer my Oma Lysbet, my grandmother, she made me a deal." He grinned at the recollection. "I thought I wanted to try the piano. So she said she'd teach me a few songs if I learned more Dutch."

"Sounds like a good bargain." Joan smiled. "Did you learn any?"

"*Ja-wel*," he replied. "*Een klein beetje.* A little bit. Not so much piano, though."

Joan waited for him to explain, and something made him continue.

"She died that fall. But I remember how she used to play. She would just throw her head back and belt out these old Dutch hymns like nobody was looking but God Himself. She had a wonderful voice, clear as a bell. Guess I never forgot that."

What am I telling her all this for? Gerrit almost pinched himself. But Joan just nodded slowly, as if she understood. As if she could.

"I would have liked to have met her," she said. "I'm sure she was proud of her Steinway."

Gerrit nodded. "I used to think every time I touched the old thing, a little bit of Oma would rub off on me. As if I would be able to play like her. Silly, huh?"

"Maybe not so silly." Joan seemed to consider the thought for a moment. "I think I understand."

If she did, that would make one of them. In any case, he'd said too much. And since he had come for a purpose, not to reminisce, he straightened up and rested his hands just over the keys, the way he'd seen her demonstrate so many times for Mal and the way he'd seen in the Alfred book.

The bubbles. Remember the bubbles.

"Okay," he told her. "I'm ready. Teach me something."

Chapter 20

Don't play what's there, play what's not there.
—MILES DAVIS

*J*oan leaned on the keys as she commanded her fingers to play faster and faster, faster surely than even Rachmaninoff had intended or was proper. But this time she didn't mind, just as she didn't care about the soft snow falling outside, filling up her yard and covering the rhododendron plants. None of that mattered today. She still had two hours until Gerrit and Mallory were supposed to show for their lesson. No one else was scheduled in between.

Two hours to pray for Randy, to beg God for her son.

Yes, he still had his choice, his free will—a commodity on which Joan had learned to place such a high premium. So Randy returned her calls or didn't. He was going to church or he wasn't. He would get another job or he wouldn't. Ever since he was a little boy he had always been bright, quite intelligent when he applied himself. He would land on his feet.

But if that was so, why was she still losing sleep about it?

Losing sleep and losing money. Because at least one thing was predictable about Randy these days. He always cashed her checks, which was fine. They'd even had a chance to chat—briefly—just after Christmas, though he'd sounded disturbingly groggy and said he had to run after only ten minutes. Don't worry, Mom, I'm fine. So now what?

She leaned her head and swayed slightly, letting her eyelids droop as she reached for the familiar notes of Rachmaninoff's Concerto no. 1 in F-sharp Minor. If only her life was as orderly as her music, or as lovely. Or even as orderly as the yards in Van Dalen, each one now buttoned up with neat white Styrofoam vent covers along the foundations and white Styrofoam faucet covers to protect against the freezing January winds that were sure to come any day now. Surely Van Dalen homes and churches would weather the winter just fine, no matter how cold it got, and no matter if they were blasted by a northeaster from the Fraser River Valley this year or simply subjected to the usual forty-degree, four-month dark rain that kept everyone indoors until April 1. Either way, they were protected from the unending gloom everyone had warned her about.

She supposed that was one of the things that had charmed her about this town, about these people. They were orderly, lovely, good, and buttoned up. Unlike her, they were prepared for whatever came and were resigned to the fact that God was firmly in control. They had nary a twinge of guilt. Of course, she knew enough to recognize that this outlook on life had not sprung from a vacuum but from the pulpits and pews of the dozen Dutch Reformed fellowships sprinkled throughout the town. From the little glass-enclosed reader board in front of Second Church: "All that the Father giveth me shall come to me," John 6:37. Even from the big sign in front of the Bloemendaal Nursery at the end of Main Street: "God's will is the final cause of all things, even the smallest details of life."

The quote made her think of Gerrit Appeldoorn, the handsome dairyman who could very well have said the same thing. And though he carried himself with the same blessed assurance as so many other Calvinists she had met, he also displayed a hint of wildness and a touch of sadness that seemed to keep his nose from pointing too high. She suspected he wasn't as rigid as he had first seemed, which could be a good thing. But beyond the obvious fact that they had both lost spouses, they were really not at all alike; they held very little in common, and...this second movement was much harder than the first. Finishing was harder than starting.

But she launched into it with a feverish, blistering attack that could only help clear her mind and help her not worry. After all, that's what playing usually did for her, since playing and praying were separated by only a single letter and usually brought her to the same place at the feet of her Savior.

Only not today, no matter how hard she played or how desperately she prayed. Her fingers fumbled across the Andante she'd breezed through perfectly dozens of times before, so she stopped, backed up, and tried again. But this time names and faces kept popping up to distract her, so she decided to dispatch them with a prayer. For Randy, her prodigal: protection. For Mallory, her reluctant student: perseverance and help with discouragement. For…Gerrit? She still wasn't sure what this simple, complicated farmer was looking for. In any case, he wasn't going away, and neither were the others.

They doggedly followed her through crescendos and counterpoints, across the undulating, measured landscape of harmonies where she had hoped to lose them in a forest of melody. Still they refused to drop the chase, so she played faster and faster, jumping across rests and arpeggios until her fingers knotted up and crossed themselves and she gave up the breathless escape.

Enough. She dropped her forehead to her hands, trying to catch her breath but still mindful of any stray tears that would mar the keyboard. What was that for? The midafternoon church bells sounded from Second Reformed's bell tower, sure of themselves, sure of the time, clear and true. Just like their builders. Mallory and her grandfather would arrive soon, but she still had time to clean herself up and straighten her hair. After all, she was the cheerful, sophisticated music professor who had all the answers and who was supremely confident in her abilities. *Professor* Joan Horton.

Joan wondered how she had become so skilled at convincing everyone around her that she was just as orderly, lovely, and good as they. Because she was certain now of one thing: She was not now, and had never been, good enough. Never the good-enough wife. Look at Jim. Never the good-enough mother. Look at Randy. Never… She pulled a handful of tissues from the box beside her and cried for the fraud she had become.

≈

Gerrit hit the playback button once more on his new CD player so the music scrambled back to the opening notes of Grieg's Concerto in A Minor. Too bad the Norwegian couldn't slow it down a little so Gerrit could follow along. But he'd already been through all the "Yankee Doodles" and "Old MacDonalds" he could take, and Joan had told him at their last lesson that he'd learned more in a few weeks than most students could in a year. Things like harmonic and melodic intervals, beginning dynamics, and basic meter. And how to tell the difference between *crescendos* and *diminuendos*. He tried not to practice when Mallory was home, so as not to remind her of her own struggles, except that when he worked at the piano two or usually three hours a day, keeping it secret was a constant challenge.

"From the top." Grieg started his concerto once more while Gerrit made his own attempts to follow along with the John Thomson *Modern Course for the Piano* book Joan had given him. His efforts didn't quite match the CD, of course, but Gerrit didn't mind. And once in a while he was even able to hit a simple chord that sounded like the master, sort of.

"Hey, not bad, eh, Missy?" He gave the old dog at his feet a good scratch behind the ears before waving a free hand as if he were riding a rodeo bronc. But he quickly recoiled his hand and snapped the CD player off when the doorbell rang. Rick, the curious UPS delivery man, made a point of peering inside the living room before he handed over a small package of cosmetics stuff for Liz.

"Nice playing in there, Mr. Appeldoorn." He wore the kind of silly grin seen only on guys who had survived the holiday rush and now wore shorts in January. "Sounds like you're just about ready for prime time. I hear that—"

"Thanks, Rick." Gerrit handed back the clipboard with his initials. "Love to chat, gotta run."

"Oh, you bet. Keep it up, sir." Rick waved his clipboard and dashed down the slushy gravel path to his idling brown truck. "Too bad I can't keep this original signature. You know how things like this from famous people get valuable after a few years. I hear a signed guitar from Paul McCartney got auctioned off for—"

Shoot. Gerrit closed the door and imagined Rick the delivery guy telling everyone in the north county that he'd just come from a piano concert at the Appeldoorn farm. But that wasn't what Gerrit had in mind when he'd agreed to take lessons from Joan Horton. At least that's what he tried to explain to her a couple hours later, toward the end of his four o'clock lesson.

"I know you said performing was important," he lowered his voice so Mallory wouldn't hear from across the room. "But—"

"Don't think of it as 'performing,' Gerrit."

"I'm still not playing in the spring recital."

"And I'm just not sure how you're going to explain it to…her." This time it was Joan's turn to lower her voice as she glanced across the room. "You know how much we've had to…well, you know what I mean."

Right. He knew how much they'd had to lean on Mal to even agree to play in the upcoming spring recital. Maybe because it was still over three months away. He just prayed his own argument wouldn't be turned on him so quickly.

"I know you're concerned about playing in public." She only paused for a moment before going on. "But remember what I said about just 'sharing' the music with people who know you? That's what I tell all my students. We share our music because we can't keep it to ourselves. Music is for everyone, not just a chosen few. Just like the gospel, I suppose."

"Hmm." Gerrit ran a hand through his hair and thought about letting it pass. But no. Not again. Perhaps it was time to get everything out in the open, to find out what this piano teacher *really* believed, to make sure she didn't pass along any more heresy to his granddaughter. "That's another place where you and I disagree."

"Pardon me?" She looked confused, as if she hadn't realized she'd just challenged him.

"You said music is like the gospel, that it wasn't for just a chosen few."

"Ohh." She nodded and pressed her lips together. "I didn't mean to—"

"No, no, that's all right. You, your church has its own beliefs, I understand that. You're not Reformed."

"No, I'm afraid not." She smiled. "Though in a town like Van Dalen sometimes I wish I were. At least I imagine I'd find a few more doors open to me if I weren't such a minority."

"You make it sound as if you're discriminated against."

"Oh no, not at all. People have been more than friendly to me. They've been lovely. No, it's not that."

"What then?"

"Well, I suppose in a very small way it's like..." She seemed to grasp for the words. "Like being a missionary to Africa, being the only outsider."

"Oh, so you see yourself as a missionary to Van Dalen. Here for a one-year assignment."

"No, no, no. That's not what I meant to say at all. It's just that I feel like a complete outsider sometimes. I don't have a Dutch name. I don't have the little Dutch windmill on my front lawn or even the kissing-

Dutch-children-with-wooden-shoes statues. My car doesn't have a window sticker for Calvin College. And I believe..." She paused for a moment and changed course. "No, actually perhaps you should tell me first what *you* believe."

Chapter 21

Too many pieces of music finish too long after the end.
—IGOR STRAVINSKY

"What *I* believe?" Gerrit could certainly unload his considerable truckload of theology on the unsuspecting piano teacher. He hadn't exactly come to the piano lesson prepared for this kind of thing. But..."I thought you already knew. Didn't you say you studied us in college?"

"Well, yes, a little." She paced in front of her bookshelf, the one with *Principles of Debate, or How to Win Any Argument.* "It's just that most Calvinists I've met don't really know what they believe, and if they do, they tend to contradict themselves."

His raised eyebrows must have signaled her to back up. The metronome still kept time with their parrying, back and forth, and no one made a move to stop it.

"Not you," she stammered. "Not necessarily, of course. I only meant that—"

"Give me an example."

She swallowed hard. "All right, then. We were talking about missionaries. Does your church have any?"

"We support nine families."

"Good. But at the same time you believe that Christ died only for the elect, and that God decides who are the elect and who are not, and that nothing you can humanly do will change whether you are elect or unelect. Am I right?"

"I would have put it a little differently, but basically right. So far."

"So if I understand correctly, what's the point?"

"Of missionaries? The point is that God is sovereign, and that it's not up to me to decide."

"No. The point is that some Calvinists say they believe Calvin's Five Points, but in their hearts they know the Bible is true and they send out missionaries anyway."

"Oh, come on." Gerrit shook his head. "I can tell you don't get it."

"That's why I asked."

"And there's a difference between asking and listening."

Gerrit might just as well have slapped her across the face, and he knew it instantly.

"Look, I'm sorry. That was out of line. I…didn't mean to get personal." He started to rise from the bench. "Fact, I shouldn't have said anything about all this, and we should have stuck to music. It's none of my business *what* you believe. I think you're a nice person, and you're obviously a good teacher, who…"

"Who doesn't believe the right things." She finished his sentence and straightened out the perfectly straight stack of music books in front of her face. Gerrit thought he could see a slight quiver of her lower lip. Not a good sign. He remembered Miriam getting that look. If he could have apologized any more, he would have, and if he could remove the size-thirteen foot from his mouth, he would have done that, too. All he could do now, though, was bail out. And quick.

"My time is just about over anyway. I'll just shut up and get a few things checked off your to-do list while you two have your lesson."

He glanced over at Mallory, who was following them with the wide-eyed look of a marathon Ping-Pong spectator. Maybe it hadn't been such a good thing they'd swapped lesson times this week.

"I think you should visit each other's churches," Mallory told them as she approached the piano for her turn. She looked from one adult to the other; for a moment neither would volunteer the first word. "That way maybe you'd understand each other better, whatever it is you're arguing about."

Finally Gerrit broke the silence. "I've been to a Methodist church before," he blurted.

"When?" Mallory wanted to know. "I don't remember."

"Before you were born. My cousin Jake's wedding."

"I don't think that counts, Grandpa. Mrs. Horton goes to a Nazarite Church, don't you?"

Joan smiled and cleared her throat. "That would be *Nazarene.* I tell you what, let's see what you remember from last week, shall we?"

"But what about the visits?"

No one had ever accused Mallory of not being persistent when she wanted to make a point.

"I can't promise anything." Gerrit shrugged his shoulders. "Usually I have to count the offering. But…"

Mallory flashed a smile and looked to her teacher, who nodded as well.

"I suppose it wouldn't hurt to visit the church where my students attend."

"It's settled then." Mission accomplished, Mallory finally scooted onto the bench. "You each take a turn visiting the other person's church."

Before Mallory could conduct further ecumenical peace talks, Gerrit hurried into the kitchen with Joan's list.

"Wait a minute," he whispered to himself, and the feeling was vaguely familiar, as if he had just walked away from a carnival attraction with a stuffed bunny after having spent more than he'd intended. "Did I just agree to do something?"

While Mallory played her opening scales with Joan Horton, Gerrit retreated to the relative safety of the piano teacher's kitchen to scan the list of January to-dos: touch up the trim paint, check the funny noise in the furnace, fix two leaky faucets, pull out the old broken dishwasher before the appliance guys show up with a new one sometime tomorrow. Routine stuff, except he guessed the washer was probably an armful. He would tackle that first, even if it might be a little more than he could carry by himself out to Gomer.

And he was right about that. No problem yanking it out of there and disconnecting two hoses and the power cord. He finished that in twenty minutes. And it really wasn't all that heavy either. So he managed to hoist it to his chest and wrestle it outside without pulling the screen door off its hinges. He'd seen bigger dishwashers. Just hadn't carried them by himself. From there it was just a little awkward getting it down the back porch steps, holding it out in front of himself and not falling on his face. He paused and pointed a toe to locate the next step when he felt a familiar stab in his chest.

Not now. Please not now.

⁀⁀

Joan did her best to concentrate as Mallory plodded through a minor scale, but despite her best efforts, the music faded to the background. Had she really agreed to visit Gerrit's church, as in some kind of student exchange program? She knew Mallory's intentions were pure as snow, but she couldn't help feeling as if she had just been enrolled in some kind of *Choose the Bachelor* reality television show.

And what would she find at Gerrit's church? Would they sit together? Well, yes, of course. How formal would it be? She wouldn't be expected to wear a head covering, would she? What dress would she wear?

She scolded herself for worrying. It was, after all, just a visit to another church. A friend's church. Or rather, a student's church.

"Mrs. Horton?"

"Oh yes." Joan woke from her daydream. "What? Did you want to try that again?"

Mallory looked toward the back door.

"I've done it three times. But I was just thinking of Grandpa. It sounds like he's maybe having trouble getting out the back door."

"Hey, Maestro!" Someone had stopped his truck out on Delft Street to holler. Of course Gerrit didn't need to see to recognize Ben Kootstra's voice. Probably everybody back at the Kup could hear him too. "I see she's put you to work now. Pretty nice of you to help."

Maybe if he ignored him, he would go away. But despite the growing pain, he couldn't resist returning the volley. They'd been at it since the third grade, after all. Good-natured ribbing from Ben Kootstra was just part of the spice of life.

"Listen, Ben, if I didn't have my hands full, I think I'd just break your neck, put you out of your misery."

"No misery here, buddy." Ben sneezed. "I just think it's real nice of you to help out a widow lady the way you do. Very extremely sweet."

Gerrit tried to get a better grip, but by this time the edge of the old dishwasher was digging into his fingers, cutting off the circulation. His forehead dripped with cold sweat. This was not good.

"So why don't you be a little very extremely sweet yourself and give me a hand with this, huh? I'm about to..."

Lose his grip.

As if in slow motion, he felt the big plastic-and-sheet-metal box slip from his fingers, and for an instant that was good. But only an instant. After that he wasn't so sure what happened, exactly, especially not how he found himself falling with the dishwasher. But the machine exploded into a hundred pieces with a bang. Brittle plastic and pieces of the wash arm flew up in his face while twisted pieces of sheet metal and dish racks wrapped themselves around his arm and neck like a General Electric anaconda. He hit the ground—hard—wrapped in the whole gnarled mess.

And he must have yelped, too, or grunted or groaned. Gerrit really wasn't sure what kind of noise he made, except that he made one. Loud enough to bring people running. Ben Kootstra from his truck out front, Lulu DeLeeuw from next door, and Mal and Joan from inside the house.

Now I know what it's like to be in a car wreck, he told himself, momentarily facedown and helpless in the broken mess.

"Holy smoke, Gerrit!" Ben was the first to reach his side. No one had a bigger mouth than Ben Kootstra, but he could move his tail when he wanted to. "Why didn't you wait for me to help you?"

The back door slammed, and Gerrit felt another hand at his shoulder, beside Ben's bad breath. What, did the guy gargle with fish oil?

"Heavens, are you all right, Gerrit?" With a soft but firm grip, Joan helped him up.

Was he all right? His chest hurt. His face hurt. His right arm had twisted behind him and should have been broken.

"Never better."

"I'll call the doctor," offered Mallory, turning to go back inside. Gerrit held up his hand.

"No, you don't, girl. I'm not anywhere near doctor material just yet. He'll just tell me what I can and can't do."

Mallory wavered in the doorway.

"And that's a bad thing?" wondered Ben. He coughed again.

"Mallory's right," countered Joan. "I think we should at least take you in for a checkup. You never know about these things. Look at your face. You've scratched yourself pretty badly. And how's your arm?"

Gerrit flexed his muscles. Sore but unbroken. There, see?

"I'll throw him in the back of the truck, and we can take him to the hospital." That was Ben's contribution, for which he would surely receive a tongue-lashing from Mrs. DeLeeuw, the neighbor.

"Ben Kootstra," she scolded him. "I can remember how much you carried on when *you* broke your arm falling out of that tree at the playground. Now don't you be an uncaring dolt when someone else is hurt."

Even at eighty-something, Mrs. DeLeeuw still had a way of putting little boys in their places.

"I'm not hurt." Gerrit did his best to convince them, but it wasn't working extremely well.

"Let's at least bring you into the house and clean you up." So when Joan took Gerrit's arm and led him up the back steps, he let her. Only one problem remained.

"I can't leave that mess on your driveway." Gerrit paused before stepping back inside. "Looks like a junkyard."

"I'm sure Ben will pick it up for you," volunteered Mrs. DeLeeuw. "Won't you, Ben?"

Ben said nothing for a moment, and Gerrit thought he could almost hear the jab to the ribs.

"Ow! What? Sure." Ben cleared his throat and sniffled once more, louder this time. "Anything for an old friend."

Chapter 22

We don't believe in rheumatism and true
love until after the first attack.
—MARIE E. ESCHENBACH

Gerrit could read the *Farmers' Almanac* as well as the next guy, and he
knew that by February the days were supposed to be getting longer
and lighter. Of course, if you believed all that stuff about how fuzzy cater-
pillars in November meant more snowstorms that winter, then they were
due for some record cold temps as well. Gerrit had no way of knowing
how cold it was from the vantage point of his La-Z-Boy, though. One day
it rained nonstop; the next even more. Even so, he had his lifeline, peeking in at the front door just after dinner on a Friday evening early in the
month. He waved her inside.

"You ever feel like Little Red Riding Hood, coming to help your old
grandpa when he's sick?"

"You're not sick anymore, are you?" Mallory studied his face as she
jerked off the red hood of her parka, sending a spray of water all over the
entry. "You've been stuck in this little house for a week with no e-mail and
only Missy for company. I'd go nutsies if I were you."

"Eight days." Eight of the longest days of his life, and yes, he was
going nutsies, too. "And all Missy does is sleep anymore."

But granddaughters were wonderful day brighteners, eh? From underneath her dripping raingear, she pulled out a plastic-wrapped plate, bulging
with…

"*Speculaas* cookies!" He straightened out from under his crocheted blanket and swept the tissues from his TV tray. "That's enough to bring an old Dutchman back from the dead."

Even Missy raised her head and sniffed the aroma.

"Dad says he can't understand why you didn't get a flu shot so this wouldn't have happened."

"You tell your father…you tell him I've done just fine without a flu shot."

Well, he had. His kitchen trash bucket bulged with an assortment of aluminum dinner trays and pie plates, evidence of the care packages from church folks he'd enjoyed the past week. Who said he couldn't take care of himself? The embarrassing fall at Joan's house hadn't given him anything but a couple of silly little bruises on the cheek. At least he could say there was no harm done, despite all the mess on the driveway and all the theatrics and noise when people came running.

No harm done unless you counted Ben Kootstra, whose fault it was in the first place that Gerrit had gotten sick. And oh yes, he was certain of that. One hundred percent. Who else had been coughing and hacking just before Gerrit came down with this bug? Who else had breathed on him?

Thanks for sharing, Ben. Next time you're sick, you just stay home so you don't infect the whole town. Or if you do venture outside, keep your germs to yourself. Hold your breath or something.

"I'll bet he was in church last week, eh?"

Mallory paused from munching her cookie to give him a puzzled look. "Who?"

"Oh. I was just wondering if Ben…Mr. Kootstra…was in church last Sunday, getting other people as sick as he did me."

"I didn't know he got you sick. But people were asking about you, Grandpa."

"They were, eh?" Gerrit arched his eyebrows, but his forehead still ached when he did. He would need some more of that horse syrup.

"Yeah. I heard someone tell Dad it was the first time he could remember that you weren't there to help pass around the offering plates. Not since Grandma died. And…"

She went on and asked him about something he could not recall, so he just nodded blindly as the words echoed in his brain: *Not since Grandma died.* She had said the words with the same detachment as someone talking about the death of Abraham Lincoln. As in, "Sorry to hear it, but that was before I was born." He couldn't expect her to understand, and he couldn't blame her.

He also couldn't help resting his forehead in his hand, couldn't help recalling that other Sunday he had missed, couldn't help remembering the darkness and the way people brought him food that time, too. Only that time he could not take horse syrup for the pain, and at first he had not expected it to get any better, such was the depth of the exit wound he felt when Miriam had been taken to the hospital and never brought home. She'd been way too young for that kind of thing.

He still remembered all the sappy yet well-meaning cards, too: "In your time of great loss, remember that…" What was he supposed to remember? If it was all the same, he'd much rather forget. Everything. He'd much rather bury himself in his work than bury his forty-three-year-old wife in the Dutch neighborhood of the Van Dalen Cemetery, in line with three generations of Appeldoorns.

"We're so sorry, Gerrit." He'd come to expect the usual words from people whose spouses were still breathing, whose spouses still gripped their arms as if by squeezing harder they could ward off what would sooner or later come to them, too. Probably later. They were all still young. Those people with live husbands or wives had looked at him with that terrible expression of pity that had made him so ill he'd had to look away.

"Let us know if there's anything we can do for you."

Yeah, there is, he remembered thinking. *Put me out of my misery, the way Dr. DeGroot did with a sick heifer a month ago.* But of course he had never voiced the words, not even a whisper. There would be no clue to anyone that such a morbid thing had even crossed his mind, no matter how fleeting it had been. Truth is, he had barely formed the thought, had barely let his mind go there at all, and then only during his most unguarded moments after the funeral. So it wasn't really his thought, and he laid no claim to it after those fragile days. It's just that he didn't want to keep Miriam waiting.

And she would wait, he knew. She would wait for him just inside the east gate of the heavenly city, if there was an east gate. No matter the crowds, no matter how long it took. He'd never told anyone else about their agreement, never would. He'd barely allowed Miriam to speak of it, not until she'd held on to his sleeve, not until she had begged him to listen, pleaded with him to promise her, and he could not tell her no. What kind of husband would have refused?

Then she'd let go, leaving him to live the unanswered questions. For a short, private time, he had allowed himself to ask God why he had been left behind. Yet thinking of the questions once more only brought to the surface the shipload of one-sided prayers that God seemed happy enough to ignore, to let sink below the surface of his deep sorry pond. He remembered he didn't repeat the question, figuring that God had heard him the first time and that an answer wasn't on the way. He would let the question sink by its own weight, and if he could not see it, then he could pretend it had never been. Besides, if God could decide who would join Him in glory and when, Gerrit supposed He could decide which prayers to answer and which to ignore. But, he admitted to himself, knowing that kind of God did little to ease the raw pain, the big brother of the throbbing headache and fever that had kept him in bed for the past week.

Like comparing lightning to a lightning bug, to borrow a phrase from Mark Twain. But it fit, in a way, since the lightning that struck his life when she died had left him dumb and dazed and scarred. Only work and keeping up the farm had made sense, his only sinful pleasure, his born-again purpose that connected his past with his future, and now that had been taken away too. Only Warney could redeem it, and at the moment that seemed like a poor bet.

That was about all Gerrit remembered from those numb days, mainly the aching emptiness of their bed and the silence of the nights and the awkward things people would say. There were also the kindnesses and the casseroles he didn't notice until later, when someone would come by and collect an empty pie tin or Pyrex dish. Many of the dishes were probably still at the house, seeing as how he hardly knew the difference between what Miriam had cooked with before and what had later collected in their kitchen of dirty dishes.

Warney didn't ask questions, and that was either because he was Warney or because at the time he had been a seventeen-year-old who already knew all the answers. Gerrit wasn't ever sure and didn't know how to find out. Because if Warney ever did have questions, he never shared them; he just found more and more reasons to be somewhere else, to borrow Gomer, or to do his homework at a friend's house. And even though it meant he rarely helped with chores, at least he had friends—and Gerrit supposed that was a good thing. No one complained, and no one questioned the way their lives changed, at least not aloud, and the silent distance between them began to grow greater when Warney went off to WSU.

But whose fault was that, and who had time to think about it anyway? The cows needed feeding and milking, the stalls needed cleaning, the machinery needed fixing, and a thousand other chores around the farm needed doing. That turned out to be a good thing. Because the harder and the longer he worked, the easier it was to forget what they had lost. The less time he spent in the house, the less he was reminded of her. Besides, when had he ever minded hard work? Unlike other slackers, he wasn't going to pay somebody else to do work that he himself could do just as well or better. Where was the sense in that?

He did return to church soon enough, though. The week following the funeral. But even by that time, Gerrit still remembered asking God to take him, pleaded with God to take him. Why shouldn't He? Why wouldn't He? He remembered shouting out his anger early one morning, in the middle of a 3:00 a.m. milking, alone in the milking parlor. But the girls had jumped and kicked, and he told himself he wouldn't do that kind of thing again. Where was the sense in that? God had apparently given him His answer. So just like the cows waiting outside the door, udders full of milk, he would have to wait his turn. He would join Miriam when God was good and ready to open the gates, no sooner and no later. It would do no one any good to shout or carry on, no matter how good it felt at the moment.

"How did Mr. Kootstra get you sick anyway, Grandpa?"

Gerrit hovered for a waking moment between the memories and Mallory's question, between the past he couldn't change and the future he could not control. He shook his head to clear the words, but his brain still rattled painfully when he did. The pain was good if he could use it like a crowbar to pry himself away from the memories and back to the present.

"I'm sorry." He wondered how long he had been dreaming. "What did you say?"

"Mr. Kootstra. How did he get you sick?"

"Oh, that. Well, he went out when he shouldn't have. Should have stayed home."

Gerrit tightened the wool scarf around his neck and hunkered down again.

"Does that scarf help you feel better?"

"Keeps my throat warm. Works better'n that stuff anyway."

He pointed at his nearly empty bottle of medicated cold, cough, and flu syrup on the floor next to all the tissues.

"Black cherry flavored," she read the label. "Mmm. Sounds pretty good."

"Can tell you haven't had any lately. Tastes like fermented silage, and doesn't work worth a fig for humans."

"Cool."

It was better than nothing, though it did tend to make him drowsy, and he did need some more, which was part of the reason he found himself wandering the aisles of the Deelstra Market forty-five minutes later. While Mallory ran to the produce section for three apples, he checked his crumpled list for the rest: another Hungry Man mac-and-cheese dinner, a can of OJ, a loaf of bread, and some chunky peanut butter. That would last him for a while. He looked around the end of the Dutch food aisle for Mallory, then held back and scolded himself for not shaving before he'd left home. Shoot. He should've known he'd run into Joan when he looked like death warmed over.

He could probably come back for the rest of the list later. But this time he could not have avoided her even if he had wanted to. Not with Mallory leading her his way.

"Doing a little shopping, Gerrit?" Joan pulled up next to a pyramid of d'anjous. Like him, she held a plastic basket and a list, only hers was written on some kind of Palm Pilot thingie, not paper. Impressive. She could probably teach him how to run his e-mail, too. "Mallory tells me you're doing better."

"I've been trying to practice." He swallowed and wondered why his answer sounded like a little boy in grade school. To his credit, he avoided clipping the end-cap display of Tide.

"Oh." She stopped for a moment. "Good. But actually, I meant your flu."

"Right." He knew that.

"Mom makes him chicken noodle soup when he comes in and practices. He's good, not like me."

"Now wait a minute, Mallory," the teacher spoke up. "Don't sell yourself short. No one's an expert right away."

"He is."

Gerrit could only shrug. "Nice to have a fan, eh?"

She smiled, but he could not make out exactly what lay behind it.

"Oh, and Mrs. Horton?" Mallory almost looked as if she had rehearsed this line, the timing and the delivery. "Is this Sunday a good time to start visiting churches, the way you both said you would? Is that okay with you?"

Gerrit nearly choked. Mallory hadn't forgotten.

"Well…" Joan arched her eyebrows at him for confirmation. "If it's all right with your grandfather…"

The line ahead of them moved, and the young checker parked her hands on her hips. Gerrit began to dump his goods on the moving belt. No, he still wasn't feeling great, but maybe that was really an unexpected blessing. Because if people at First Church still thought he was sick—which to some degree he still was—then they might not think it odd if he was missing again this Sunday. And they might not ask, except to inquire later how he was doing, and he would be able to report that he still wasn't one hundred percent. And that would be the truth. So he shrugged again and nodded his okay.

"All right then." She smiled once more, and Gerrit had to admit her smile had a way of making him forget things more easily. "I'll visit your church Sunday morning, and you can visit mine next week."

"Fine with me." He stifled a cough and turned away, just so he couldn't be accused of getting everybody sick. Mallory had moved off to examine a cereal display, and Joan confirmed what time services started before she resumed her shopping.

"How was that, Grandpa?" Mallory returned wearing an innocent look. "Did it work out okay?"

Now he'd done it. If anyone heard he was visiting the Methodist, no, the *Nazarene* church, he'd have some explaining to do.

"Listen, young lady." His neck still ached as he looked down at Mallory. "I don't know what you're thinking here, but it's not going to work." He slapped a package of Juicy Fruit gum onto the checkout belt, and she nodded.

"Uh, paper or plastic?" asked the young girl behind the counter, and he thought it was one of Herm Jonker's daughters. Gerrit faced her head-on.

"And that goes for you, too."

Chapter 23

I want to know God's thoughts...the rest are details.
—ALBERT EINSTEIN

Early Sunday morning Joan was adjusting her hair once more in the mirror. Funny, but for some reason the wave on the left side stood up more than the wave on the right side, even after a shower. She frowned as she sprayed a little more holding mist. It was not normally a thing she toyed with, this vanity.

She wondered at the butterflies in her stomach. It wasn't as if she had never visited new churches before. Perhaps she needed another cup of coffee.

She brushed past the black ankle-length dress that still wore dry-cleaning plastic and wondered why she had hung it up to take space in her modest closet. To remind herself? Some people kept pictures of their dear departed ones hanging on the wall, and that would have been far better than the dress that always reminded her of the event she had worn it to.

His funeral.

She picked it up by its plastic hanger and held it up to the morning light streaming in from the bedroom window. Held it at a careful arm's length as if it had been laced with cyanide or some kind of poison that could not be dry-cleaned away. *Come on, girl,* she chided herself. *How many years has it been?* But she desperately wished it didn't still fit her, wished it wasn't flawless, wished for a stain or a rip, a stain of tears, anything to make it easier to simply toss it into a paper sack and leave out on the front step for the Van Dalen Hope Chest to collect on Tuesday and

Thursday mornings. But like the Vietnam War Memorial, which she'd once visited with Jim to honor the memory of an old college buddy, this black, widow's uniform had his name indelibly etched on it. And though it would be invisible, she knew it was just as permanent as names etched in granite, just as real as the names of the people who had been killed in action during a horribly tragic war.

She stopped the analogy there, afraid of stumbling upon too many common threads, too many uncomfortable ties, even knowing that his memory would not unravel so easily. Yet the thought of giving away this dress seemed profane, and she knew she could not allow anyone else to wear his name unknowingly, even if it meant nothing or was not obvious to anyone but her. She would know, and that was enough.

So what then? She pulled aside a place on the clothes rack and jammed the dress back in, wishing the memories could be stuffed away so easily. If only she could pack them in the closet of her dark memory, comforting herself with the promise that, yes, she would dispose of it properly someday soon. She would quietly destroy the dress someday, burn it perhaps, like a worn flag that has outlived its honor.

If only it were that easy.

She looked at her watch and felt a catch in her throat. Just forty-five minutes before the eleven o'clock service began at Van Dalen First Dutch Reformed Church.

"Woo-hoo. You look pretty spiffy, Grandpa."

Mallory waved from the barn as Gerrit emerged from his little house. Spiffy? Shoot. Maybe they didn't wear ties and suit jackets at the Nazarene church. Maybe they didn't sing hymns or read the Scriptures. Maybe it was the kind of place that had a drum set in the front of the church and a loud young preacher named Brother Ralph roaming the platform the way they did on the television shows, with tight camera shots of people waving their hands like lunatics shooing flies.

That would never happen at his First Church. For one thing, their janitor, Agnes Oostdorp, would never stand for flies in the sanctuary. And as he adjusted his tie, Gerrit decided he probably wouldn't either. First sign of anybody rolling on the floor or hopping up and down…well, he was out of there, Joan Horton or no Joan Horton.

He felt his chin to make sure all the stubble from the past few days was double-shaved, checked the shine on his shoes, and headed for Gomer. Who said farmers couldn't look spiffy when they wanted to?

Mallory, too. But this morning she looked more like her usual self, with muddy rubber boots up to her knees and a frayed, grease-stained tan corduroy coat over her blue church dress. The coat had once belonged to her father and had probably crawled under one too many tractors. She'd managed to roll up one sleeve, but her left hand looked amputated, poor thing.

"Looks like you're going on a date or something." She trotted over to admire or tease him—probably the latter while pretending the former.

"Watch it, girl. I'm just going to church." He checked his watch again. "Speaking of which, you'd better be ready pretty quick or your folks are going to leave without you."

Sure enough, Warney had just stepped outside to warm up the Explorer. He waved at them while Mallory twirled in her boots.

"Okay, but say hi to Miz Horton for me. Do they start the same time you do?"

He thought about their conversation at the market a couple days before, did his best to remember what Joan had told him, tried to recall the arrangements. Mostly it was a blur. Shoot. He'd have to stop taking so much of that strong cough syrup, seeing as how it had fogged his remembering. Or maybe not.

"I think their Sunday school is at ten," he told her. "Services at eleven. And say, Mallory…"

She stopped and looked back over her shoulder. And she must have read his mind.

"Don't worry, Grandpa. I won't spread it around."

"You make it sound like—"

"On account of you're still supposed to be sick and all, and that's why you want people to think you're not at church, right?"

"No!" That girl could hit a little too close to home sometimes. "I mean. I'm not asking you to lie or anything. You just don't have to go around announcing to everybody you know that your Grandpa's off with some lady friend, okay?"

She giggled. "Even though you are."

"All right, you." He grabbed for her hood to give her a good squeeze, but she was too quick. "If anybody asks, you just tell 'em the truth."

"And what's that? I forget."

"Truth is, your grandfather is feeling better today, thank you, and that he expects to be back in church next week. How's that?"

"My grandfather is feeling much better, thank you." She hopped over Missy on the back step and skipped off to the shed where her dad was warming the SUV. "So much better, he's off visiting his lady friend."

"Shoot." Gerrit gave up and yanked Gomer's driver's-side door handle. "I have no idea why I let her talk me into this."

⌒

Surprisingly nice, she thought.

Joan settled into a padded pew about a fourth of a way into the lofty sanctuary of the Van Dalen First Dutch Reformed Church, the same church where she'd had their recital, and right where the ushers had seated her. She hadn't been seated like that since the last time she had been to a wedding back in New York. But she breathed a sigh of relief that she hadn't been asked for her Dutch identity papers at the door or asked to swear allegiance to the memory of John Calvin, though while she waited in the foyer for Gerrit, she had once again been asked the question, "Where are you from?"

In the South the equivalent would have been "Who are your people?" and it would represent a curious search for a pedigree, a family connection that would guarantee her a ticket for a smooth entry into this society. But of course she had none, only a half-stub that said she was Alison's mother, who was married to the county agent who, by the polite smiles and nods at his name, appeared to have a favorable reputation among the farmers. But Shane and Alison were not Reformed either (Shane was Free Methodist), and they had not been born and raised in the same house out on Van Akker Road, as had Joan's inquisitor.

Until she had safely made it past the official greeters (an older couple with name tags and warm hands who asked if she was with someone), she might as well have planted herself in the middle of the foyer and announced in a loud voice, "NO I'M NOT FROM AROUND HERE, AND NO I'M NOT RELATED TO ANYONE IN THIS CHURCH!"

Even so, she felt an unmistakable warmth here, more than just the hot air pouring occasionally from the heating vent at her feet and tickling the hem of her skirt. Despite her inability to claim the native-born connection—and she had anticipated that considerable handicap—doors had swung open to her, and smiles had been real. If anything, people were perhaps a little on the curious and tentative side, but altogether genuine, as if they really were glad to meet her after all.

At least she seemed to have chosen the right uniform: a modest black pleated skirt, white blouse, and matching plaid blazer. In fact, one of the women drinking coffee in the foyer when she'd arrived ten minutes earlier had been wearing a twin outfit, only with a cream-colored blouse instead. Nordstrom's must have sold quite a few of them.

Joan managed to avoid her twin, but so far her only other apparent faux pas had been bringing her own large leather slipcovered *NIV* Bible. And though it seemed odd to her, she quickly realized that the people of First Church relied on their black *King James* pew Bibles instead. Of course that was fine, but just not what she had been used to in other churches that tended to meet in storefronts and shopping centers rather than beautifully landscaped brick buildings with designer interiors like this one.

Was everything really that different from the little Nazarene churches her father had pastored and where she had grown up? It could have been the music, since there was certainly no praise band here and most approved music seemed to have been seasoned a good seventy-five years or more. Up front a woman about her own age was doing a commendable job on a quiet version of Bach's Prelude in C Major, though she missed the sharp in measure eight and passed over the B-natural toward the end, measure fourteen—but nothing serious and probably nothing that anyone else would notice. The woman's instrument, a newer Baldwin baby grand, had been kept spotless and in proper tune.

Joan sighed and wondered if cooks felt this way if they ever ate out at a restaurant, or if editors ever read for pleasure without obsessively picking out typos. Probably not. She pursed her lips, forced herself to just listen to the music for its beauty, and tried to pray.

But where was Gerrit? She breathed only a little easier when others began filling into the pews around her, naturally allowing a bubble of personal space and a spot to the left for her presumed husband. Several more people smiled their welcomes, and one older man with a name tag even reached over the back of the pew behind her to whisper a hello and "We're glad you're here."

Perhaps *that* was the difference. Instead of the friendly preservice chatter she was used to at her home church, here she heard only the whisper of an occasional discreet comment and the hushed piano prelude. Dim rays of late-morning sun found their way through the crimson-and-gold stained-glass depiction of the life of Christ, alternating with scenes from rock-solid church fathers like Knox and Calvin. She recognized a bearded Jesus, of course, but knowing the reformers would have been much more of a stretch without the labels below their respective windows.

All in good taste. She sunk her toes into the plush royal red carpet and skimmed the bulletin. First on the agenda: a responsive reading from Psalm 90, followed by hymn number 170 ("O God, Our Help in Ages Past") from the Psalter Hymnal in the pew racks. Verses 1 through 6. Assuming Jesus didn't return in the meantime, after that they would recite the Confession and Assurance, followed by a prayer (printed in bold so worshipers could follow along). Next came a hymn from the choir, a Scripture reading from the Common Lectionary emphasizing the sovereignty of God (page 1243 in your pew Bibles), and the congregational reading from the Canons of Dordt—which the bulletin explained asserts that we cannot save ourselves or come to faith by our own strength.

So far so good. At least it was all in English, something that probably would not have been true a few years ago. The message from the Reverend Jongsma, titled "Our God Reigns," would be based upon Psalm 2:4, which seemed appropriate, followed immediately by the benediction and hymn number 603, verses 1 and 4. Of course, all the hymn numbers and verses were listed on the reader board, too, so she couldn't go wrong.

Well, perhaps this wouldn't be so intimidating after all. In fact, the service looked downright bulletproof, and it occurred to her that she could get used to this very easily. So she began to smile to herself and even allowed her shoulders to loosen a notch—until she remembered again.

Where in the world was Gerrit? She allowed herself a small taste of sour grapes. Is this how he treats guests at his church? Invites them to the service, and then never bothers to show up, or ignores them in front of everyone?

Two rows back she recognized the Vanderstraats from next door, and Judy brightened to see her. Judy seemed like a very nice lady, never at home until late in the day, but one person whom Joan thought she wouldn't mind getting to know a little better. Perhaps she should ask her over for coffee one of these days, perhaps after church sometime.

Joan didn't recognize most of the other faces until Mrs. Velkomvagen stepped in with her Earl in tow just as the organist was finishing up a pleasant but unevenly paced Handel sonatina. The older woman swept up to an empty spot two rows from the front that not many generations earlier would probably have listed her name as the owner. Joan breathed a sigh of relief that she herself hadn't tried to park there. Finally, the Reverend Jongsma swept into his place on the platform. He was dressed in a proper black suit and a conservative navy blue tie. But still no Gerrit.

Perhaps she had missed him. In a church this size, seating three hundred or so, he could have slipped in, not recognized the back of her head, and believed her not to be there. Perhaps. But as she discreetly scanned the crowd behind her once more, she saw no evidence of his sturdy face or profile. Head and shoulders above most men, he would be hard to miss.

She did notice a fair number of young families, though, which was nice, and quite a few young children perched beside their parents, quietly coloring their bulletins as they waited for the service to begin. Several more families slipped in late, including one that reminded her of Warney, Liz, and Mallory. She nearly waved at them before she remembered that Mallory and her family attended the Free Methodist church on the other side of town.

Joan turned back to follow along in the responsive reading, responding at the right times and listening at others. No, it was not the first time she had been in such a formal service, but she had to admit she slipped comfortably into the structure and form of the worship. Still, every few minutes she glanced back to see if Gerrit...

Where in the world *was* that man?

By verse 6 of "O God, Our Help in Ages Past," Joan decided she had either missed him entirely or he wasn't going to come. With a twinge of concern she looked back one last time.

And still Gerrit was nowhere to be seen.

Chapter 24

I never knew how to worship until I knew how to love.
—HENRY WARD BEECHER

*Y*ou say she's usually here by now?" Gerrit whispered to his neighbor. He loosened his tie and looked around to see if anyone else had stepped into the room dressed like him. One thing was sure: He would not be mistaken for a regular attender at Cornerstone Church of the Nazarene.

"Usually Joan is early." The guy in the folding chair next to him, Mark Something (definitely not Dutch), bounced a wiggly little girl on his knee while his wife fed an infant from a bottle. But no, he hadn't seen Joan all morning, not in Sunday school and not in the preservice prayer time. He thought maybe she helped out with children's church sometimes, but that didn't start until usually about fifteen minutes into the service. So nobody had seen her yet this week. Was Gerrit a friend of hers?

"Oh, ah, she's my granddaughter's piano teacher. And since I usually drop my granddaughter off, well, the subject of church came up, and I was...Mrs. Horton, Joan, invited me to visit her church, and..."

Mark tilted his head to the side, like a golden retriever trying to make sense of the words as Gerrit continued his roundabout story.

"And then when I didn't see her, well, I started to wonder if I'd come to the right place."

"Oh, you're in the right place all right." Mark had grease under his fingernails, probably a mechanic. "Ever since she moved here, I don't think she's missed a Sunday. And she's an incredible pianist. She can play anything blindfolded. Composes her own stuff, too, burns CDs, incredible. Too bad she's only here for a year."

Give her a gold star. In the meantime, what kind of place had he just stepped into anyway? The small North Valley Grange Hall had been crammed full of folding chairs and a small platform erected up front. And all the stuff up there made him think he had come for a rock concert rather than a church service. They would probably be leading a swaying throng in three-word worship choruses, chanting hallelujah over and over and over. The only reminder he could see that this would really be a church service were the three banners hanging fairly high up on the side walls between the windows, which did a pretty good job of covering up most of the water stains from what had to be a pretty leaky old roof. Each banner had a different Scripture saying, like "I Am the Way" or "Holiness Is What I Long For." Which was all very nice, but the thought occurred to Gerrit that maybe they should have been longing for a real building, too. And maybe they didn't have enough money for a real pulpit after they'd bought all that fancy sound equipment, the big chrome and black drum set with five cymbals and three electric guitars on their own stands.

He'd actually been here once before, years ago, when the pudgy old building with the peeling yellow paint had still been used as a real Grange hall. Apparently, that had been longer ago than he'd thought. From the look of things, he doubted the kids here knew what the Grange even *was*.

Gerrit would wait just a little longer. At least the coffee tasted pretty good, and drinking a second cup gave him something to do with his hands, something to make him look occupied in the middle of all the chatter. Joan would have no trouble picking him out of the little crowd when she finally showed. He would be the Dutch guy wearing a suit and tie, sitting in the middle of all the folks chatting and carrying on like this was some kind of a potluck dinner, not a worship service. That was what he came for, wasn't it? A worship service?

He turned the bulletin over and checked the back page again, convinced he'd missed something. He scanned the usual announcements, like an upcoming youth group trip to play paintball. Okay, these looked familiar: A thank-you from Tillie Johnson to all the people who brought her casseroles while she was laid up with a broken hip. A note from the Awana kids program that they needed another Sparks leader; contact Steve Porter right away. That sort of thing. But where the order of service should have been, all it said was that Pastor Kevin was bringing a message from the Word today, something about discipleship.

That was it? What about the hymn numbers, the Scripture references, the responsive readings? Either the church secretary had the week off, or something was very wrong here. He checked his watch and saw that it was already three minutes past eleven, but the pastor was still nowhere to be seen.

What happened to Joan?

"Hiya!" A young kid of maybe twenty-five or thirty stepped up to him with his hand out. No way was this guy wearing a tie to church either. Fact, Gerrit wore those kinds of jeans to milk cows in. "Name's Josh Miller. You new to the area?"

Gerrit shook his hand, but he would have laughed if they'd been anywhere but the inside of a church. Grange hall or no Grange hall, it just wouldn't be right.

"I suppose you could say that," Gerrit whispered back. "My grandparents came here from Holland not too long ago."

"Really?" The kid leaned forward but wasn't following. Add it up, kid. Grandparents?

"Eighteen ninety-five, I think."

"Eighteen…" The kid pulled an ear as if that would help him realize his leg was being pulled too. "Oh, wow. I get it. Awesome. Like, early settlers or something."

"Or something."

As Josh Miller sidled off to talk with somebody else, Gerrit guessed that probably only a handful of people in the room had lived in this county for more than a few years. This was the odd part: In a town where he thought he knew just about everyone, he'd stepped into a room full of strangers at Cornerstone Church.

Although that was actually good news when he thought about it. If no one recognized him, there was less chance of word getting back to First Church about where he'd spent his Sunday morning. So this was good in its own way.

Actually, he did recognize a few people. The guy over in the corner swigging coffee had moved up from California a couple years back, bought the local Radio Shack. Benson or Swenson and also definitely not Dutch. Was anybody else seeing a pattern here? As for the family with the passel of stairstep kids, Gerrit thought maybe he'd seen the guy at the lumberyard, driving a forklift. And now the rock band was starting up. Oh, man. Joan was either going to have to show up in a hurry, or he was out of here. The pastor finally arrived (six minutes late!), and the little congregation started to sing.

And sing.

By the time fifteen or twenty minutes had passed, Gerrit had lost his window of opportunity to slip out gracefully. Sure, he could still head out to the restrooms in the foyer, but the only way out from there was through the main double doors, and he would be carrying his coat besides. So that was out; he was stuck. Everyone could see and hear those doors plainly.

Joan was nowhere to be seen.

Even if she were here, what could he do but follow along on the overhead projector? There wasn't a hymnal in the house, and for that matter not a pew Bible either. Russ or Gus on his right side was belting out the words, making up in volume what he lacked in pitch.

"One day every knee will bow. Still the greatest treasure remains for those who gladly choose you now."

Gerrit cringed at the lyrics. As if people had any choice. Every good Calvinist knew it was God who did all the choosing.

Aside from that major typo, however, he did have to admit most of the tunes were catchy. Louder than he was used to, but catchy, and maybe the words weren't quite as shallow as he'd been expecting. He wouldn't want to be quoted on that, though, especially not so early in the game. He even caught himself singing along on a couple, tapping his toe once. Joan would have been proud of him, he supposed...as if that sort of thing mattered a fig.

What irritated him the most, though, was the odd feeling that everything here was in order, no less than if he had been sitting in his usual pew back at First Church. He didn't quite understand how that could be, especially not in the middle of this crowd of strangers named Miller and Gardener, Wilson and Johnson and Porter. Shoot, there probably weren't more than one or two Dutch folks in the entire congregation, if a person could believe that.

Gerrit himself wasn't sure *what* to believe. Because although he kept an eye out for weird stuff going on, the worst thing he noticed was two or three younger people (weren't they all?) raising a hand as they sang and swaying with the music. They hadn't been shown the door yet. After a while he grudgingly had to allow the remote possibility that maybe this wasn't a wild cult after all.

Shoot. Because if they had been, this visit would have been a whole lot easier. As it was, the longer he stayed, the harder it became to dismiss this little congregation out of hand.

Even more surprising, Pastor Kevin Gardener's message was the best he'd heard in years. Well, one of the best, and Gerrit wouldn't want to be quoted on that either. For one thing, it wasn't Reformed, and the man drew his water from another theological well. But you had to admit it was easy to follow, straight-shooting, and marinated in Bible verses. At times Gerrit almost nodded until he realized how that would have looked if word ever got back to First Church. But the way Kevin milked the Scriptures, it was almost like talking to somebody out in the barn, somebody you had worked with for years. Nothing at all like what he'd expected from seeing the occasional fire-breathing televangelist.

"Little longer than I'm used to," he admitted to the pastor as they shook hands on the way out. "But can't say I minded too much."

"I'll take that as a compliment." Pastor Kevin gave him a crooked grin. Gerrit probably had ten years on him, but the reverend looked to have lost the last hair on his head long ago, so grayhead beats domehead. A hat would have made a lot of sense for the guy, especially while he was standing there in the doorway and chatting with everybody as they left. Gerrit introduced himself and pulled his own coat over one shoulder.

"So you're the Gerrit we've been praying for," the pastor boomed. "Well, we're sure glad you came even though Joan wasn't here. She usually is. Feel free to come back any time."

Fat chance of that. But the pastor's words didn't sink in until Gerrit had hit the gravel parking lot and pointed himself in Gomer's direction, the far corner of the lot behind a storage shed.

The Gerrit we've been praying for? He supposed people had done that years ago, when he'd lost Miriam. Such a thing could be expected during a tragedy. But he hadn't even asked for it then, and he sure as original sin hadn't asked for it now. Even if he had, that would be his business, and his alone.

"I'll be sure to tell Joan you were here." The pastor's words drifted across the lot on the wind.

"Don't bother," Gerrit called back, his teeth grinding. "I'll catch up to her."

He did catch up to her the following Tuesday afternoon at their regular lesson, right on time, and boy, he was ready to tell her what for. His jaw worked an invisible piece of gum as he sat down at the piano bench. But she didn't give him a chance.

"I am so sorry about the mix-up last Sunday." She was? He looked over sideways, just to be sure he'd heard right. "I heard you visited my church while I went to yours."

He cleared his throat, a little off his game plan, but oh well. Yeah, that was true, just the way they'd agreed in the market.

"I am so sorry." She repeated herself, hiding a smile. "But can you imagine what we must have looked like?"

"Well…" He hadn't.

"I mean, here we are, both of us uncomfortable in a new church, both of us waiting for the other to show, and…"

Her chuckle turned to a soft laugh.

"I suppose," he admitted. "When you look at it that way."

Well, he never delivered the lines he'd prepared about whose fault it was and it being the last time he would ever do such a thing and the rest of it. All he could do now was laugh with this woman, and they laughed as he forgot more and more of what he had meant to say.

"So did you enjoy Pastor Kevin's sermon?" She wiped a tear from her eye with a tissue. "He's been talking about being a disciple."

"It was half-decent, and I told him so."

"Really?" She turned her head to the side as if she didn't believe him.

"He left out a few key verses, though."

Which key verses? Well, since she asked, Gerrit reminded her of how many scriptures revealed the sovereign God of the Five-Point Calvinists. Don't forget, "Ye have not chosen me, but I have chosen you" (John 15:16), and "He hath chosen us in him before the foundation of the world" (Ephesians 1:4), and…well, he could go on about how disciples are chosen, not the other way around.

"I don't entirely disagree with you." She crossed her arms and nodded.

"You don't?" It was his turn to look at her sideways.

"Well, no, except—"

"Aha!" He smiled. "I knew there was a catch. Except what?"

"Well, what about when Jesus asked his disciples to follow Him? Was that a choice, or did they have to?"

"None of them would have refused."

"But even Joshua had to make a choice. Remember? 'Choose for yourselves this day whom you will serve.… But as for me and my household, we will serve the LORD.' "

Okay, so she could quote Scripture too. So for the next hour they chased a theological merry-go-round, around and around. Never mind the piano lesson. If people were predestined, how could they still be accountable? Joan wanted to know. Could people resist being saved? No? Then did Jesus really die for everyone, or were some people just born for hell? And if that were the case, why not just sit back and let it happen? If your friend was in trouble or sick or distressed, why not relax and say, "That's God's will"? Wasn't it their destiny? Their karma?

Gerrit looked at her as if she'd just sprouted a nose ring.

"We're not into New Age stuff around here."

"Oooh!" Joan finally threw up her hands. "You are impossible, Gerrit Appeldoorn! In a nice sort of way, of course, but…you know I was just trying to make a point."

He paused for a moment and couldn't keep the corners of his mouth from turning up.

"In a nice sort of way, eh?"

This time she didn't giggle, she just threw her head back and laughed.

She said, "Well, I'm glad I had a chance to soak up some good theology at *your* church."

"No argument from me."

"And at the same time, you were over at Cornerstone, swaying to the worship band and probably clapping your hands. Am I right?"

Gerrit opened his mouth to defend himself, but it was no use. This woman did not play fair. And besides, wasn't it time for Mallory's lesson?

Chapter 25

Well, all I know is what I read in the papers.
—WILL ROGERS

$\mathcal{T}$ hank you." The middle-aged woman nodded at Warney as he held open the door to the bank lobby and let in the February chill. But she was only the first in the parade. Who else would hold it? He stood there as a young mother in a hooded coat passed through with her stroller, then another couple he recognized.

"I hear doormen get the big bucks," Scott Van der Brug joked as he scooted through. Scott had graduated from Van Dalen High a couple years ahead of Warney, never went to college, but was making decent money selling berry harvesters for his dad. At least it looked as if he was, judging by the new four-wheel-drive Ford pickup he drove.

"Yeah, I wish." Warney could chuckle now, and actually he didn't mind dragging his feet a little. He was in no hurry to meet with Herm Jonker, no hurry to step inside the Van Dalen Savings and Loan.

No hurry at all.

He paused to check out the travel magazine in a rack just inside the lobby door, right next to the rack of brochures on IRAs and SEPs and 401(k) accounts. Retirement? What a concept. He slipped a gumdrop into his mouth from the bowl on the counter and nodded at the investment gal buried behind a mound of file folders. He and Liz had talked to her once, a few years ago, when they were first taking over the farm and thinking that anything was possible. Now, of course, he knew better.

And speaking of knowing better, the person behind the farm-loan desk in the corner of the bank knew him all too well. Lisa Van Ooyen knew his date of birth and Social Security number, and she knew (probably to the dollar) how much he owed on each piece of new equipment they'd bought and how far behind the payments happened to be. This was not someone he would want to challenge to a poker game, even if he had been a gambler.

Being a farmer was the same thing, a literal crapshoot, but that was a bad joke he had only tried once and never again, so never mind. He chewed his gumdrop double-time as he dragged himself over to the loan reception desk, where Lisa had already picked up her phone to warn Herm that another victim…*client* had arrived.

"I'll tell him, sir."

She smiled at Warney as she replaced the phone. And the back of Herm's head nodded in unison from where he sat behind his medium-size, imitation oak desk, lost in a jungle of papers behind the row of glass-panel windows that separated him from the rest of the world.

"Mr. Jonker will be right with you. Would you like to sit down for a moment?"

Warney shook his head no; he could reread the latest *Sentinel* just fine standing up, thank you. Maybe skim the obits. Which reminded him that Lisa's sister-in-law had the same job over at Van Grootveld's Mortuary and Funeral Home, two blocks down and around the corner. Those two ladies had to know how similar their jobs were. Take in the victims, greet the survivors.

And sure enough, there was the big, black, serious half-page ad from Van Grootveld's right there on page 2 where he was reading: "Pre-Need Arrangements, Giving Your Loved Ones Peace of Mind."

In other words, buy your funeral now and save a few bucks.

Not that it was such a bad idea for some people. And standing here in Herm Jonker's office gave him the feeling that maybe he should consider it after all. If he couldn't afford an IRA, a prearranged funeral could be the next best thing.

"He'll see you now, Mr. Appeldoorn."

Mr. Appeldoorn? He took a deep breath, knocked on Herm's door, and pushed his way into the dark-paneled den.

Den, as in the kind of place where good ol' boys from the local chapter of Ducks Unlimited sat around with their feet on the desk and swapped yarns about the buck they brought down last season or the fifteen-pound steelhead they caught. Herm Jonker had plenty of proof on that account, with two mounted leaping fish gracing one wall and a five-point buck dominating the other. He'd also dispatched scores of local ducks, a couple of which were mounted on the wall in realistic midflight, as if they were just about to set down on Koster Lake but had been condemned to an eternity of almost. Warney thought he knew how they might feel.

"Warney! Thanks for coming in. Here, have some hearts." Herm Jonker's bear-claw grip made Warney almost wince as he pointed with his free hand to a bowl of Valentine candies on the corner of his desk. "How are ya, buddy?"

"Not bad."

That's what he was supposed to say anyway. Truth is, he felt like a little kid with a hall pass to see the principal, even though Herm had graduated from Wazzu less than ten years before Warney. Warney did help himself to a couple of pink and green hearts though. One said "WALK ON BY," the other "AS IF."

How appropriate.

At the banker's waved invitation, Warney settled himself on the edge of the crinkly leather side chair, crunching on his hearts and waiting while Herm peered over his bifocals and riffled through a well-worn file. Part of the label had been inked out (the "Gerrit" part), and "Warner K." had been added underneath. Herm riffled and riffled, as if he wasn't quite sure what he was looking for. Finally, he set the file down, pulled off his glasses, and stared over at Warney with red-rimmed eyes.

"Listen, Warney, I appreciate you coming in when I called. I don't know exactly how to say this, so I'll just, uh…"

The phone buzzed, and Herm swung on the innocent machine like one arm of a steel-jaw trap.

"I'll take it later, Lisa," he barked. "Not now."

Yeah, thought Warney, *we're in the middle of my funeral arrangements here. Important stuff.*

Herm squirmed as if he thought so too. And his considerable bulk bulged out of both sides of his overburdened office chair. It creaked when he leaned forward.

"Let me just put it this way, Warney. Your dad was a good operator in his day."

Warney heard it coming. The history lesson. He nodded.

"What did he use to run, about a hundred head? Closed herd, raised all his own replacements. Feed costs were decent. Made a pretty good living even at that level. Milk blend prices were thirteen bucks a hundred-weight twenty years ago."

Warney nodded again. If Herm wanted to go through all this again, he was welcome to go ahead.

"But hey, you know all this."

"Yup."

"You've added a few head. And you know milk prices are still the same today as they were back then. Almost to the penny."

"Only difference is everything else costs us three or four times as much."

"Ain't it the truth." Herm shook his head. "Yeah, sometimes I wish I were doing business back during your dad's generation, 'stead of ours."

By *ours,* he had cut a fairly wide generational swath. But okay. Warney waited for the point, which came swift and unexpected like a shotgun blast to the wings.

"Warney, when was the last time Darigold paid you premium prices for your milk?"

Warney sucked in a breath and tried not to cough. Where had that come from?

"Uh, I'm not sure." He stalled, looking for a way out. "I'd have to check my records."

"Save you the trouble. You guys haven't been able to deliver a quality product for the past four years."

"That long?"

"And your somatic count has been well over three hundred thousand all that time. You have some serious, chronic mastitis going on."

"I know how to clean it up."

"So do I. So does every kid in the FFA program. But we both know you can't afford to put in all new barns, make 'em more state of the art. You can't afford to tear out those old stalls. You can't afford to start all over again."

"Our breeding's a lot better than when Dad ran the place. We do A-I, and—"

"I know, I know." Herm put up his hand as big as a stop sign and louder. "But it's not going to be enough. Let me just ask you this."

By this time Warney was wiping the sweat from his forehead. By this time he knew why he had dragged his feet coming to this meeting. By this time he wished he'd stayed in bed that morning.

"How much did we lend you for that fancy four-wheel-drive tractor Van Breemen sold you?"

"You're the one with the file." Warney shook his head. "One thirty or something like that."

"One hundred thirty-two thousand, six hundred forty-nine dollars and twelve cents."

"And twelve cents. Seemed like a good deal at the time."

"It was, for somebody with a little more capital than you, for somebody with a real need for a machine like that. And how much did we loan you to put in that waste lagoon?"

"Oh, I remember that one. Fifty thousand, even. That was one expensive poop pond."

"Cheaper than most. But what about that new refrigerated tank you had to replace?"

"Dad had a cow about that one. Eighteen thousand for a new tank when we have a perfectly good one already? 'What are you, crazy, Warney?' You should have heard him."

"I did. Everybody at the Koffee Kup did. You should stop by there sometime."

"I would, but I'm usually too busy working my buns off, trying to make the payments on all this stuff."

"Exactly. This is my point."

"Reminds me of one of those 1970s farm disaster movies. Remember those? I think one was called *Country*, the other one was...I forget."

Yeah, forget it. Herm shook his head. "Me and the missus don't get out much to movies. She watches *Oprah*."

"You can get 'em on video. Anyway, if this were the movie, you would probably be telling me it's all over and we have to auction off the farm."

"I'm not telling you that, Warney."

Warney took another heart and almost traded it in. The message: "YEAH RIGHT."

"Is that the good news?" Warney finally whispered, but Herm's face remained stone serious.

"Honestly, I don't know what the good news is, except that we're still in this fight. But this month I've had to close the accounts on two farmers. Two. And they were good operators, just like you and your dad. But they let things creep up on them, just like you. They didn't make the big changes quick enough, and then when it came time to pass the baton, all they could do was put expensive Band-Aids on the problem until their operational blood ran dry. I mean, they ran out of equity."

Warney stared straight ahead. He remembered when he was in the third grade and Marci Middelkoop had told the teacher he was the one who made the spitwad stick on the ceiling. When the principal, Mr. Van der Klock, made him bend over and grab his ankles. He felt the same way now.

The same exact way.

"Are you following what I'm telling you, Warney?" His voice rose a notch, two notches.

"I'm following. But what are you saying?"

"I'm not saying you have to sell out, and I'm not saying they're going to make some disaster movie about you."

"Not yet."

"That's right. I'm just telling you that we're getting mighty close here. Your equity's bottomed out, and I'm not even going to mention your water issues out there. I just don't want you to be the next casualty. That's why I wanted you to stop by. So we could talk about this."

"I know. And I appreciate what you're telling me."

Like he appreciated the "idiot light" on the dashboard of his car, the one that told him the car was overheating—but only when it was too late to do anything about it.

"If there's anything we can do. I mean, apart from giving you another loan."

"Right. Does Dad know about this? I mean, do you guys talk about it at the Kup?"

"Uh-uh." Herm shook his head. "No. I thought you knew me better'n that. You own the place now, not your dad. It's your show. You'll do the right thing. You're the college boy."

The college boy who was running his father's farm into the ground. He watched Herm pick out his own heart and grin at the message. Was that all? Spanking over. Warney stood to go. But one more thought grabbed him as he patted the wall-elk on the nose.

Maybe Herm would want to mount another turkey on his wall.

Or a farmer.

Same difference.

Chapter 26

You should always go to other people's funerals,
otherwise, they won't come to yours.
—YOGI BERRA

 o you understand what your mother and I are trying to say?"
    Warney stabbed at his cold Tater Tots, wishing they would go away. Wishing this entirely awkward family discussion would go away. But after his last meeting with Herm at the bank, he knew he had no choice. He and Liz both knew it.

"Not really," mumbled Mallory, tears dropping to her lunch plate. Sloppy Joes were her favorite Saturday lunch. She hadn't taken a bite. "I don't see why we just can't stay here."

"Honey, we've been doing everything we know to do." Liz scooted closer to her daughter and wiped a tear from Mallory's cheek. "I've been working and your daddy's been working, but it's just not...the farm's not..."

"We just can't make enough money here at the farm to keep it going." Warney searched for another way to say it. So far, he and Liz weren't doing too well. "It's not anybody's fault. It's complicated. And we're not the only people who have to sell."

"Well, we don't have to be rich, do we?"

"It's not a matter of being rich." How could he explain failing farm economics to a ten-year-old? "It's a matter of not even being able to pay the bills. We're standing on the edge of the cliff."

"I'll eat beans. I'll eat goat food."

They couldn't help but chuckle.

"If that would make a difference," said Liz, "we would too."

"Then can't you just borrow some more money?" Mallory stroked Missy under the table and looked from Mom to Dad with pleading eyes. "Grandpa has lots of money."

"That's part of the problem, Mal." Warney had run out of ways to explain. "We can't borrow any more. The bank won't let us, and I don't think that would be a good idea, even if we could. We're way too far in debt, we can hardly pay it back, and we can't borrow any more from your grandpa, even if he did have it, which he doesn't."

"So we're really going to sell the farm? What about Lilbit? What about 4-H? What about—"

"I'm sure the Kroodsmas will let you keep your animals on their place. But I've already talked to the real-estate guy. And you have to promise us one thing."

Mallory didn't nod, didn't take her eyes off her plate, her untouched lunch.

"We're not going to tell Grandpa about this just yet, since it's his birthday and we're having the party tonight and everything. It would just ruin it for him. Do you understand?"

That much she did. Warney went on.

"I'll break it to him soon. But you have to leave it to me, okay? Promise?"

This time she nodded, slowly and silently.

"Look at it this way, honey." Liz struggled to find the silver lining too. "God's taking care of us. And if your dad can find a job close-by, maybe we'll be able to live in town, closer to your friends, like Gina. Wouldn't you like being able to ride your bike over to Gina's?"

"Uh…" Warney shot Liz an eyebrows-up glance, and she had to know she was promising too much. *As if* he could get another job, just like that.

"Well, anyway," continued Liz, "let's get these dishes cleaned up before Grandpa wanders over here and wonders why everybody's making such a fuss."

~

"You look down, Pumpkin. Something eating you?"

Mallory looked at her grandfather and opened her mouth, then seemed to change her mind as she clamped it shut with a shrug. She dragged herself from the picture window and crawled across the living-room carpet to hover behind Gerrit, where he sat playing the piano after dinner on a Saturday evening in late February.

"I think lots of the snow melted earlier today." She finally said. "No fair."

"Who said weather was fair? It is what it is. But is that what's really bothering you?" He squinted at the music and set his hands to repeat the measure he'd been practicing. Four-four time. No sharps or flats. He could do this as long as he didn't get too distracted by the wonderful smell of warm birthday cake drifting from Miriam's…make that Liz's kitchen. No matter how much time passed, he couldn't shake the memory of Miriam in that kitchen, wrapped in her ridiculous cow-print apron.

But Mallory didn't answer his question. Something was wrong with that girl. Probably a good case of cabin fever. Well, that was typical for late February. He didn't blame her.

"I'm glad you don't just practice in secret anymore." Mallory watched him repeat a measure, then once again. "But is that the way the song is really supposed to sound?"

"No comments from the peanut gallery. You're next, you know, after we finish with the dishes."

"How much longer until I can help with the frosting?" Mallory retreated toward the kitchen while Gerrit listened for the growing whistle of the wind. Meanwhile, Liz tried to keep ahead of her whirlwind daughter.

"Why don't you go out and check on Lilbit?" she suggested. "People aren't going to be here for about an hour, and this cake needs a few more minutes before it's cool enough to frost. Your pregnant goat needs you."

"When you come back in," Gerrit added with a grin, "remember it's your turn to practice."

"Oh, Grandpa." Mallory groaned and covered her head with her hands. "I've been playing horrible lately."

"Mallory Ann Appeldoorn." Liz had obviously heard every word from the kitchen. "First of all, the word is horri-*bly*, and second of all, we already talked about that. You are not playing horribly, but you do need to have a better attitude if you're ever going to improve."

Mallory sighed as her mother went on.

"Look at your grandfather. He even practices in public now."

"Hey, I wouldn't call this 'public' exactly." Gerrit kept his eyes on the music but let himself grin. "It's in honor of old Johnny Cash's birthday. And besides, I just got tired of sneaking around."

"There. See, Mallory? Maybe you'd like to play something easy for all the people coming to your grandpa's party tonight. Assuming they all make it."

Gerrit shook his head at Liz. Bad idea. The lights flickered, and she paused a second.

"Or maybe not." She shrugged and licked her frosting spoon. "I was just thinking, since it was mostly church people and family, maybe you wouldn't think it was so threatening or scary."

Liz meant well. Mallory didn't answer but ran to the little mud room connected to the kitchen, threw on a coat and hat, and jumped into a pair of boots. She nearly bowled over her father as she tried to escape out the back door.

"Whoa, hold up there, pardner." He reached down and lifted her a foot off the floor with a grunt. "And how did you get to be such a heavy-weight all of a sudden?"

"Warner!" scolded his wife. "That's not the sort of thing you say to a lady. And take off your boots. You're a mess."

"Sorry, but it's starting to get really nasty out there." He smiled as he stepped aside to let Mallory by, but then his voice turned dead serious. "Everything that melted this morning is freezing again, just like that. Like the wind changed and somebody switched on a flash freezer. Has anybody been listening to the radio this afternoon?"

"We've been listening to Grandpa," explained Mallory.

Warney nodded as he stepped over to the little clock radio on the kitchen counter and flipped it to the local news. A commercial for Speedy Lube repeated their phone number twice before the voice of an urgent-sounding young female announcer filled the kitchen.

"Winds of up to seventy miles an hour are now predicted, and with the unexpectedly fast-moving Arctic cold front blowing through the Fraser River Valley will come temperatures down to minus fifteen, with wind chills down to minus forty-five, temperatures which are extremely dangerous for animals. All previous weather advisories have been updated after yesterday's mild conditions."

"In other words," Gerrit translated for them as if they didn't know, "those weather guys had no idea this Arctic Express was coming so fast."

"Shh, Dad!" Warney turned up the volume.

"Anticipating the storm, Nooksack County sheriff's office is now advising travelers to stay off the roads, which are already turning into sheets of ice in northern parts of the county, while Puget Power emergency crews are gearing up to remove dangerous ice accumulations from power lines as quickly as possible. Stay tuned to KGMX for the latest updates. We'll be reading a list of closures and cancellations as soon as they come in."

Finally, Warney turned the volume back down a bit.

"We haven't had a silver thaw like this for what, ten years?" He tried to remember.

"Since I was pregnant with Mal." Liz stood over her cakes with her hands on her hips. Already she had written "Happy 60th, Grand" on the top with green frosting.

"Well, there goes the party." Gerrit padded to the window to look out, but the sun had already set, and he couldn't see much. Couldn't hear much, either, except now the windows had started trembling with the growing wind, and snow pellets started pinging on the north-facing windows. The thaw had long since stopped. It was as if someone had suddenly opened a massive deep freeze, and they were standing in the door.

"You don't sound too disappointed, Dad." Liz finished up her lettering.

"We can still take care of that cake, if you want." He winked at her. "But what about the cows, Warney? We'll need to get them all out of the wind, out of the loafing sheds."

Obviously. Though the loafing sheds had been designed to shelter their cows from the Pacific Northwest rains, they weren't much help in extreme winds, especially not after Warney had removed the shutters for maintenance. Good timing. The only alternative was herding all 189 head into the small dry barn, where the dry cows and calves normally spent their time. It would be extra crowded but better than the alternative.

"Not *we*, Dad." Warney headed for the door. "You don't need to worry about it. I'll call a couple people."

"And you think they're going to be able to get through on these roads? Are you sure that's what you want?"

"I'm sure they'll be okay, Dad. I'll take care of it."

"Warney, listen to yourself. Time like now, you better not be too choosy about your help, boy."

Warney opened his mouth but seemed to change his mind when the lights from a pair of headlights flashed through the window.

"Look," he told his father. "They didn't even wait for a phone call. My help is here already, see?"

They pressed their noses to the now-frosty kitchen window on the west side, but at first they could not make out who was approaching through the growing blizzard.

"Doesn't look like a pickup to me," grunted Gerrit. "Fact, looks like they're drunk or something by the way they're weaving around."

"I think the ice is getting pretty bad out there on the driveway, honey." Liz agreed as she put her hand on Warney's shoulder. Then she gasped. "Oh! They're almost off into the ditch!"

"Almost?" Gerrit chuckled. The headlights had made it halfway down the drive to the big house from Vanderkrans Road, just past Gerrit's little place, and each beam seemed to hold white streaks of snow comets suspended in the darkness. "Looks like we'd better fire up your fancy tractor and help your help out of the ditch."

But KGMX didn't know the half of how slick it had become or how fast it had turned from fluffy white to a crusty ice rink. Almost like Liz's cake, topped with white frosting and sprinkled with little colored candy things.

Did somebody say *sprinkled?* It was more like sandblasted. Because of this growing wind, the powdery white didn't so much fall to the ground as it laser-beamed sideways, looking for any exposed flesh to pepper with ten thousand stinging nips.

But this time Warney didn't say anything about doctor's orders or "Dad, you'd better not strain yourself." He just mumbled as they bundled up and stumbled outside to see what had really happened, or maybe it was the howl of the wind. One thing Warney was right about: It didn't get this cold around here too often. Gerrit could count on one hand the times he remembered: In 1949 and '50, when he was a kid about Mal's age, and the nor'easter piled up so much snow, it buried his dad's chicken coop. Then again in '60-something, when power was knocked out for weeks. It hadn't mattered so much then because most folks still heated with wood.

The blast in 1989 included a wicked silver thaw as well, and the weight of the ice snapped so many power lines that it stayed dark for a week of the coldest weather in years. Then, as now, the combination of partial melt-down and quick refreeze was the worst. But then it didn't do anything to e-mail and all that nonsense, since people didn't have e-mail and all that nonsense. Still, it had hurt a lot of farmers pretty bad, besides killing the local strawberry crop overnight.

And speaking of killing off strawberries, after five seconds in the cold, Gerrit's nose felt as if it had just been dropped into Marty Middelkoop's liquid nitrogen IQF warehouse, where they flash-froze local raspberries and strawberries for Smucker's jams, but mostly during the summer harvest. He'd been inside there once, and it had felt like a picnic compared to this. He didn't dare wiggle his nose for fear it would fall off.

"We're not gonna last too long out here, Warney," Gerrit yelled into the wind. It was all he could do to move his blue lips. But his crystallized words were blasted from his mouth, shattered into a thousand syllables and tumbled into the next county before they had a chance of reaching Warney's ear. Kind of like throwing a fistful of Alpha-Bits into a frozen hurricane. It would be a wonder if his son heard anything he said, but Warney nodded as if he had.

Meanwhile, the driver of the car in the ditch was trying to rock and roll his way out, backward and forward, forward and reverse, spinning his wheels and kicking up ice chips like a giant blender with the top off. Only this was no slurpee, and that was too bad.

"Hold it! Hold it!" Warney hurried toward the dark car with his hands up. A faint glimmer from the front porch showed the way and cast wild shadows in the row of bare maples lining the driveway. Gerrit had planted them himself thirty years ago, so he knew they could stand up to the wind. Had before. But he could not say how many of their branches would be stripped by the unwelcome Arctic Express, especially now that they were burdened with a heavy coating of ice. He labored behind his son, but each stride broke through the crust of frozen snow, which in turn grabbed his boots up to the shins and forced him to wrestle back his footing step by step.

Something about the stranded car, too, grabbed Gerrit when he drew close enough to make it out, though it hung at a crazy angle, shining its twin headlights blindly into the storm, straddling the edge of the driveway, and dipping its two right wheels into the little gully. How many people did they know who were fool enough to be out driving in a storm like this? And how many people did they know who drove a late model black Volvo sedan?

"Warney!" he shouted. "Warney, it's Joan!"

She looked out at them with wide eyes, as if she might have appreciated a helping hand just about then. But opening the driver's-side door would be like opening a hatch in a submerged submarine. It took both Warney and Gerrit to help tug it open, but once they did, a gust ripped it from their grip and nearly tore the door from its hinges.

"Am I ever glad to see you two!" Joan Horton fumbled with her seat belt. "Do you think we can get my car free?"

"Maybe in the spring." Warney wrestled the door and looked around. "Right now you're not going anywhere. Hope you brought your toothbrush, Miz Horton."

"I'm awfully sorry about this." She pulled a hood around her head more tightly. "It wasn't blowing nearly so hard when I left home. And then I tried to go to the store, but it was already closed. I had no idea…"

Her voice sounded weak and hoarse, but again maybe it was the screaming of the wind that nearly drowned her out. Not that she lived that far away. But they all knew how quickly the weather had pounced on them from the northeast.

"I hate to say this," replied Gerrit, "but you're probably the only one who's going to show up for the party."

Gerrit reached in to help her out—just as a crack like a gunshot over-head told him to duck and cover the door opening.

"Down!" he yelled. Hard to tell in the darkness, but it seemed as if half a tree had split loose in the wind. A cascade of sparks lit up the night sky overhead, followed by a crash somewhere behind them

"Dad, that tree just missed us." Warney gasped as he bent over the opening next to his father. "And the power lines snapped. We need to get her out of here."

Gerrit knew his son was right, and he turned to Joan. "Give me your hand!"

With Warney's help, she didn't seem heavy at all, and she half-climbed, half-slid up out of the door and off the side of her car. The tree had missed them all right, but in the process it had cut the power feed to the farm, which came directly off a pole from Vanderkrans Road. He remembered the day a lineman from Puget Power had restrung the line too close to the elms, but had anyone listened to Gerrit when he warned them something like this would happen? Of course, that was twenty-five years ago, and the trees had been only shoulder high at the time. What did it matter now? Gerrit helped support Joan in the icy snow while Warney wrestled the car door shut during a lull in the wind. At least she'd had enough sense to wear a good, heavy winter coat and boots.

"Meet you in the barns." Warney started off into the darkness. "I'll get the generators fired up and a couple propane heaters set up in the dry barn. Good thing we just milked 'em."

"Be right there." When Gerrit turned to see where they were going, he remembered the sparks from the downed power line. The shy beam of a flashlight lit their way from the dark kitchen window, but that was the only light he could see from the big, dark farmhouse.

"I'm terribly sorry to have caused you this trouble." Joan's voice was barely audible above the howling wind. "I really should have known bet-ter than to venture out in this kind of weather."

"Wouldn't argue with you there. But take it easy, eh?" Gerrit helped her high-step through the crusty snow back toward the house, but he broke through fairly easily. Joan's lighter weight only helped her balance on top of the crust part of the time, so she broke through every third or fourth step. She stumbled more than she stepped until she started using Gerrit's footprints as steppingstones.

"You have big footprints," she told him as they made it to the back porch. "Thank you."

He wasn't sure if anyone had ever thanked him for having big feet, but this time he didn't mind.

"But what about your animals?" she asked. "Are they all right in this weather?"

"They will be. You just get inside. Wood stove'll keep it warm in there."

But they didn't make it. Even over the wind, Gerrit heard Warney's yell, saw a flashlight blink from the barn and his hand waving.

"Did he say 'hurry up,' or 'help?'" She must have heard it too, because she had already paused.

"You should go on inside." He tried to push open the back door, but ice had already glued it shut. Anyway, she didn't seem to listen as he plowed across the yard to the barn.

"Wait for me!" She bounded across the ice after him.

*I*f this was any different from the running of the bulls in Pamplona, Joan couldn't tell. Because when they reached the barn, the herd had pinned Gerrit's son Warner against the outside of the door, only he certainly was no reckless young Spaniard.

"This way!" Gerrit nearly tackled the lead cow to pull her away from Warney. Joan saw an opening in the crowd and began to push one of the chocolate brown beasts from behind. The cows gave way reluctantly.

"You okay, kid?" Gerrit yelled.

Warney gripped his chest as if he had bruised a couple of ribs, but he nodded as Joan would have expected him to. Tough just like his father, no doubt. Satisfied, Gerrit took charge.

"Okay, then, I'll pull 'em out of the yard over there." Gerrit pointed at a huddle of cattle in the distant loafing sheds, exposed to the lateral fury of the nor'easter and looking more and more like giant mounds of frozen snow in a gazebo. He frowned. "Warney, you get the generators and the heaters fired up."

"I'll guide them inside," said Joan, and they both looked at her for a moment before Gerrit finally nodded. These animals had to understand how much they needed her help, whether or not she knew what she was doing. As long as she didn't get pasted up against the barn wall as Warney had.

The work helped keep her warm, especially when the cows started coming out of the cold a few minutes later, streaming in through the half-opened double doors into the dark old barn. Gerrit followed them in, whistling and shouting like some kind of cowboy.

And it didn't matter how much slush and half-melted snow they rubbed off on her nice green Eddie Bauer coat. The big animals were warm, and even warmer when Warney finally started a couple of propane-fired shop heaters and pushed them into place on a patch of concrete behind a row of water troughs. Gerrit upended his shovel and cracked through a thin skin of ice with the handle.

"Gonna be a long night, Warney." He stirred the water before allowing several cows to drink. "We'll set up a long chute and some fencing so we can drive 'em to the parlor when it's time. But you're not going to get 'em milked by yourself next time."

Not with all the extra labor the nor'easter would wring out of them. Yet even though the wind sent shivers through the barn and piled powdery snow like rows of giant anthills along the north wall, the animals were safe in here for the time being. Joan helped Gerrit shovel cedar shavings into their stalls, carefully avoiding their hooves and udders. He told her to mind her step and not to walk directly behind them, which was good advice for a number of reasons. And still they streamed inside, now that they had others to follow.

"Are we really going to fit them all in here?" she wondered aloud. "I don't see how."

Gerrit was not asking questions as he turned to his son.

"Come on, Warney!" he shouted. "We've still got room for fifty more! Help me pack 'em in."

She wasn't sure where or how they would fit, but Joan kept pushing and prodding next to Gerrit. He whistled and slapped, begged and scolded, wrestled and this time called them by name rather than by number. "Come on, Meathead and Rosalie. Give us some room there, Jumper.

Off my foot, Fifi." And one by one, they began to park the herd in the relative shelter of the little barn.

"Ahh, the aroma." He took a deep breath and smiled at her. "Almost
makes you wish you were a farmer, eh?"

"Almost." She glanced down at her muddy boots, caked with half-
frozen manure. "But not quite."

Still she continued pulling the animals into place, saying little and
knowing they would have to reverse the entire operation in a few hours
for the early morning milking. An hour later he grinned at her from over
the back of a cow, his face almost lost in a fog of cow breath.

"See, Joan? 'Whom he did predestinate, them he also called.' They all
fit, just like I told you."

She had to laugh at the way he had mangled, or rather, applied the
verse. "I'm not sure what cows have to do with Scripture, but I suppose
you're right about them fitting."

"'Course I'm right. And cows have everything to do with Scripture.
Ever met a farmer who's an atheist?"

"Up until a few months ago, I hadn't met any real live farmers,
period."

"Yeah, I s'pose I knew that. So what do you think of them, now that
you've met a few?"

She played along. "I'm still not quite sure. Most of the ones I've met,
at least on this farm, are pretty opinionated. You know those stubborn
Dutchmen."

He frowned in mock disapproval. "Something wrong with knowing
what you believe?"

"You're impossible." She held up her hands in mock surrender. "And
I am not going to let you corner me into another argument about whose
church is better. Not this time, Gerrit."

"Actually, your church wasn't as bad as I thought it was going to be."

She looked at him a little more closely. Had he said what she thought he'd said?

"The theology might be a little off base," he went on, "but your people were friendly and they weren't handling snakes. No big blond wigs either."

"Oh, so friendly people make up for what you think is bad theology?" She wasn't going to let him off that easily.

"Didn't say that. All I said was it wasn't as bad—"

"Okay, okay. I'm just surprised to hear that from you."

"Me, too." He smiled and pointed at her in warning. "So don't you dare tell anybody, or I'll be in trouble with the board. Next thing I know you'd have me get baptized again in some kind of dunk tank."

"And then you'd *really* be in hot water."

"Which sounds pretty good right now. You guys heat up your baptismal very good?"

They both laughed, and it made Joan laugh even more to see him laugh along. But he still had another question.

"Just one thing I still don't get, though."

"About getting baptized properly? Maybe you should ask Pastor Kevin."

"I don't want to ask Pastor Kevin," he growled. "I just want to know how you fit."

"How I fit?"

"That's right." He scratched his chin, as if working up to the question. "I mean, six days a week you're totally by the book, squeaky clean, no surprises. What's the word, *percillious?*"

"Impressive. You mean *punctilious.*"

"Hmm. No wonder that crossword puzzle didn't quite turn out. But you know what I'm saying. Your recitals are polished and everybody learns how to curtsy. All that. It's almost like you set your metrodome…"

"Metronome."

"Like you set your *metronome* and then keep your life by it. Am I right?"

She bit her lip. He was more right than she wanted to say, so she just nodded as he continued.

"Then on Sunday you go to a…freestyle church in the Grange hall where they play the drums and raise their hands and don't even have the prayers written down before they say 'em. Which I guess is fine by me, if that's what they want to do, and anyway I suppose it's none of my business. But does that make any sense to you?"

"As much sense as what *you* do."

This time he waited for her to explain while he tried to slip away from two cows that had boxed him into a moo-wich. He still hadn't caught his breath, even after Joan had. And obviously he wouldn't want to hear her life story, the story of a Nazarene pastor's kid who loved the piano and was pushed in front of a church audience when she was five. Oh, look at little Joanie play. Isn't she just adorable? And as much as she resented the attention, that's how much she loved it still.

But what did all that history have to do with anything? She would give him the *Reader's Digest* version.

"Ever since I visited your church last month, I've been thinking…"

"About converting?"

"Heavens, no." She smiled again. "I loved your church, even more than I thought I would. But it just made me wonder. You lead such a mud-filled lifestyle six days a week, and yet on Sunday your church is so measured out and precise, so…so orderly."

He chuckled and took a couple of deep breaths, holding on to his chest. By the way he was carrying on, she might have guessed he was trying to climb Mount Baker rather than round up a medium-size herd of dairy cows. "Yeah, I guess we don't have too much manure at First Church. Except maybe in the flower garden."

They studied each other, as if in a carnival crazy mirror. The farmer and the city girl. The man with the Truth and the woman with the Grace. Did they each have a little of something the other wanted? Joan started to scratch her head until she realized how filthy her hands had become, which only made him laugh.

"You don't get your hands dirty much, do you?" he asked.

"Is that something new you've just discovered?"

"Nope." He shook his head. "I knew you were different. But man, the more I find out about you, Joan Horton, the more I realize you're from a different planet."

"Oh, so now I'm an alien, am I?" She put her hands on her hips.

"Sorry." He almost looked serious as he studied her with those big blue Dutch eyes of his. "I guess it's just that you're going back home soon, so it don't matter."

His eyes widened as if he had just bit his tongue, then he did some very obvious backpedaling.

"I-I didn't mean that," he stammered. "Let's just say that I don't understand you very well, and you don't understand me."

"And *I* guess you would prefer to keep it that way?"

"Didn't say that. But listen, you're from New York; I'm from nowhere." He started counting their differences on his fingers. He would not have enough digits to finish. "You drive a fancy black Volvo with self-warming electric seats; I have a dirty old pickup. You plan everything out on that little handheld computer gizmo, and computers won't even talk to me. You think God gives choices, I know He's completely in charge. You—"

"Now, wait…" She couldn't let him get away with that kind of over-simplification. It wasn't quite so, at least not anymore. But he raised his hand and continued.

"And I don't think we even want to get into politics yet, do we?"

Perhaps not. Their arguments about religion had already almost done them in.

"You're right." She broke the promise she'd made to herself to not get emotional. "You don't know who I am, and you don't want to know."

"Pardon me?"

"No, that's not what I meant." Joan realized he could have taken it another way. "I mean, not that you wouldn't want to know because you don't care about people. It's just that there's so much you probably wouldn't *want* to hear about me."

"You mean about your prison sentence and all."

Did he say *prison sentence?* She gave him a sharp look, and he held up his hands in surrender.

"Just kidding. I'm sorry, really. Bad joke."

By that time Warney had made his way through the herd to where they stood.

"We're still missing six!" he hollered.

"You sure?" Gerrit looked around. So much for this heart-to-heart conversation.

"I counted twice, Dad. There are only 183 cows in this barn."

Gerrit didn't answer. He only frowned and squeezed his eyes shut. Joan knew right away something was wrong by the way he held on to the cow next to him for balance. But Warney didn't see it.

"Dad, did you hear me? I said we're going to have to go out and bring those six in."

"Gerrit?" Joan could not reach him fast enough. "Gerrit, are you all right?"

He slumped against the cow for balance, but when it shifted, he swayed and nearly disappeared between the animals, like a drowning man letting go of the lifeboat.

"Gerrit!" She screamed and dove for him before he fell.

Chapter 28

*I have no pleasure in any man who despises music. It is no
invention of ours: it is a gift of God. I place it next to theology.*
—MARTIN LUTHER

Naturally he would say he was fine, and naturally he would resist going to the clinic. Joan wasn't in the least surprised at the stubborn Dutchman's reaction.

"Listen, Dad, you're going to see Dr. Eubanks, and that's all there is to it." Warney paced next to the couch where they had brought his father.

"And if I'm not dead now, you'll make sure I'm killed out on the road. Is that the plan?"

"No, that's not the plan. That's silly, and you're just plain bullheaded. Since when have you ever been afraid of a storm?"

"Didn't mean that. You know I don't give a fig about storms and such."

"Well, you should, if it's about to kill you."

"I've told you a hundred times, Warney. God's going to take me when it's my time and not a minute sooner. And besides that, it wasn't a heart attack. It's called stable angina. I take a pill and it gets better."

"Yeah, how about you sweating like a pig?"

"I stepped in front of a shop heater."

"You were dizzy."

"How do you know what I was?"

"The pain in your chest?"

"Went away. Fifteen minutes after I took my pill, just like it was supposed to."

"But you couldn't catch your breath."

"Just because I was turning sixty and started feeling a little old to be rassling cows. Me and Missy are about the same age. Speaking of which, is the dog inside?"

Warney nodded. "I saw her awhile back in the laundry room. But I'm telling you—I should've called 911."

"The phone's dead, Warney. Remember?" He reached over and held out the telephone receiver to his son. There was no dial tone; the phone line had been taken out along with the adjacent power line. Warney looked around at the rest of the family for help.

"He's *your* father." Liz lit another candle stub from their winter emergency kit.

"What about Grandpa's birthday cake?" Mallory wanted to know.

Joan decided this would be a good time to evacuate the combat zone. "Come on, Mallory." She took her student by the hand. "Why don't we learn a new song?"

But she wasn't going to escape that easily.

"Actually, Mrs. Horton?" asked Mallory. "Don't you think my grandpa should go see the doctor?"

"I think…it's not my place to say."

"Yes it is. You're his teacher too, aren't you? Teachers can tell people what to do."

"Mallory." Liz tried to correct her daughter. "I don't think—"

"No, that's all right." Warney interrupted. "Maybe Mal is right. So what do you think, Mrs. Horton?"

"I'm sorry, Warner." Joan shivered, and not just from the chill wind reaching its fingers under the front door. "I have no intention of coming between you and your father."

"Nonsense." This time Gerrit spoke up. "Everybody else is giving medical advice. You should too. Jump right on in."

Joan paused while the wind rattled the living-room windows. Mallory looked up with a question in her face. So all right, then. He asked. He was her student. And she had been the one to pick him up off the barn floor. Perhaps she was entitled to a small measure of input. So she turned slowly to face them once more as their candles flickered in the draft.

"All right, then. You really want my opinion?"

"I do." He put out his hands. "Let's hear it."

"This is nothing personal, you understand." Another pause. "But I think you're just caught up in that 'old man' shtick."

"Shtick?" If Gerrit had looked pale before, all remaining color had just drained from his cheeks.

"Shtick, your act. It's a good New York word. I'm not sure what you call it here on the farm. Probably 'cow manure.'"

She had just crossed the line, horribly so. Still, she opened her mouth, and still more came out. Her express-train mouth had left the station and would not be arriving at its destination anytime soon.

"The point is, just because you're turning sixty and you have a sweet grandchild doesn't mean you're old. Come on. You certainly don't look it. In fact, you're not even close yet, and I thought you would be the first one to remind us of the fact."

"I—" he stuttered but she held up her hand. She wasn't finished with him yet. Because by that time, she knew if she didn't say it now, it would never be said. This would surely be the end of her short piano-teaching career in Van Dalen, and the tears welled up in her eyes.

But here goes.

"And another thing. I cringe every time I hear someone use that old I'm-going-to-die-when-it's-my-time-to-die nonsense, because even though it may be true in a sense, people use it as an excuse to be reckless—to bungee jump or smoke cigarettes or any number of other foolish things. And you...you just give it a little spiritual coating, perhaps so no one will question you, but it's the same fatalistic nonsense. I think there's a verse somewhere, 'Shall we go on sinning so that grace may increase?' That's exactly what's happening here, and…"

The weight of her own words caught up with her, bumping hard from behind in a tumbling torrent of delayed reaction guilt. Oh, if she could only freeze her tongue sometimes! It was all she could do to choke out an apology.

"I'm afraid I've gone and said far too much, and you have every right to be angry with me, but that's just my opinion, and I'm terribly sorry." By this time she felt her cheeks flush to a fever. "I do hope you'll see your doctor, though. Your family deserves it, no matter what you think."

By that time, Gerrit was picking his jaw up off the floor.

"Romans," he croaked. They all looked at him, but he wasn't looking back, only studying his big hands. What was he talking about?

"Romans," he repeated. "That's the verse you were trying to remember. Chapter 6."

So this is what crow tastes like.

Humble pie. Here, have another helping. The piano teacher had baked up a real good one for him. Funny thing was, with Joan Horton serving, he kept coming back for more. Somehow she'd made it taste all right.

"How are you feeling now?" She put a hand on his shoulder from where she crouched behind the jump seat. He nodded. And he had to admit the inside of Warney's Model 4120 John Deere four-wheel-drive tractor was pretty roomy. Well, it ought to be, for a hundred fifty grand or whatever his son had paid. They could have all been taking the big green machine on a picnic to Silver Lake, up in the Mount Baker foothills, rather than to the Van Dalen Community Hospital, if the weather had only been a little less brutal.

As it was, this was no picnic. Because even with his four-wheel-drive and big knobby tires, Warney was crawling along at about ten miles an hour to keep from spinning out, to be able to see ahead through the blizzard, and to keep their teeth from shaking out on Highway 51's bone-jarring washboard of packed snow and ice. At least they'd made it to their neighbor's house all right, and Larry Kroodsma had agreed to help milk the herd again. And if the regular milker showed, so much the better. But now they were on their way again, and he was holding on for dear life. How was he doing?

"P-pretty g-good." His stuttering came from the r-road, not the c-cold. Fact was, he had to unbutton his coat all the way down to keep from roasting. See, if he started sweating again, Warney would think he was having another heart attack, which he hadn't had in the first place. Simple angina, that's all it was. He pulled off his coat. "Everybody warm enough?"

They were by this time, so Warney turned down the heat, while Gerrit spied another ghostly casualty along the side of the highway.

"Lookit that one!"

A state patrol car with flickering red and blue lights had just pulled up behind an upended Japanese sedan, its trunk nearly buried and its front wheels in the air.

Hours later Gerrit was still thinking about the wrecks. Maybe because they reminded him a little of himself: wheels spinning, off the main highway, a little bit lost, a little bit busted. At least that's how it would feel through the night of poking and prodding, of tests and frowns and EKGs. With only a dozen beds, Van Dalen may have had one of the smallest hospitals in the state, but no one could tell them they didn't have some of the latest equipment. They even had a big-city PA system on which they regularly made announcements like, "Dr. Hartford, line three...Dr. Hartford, line three," instead of just having a receptionist holler, "Hey, Brad, would you pick up the phone?" Either way would have worked as well, but this was a hospital, not a barn.

"So is anybody going to tell me what all these tests mean?" Several hours had passed, and Gerrit had read through four *Field and Stream* magazines, cover to cover, and was on his fifth. Warney had either fallen asleep in the waiting room or had gone back home; he wasn't sure. But he wasn't going out in the hallway for nothing, not the way they had him dressed. What kind of clown came up with these hospital gowns anyway? Finally the doorknob turned, and Dr. Eubanks stepped into the examining room.

"Well, Gerrit, we're going to have to cut back on all these night parties, eh?" At least the doctor was smiling, sort of. Of course, that could mean a couple of things. But hopefully they weren't ready to turn him over to Van Grootveld's Mortuary and Funeral Home just yet.

"Yeah, I think it's morning, all right." Gerrit checked his wristwatch, which was just about the only thing they'd let him wear. "It was my birthday today, I mean, yesterday, and—"

"And you were out celebrating in the barn with the girls." Dr. Eubanks had a dumb sense of humor, too, and he returned to his straight face. "I heard the whole story from Warney."

"Still here?"

"No, he said he had to go back and help with the milking, so I briefed him on your condition."

"Am I the last to know?"

Dr. Eubanks frowned and flipped a couple of sheets from his clipboard. No more jokes.

"Okay, here's the thing, Gerrit. Your arteries are worse than ever, and x-rays show significant blockage. You know I've never been one to say, 'I told you so,' but…"

"But you told me so."

The doctor nodded. "I'm asking that they put you on a fast track for a bypass operation this afternoon, if possible, down at the St. Joseph's Cardiac Center in Bellingham."

"Whoa! This afternoon? What if I—"

"There's no more what-ifs, Gerrit." Dr. Eubanks held up his hand. "As far as I can tell, you had a small heart attack last night, and it's a good thing Warney was able to get to you as fast as he did."

"Actually, Joan Horton was the one who caught me."

"Oh, really?" The doctor almost grinned, then returned to his serious delivery. "Well, you're going to have to thank her later. Right now we're going to get you prepped and ready for transport. I hope they're able to get an ambulance through, otherwise—"

"Otherwise Warney can run me down in his tractor."

"I don't think so, buddy." Dr. Eubanks chuckled. "I'd rather airlift you, if that's what it takes."

"Oh, man. That's expensive."

"Will you cut it out with the expensive? We're talking about your life here."

"Reminds me of an old Jack Benny gag. A robber comes up to him and says—"

" 'Your money or your life.' I've heard it, I've heard it. But listen, I know the lead surgeon down there at St. Joe's. He's one of the best in the country. And if you're lucky, they're probably going to try an EVH."

"Luck's got nothing to do with it. And you're going to have to run that one past me again, only this time in English."

"EVH. Endoscopic vessel harvesting. It's a new procedure where they use a much smaller incision to harvest a graft vein."

"Which means?"

"Which means it should hurt less, heal much more quickly, and if all goes well, you should be back home in four or five days. They'll even use the beating-heart method, which means they won't have to shut you down completely."

"Well, that's a comfort. But does this mean I still have to cut back on the mayo with my Dutch fries?"

"What do you think?"

"That's what I thought."

By this time Dr. Eubanks was obviously into his me-doctor, you-patient mode.

"Listen, Gerrit. Everything changes from here on. The way you eat. The way you deal with stress. The way you live. I don't know how seriously you've taken it up to now. But as of today you've run out of excuses."

The doctor turned to go, and Gerrit noticed for the first time his 2:00 a.m. stubble and the way his thin gray hair had been slicked down in a hurry. But he stopped at the door without turning around.

"You know the hardest part about working here in Van Dalen, Gerrit?"

Gerrit might have taken a guess or two, but he let the doctor tell him.

"You're not the only one." He tapped his pen against the clipboard. "But I keep running into this attitude that…that it doesn't matter."

"Fatalistic nonsense from a bunch of stubborn Dutch Calvinists, right?"

Dr. Eubanks looked back over his shoulder with his left eyebrow raised, probably making sure it was Gerrit who had used those words and not him. He frowned, shoved the pen into the pocket of his wrinkled white hospital smock, and left without another word.

Funny. Gerrit had always assumed it was faith. Now he wasn't so sure. He'd never felt so exposed in his life.

Oh, not just by the flimsy hospital gown, which he could cover up with his coat—and did. He tied the sleeves around his waist just to be sure and tiptoed down the hall and around the corner to his assigned patient room, Room 2. Thankfully they didn't put him in Room 4, the one where Miriam had spent a couple of weeks before they transferred her to Swedish Hospital in Seattle to… He didn't want to finish that thought, though here in the hospital it was hard to avoid. And it was also tough to avoid the fact that each room was set up identically, with a single bed and a little rest room and a television hanging from the wall in the corner.

Just like Miriam's room.

The difference in this room was that it had been decorated with balloons. Five silver party balloons tethered to the stainless-steel hospital-bed railing.

"What's all this?" he wondered aloud.

"Looks like you have some admirers, Mr. Appeldoorn." The young night-shift nurse who could have been his granddaughter steered him to his bed, but he managed to slip out of her grip. Maybe Joan had been right: Lose the old man shtick. Lose the fatalistic nonsense, if that's what it really was. Lose the skimpy hospital gown.

"Need some help with that sheet?" asked the nurse.

Stifling a growl, Gerrit steered himself into position, smiled, and shook his head no. He felt the ventilation from abaft, so he slipped under the sheets, pulled a thin blanket up to his chest, and surveyed his realm.

The balloons—and he had no idea how they had materialized so quickly—read "Happy Birthday from Warney, Liz, and Mal," with a twenty-five-dollar gift certificate from the Windmill Grill. Really, they didn't have to do that. And then the little package…well, judging by the musical notes on the card, he knew exactly who it was from. And what was taped underneath proved the woman's impeccable good taste.

A Johnny Cash greatest hits CD.

Chapter 29

What the world really needs is more love and less paperwork.
—PEARL BAILEY

*J*oan sat next to the CCU bed, watching the heart monitor and Gerrit Appeldoorn's chest slowly rising and falling. The monitor's low, muted beep reminded her of a gentle metronome, keeping the time of life. She breathed a silent prayer of thanks with each beat.

"Glad you could make it from the north county," a nurse whispered as she changed the IV fluid. "I heard the roads were still icy."

Joan nodded. "I rode in this morning with Liz, uh, Gerrit's daughter-in-law. Even in her SUV, it took us nearly two hours with all the detours and slowdowns. But that just gave us more time to talk."

About Liz's job, about their struggles on the farm, about trusting God. It was the first time Joan had ever really talked with Mallory's mom, and she hoped not the last.

"Well, Dr. Tucker pulled off another one." The nurse's name tag said "April." "I hear the triple bypass was textbook, though it was a good thing they were able to bring him in when they did. We'll have your husband home to you in no time, Mrs. Appeldoorn."

"Oh." Joan shook her head and felt her cheeks flush. "He's not my husband. I'm just a...friend."

"Oh, I see." The nurse smiled and nodded as she scribbled a note on Gerrit's chart. Joan glanced down at her left hand, resting on the bed railing, but she wasn't able to pull it down into her lap quickly enough to prevent the nurse from noticing her wedding band. Before Joan could explain, the nurse had already turned on her heel and hurried out.

"Oh, dear," Joan sighed, but it also hit her as a little funny, funny enough to giggle softly as Gerrit's heartbeat metronome continued to play. It could have been Beethoven, that strong regular rhythm, punctuated by…giggles.

Mrs. Appeldoorn?

Still, Joan kept watch while Liz talked to the doctors and Gerrit continued his nap. Warney had promised to come a little later that day, as soon as Mal was out of school. Until then, it seemed a good time to pray, thanking her Savior for Randy and Alison, for little Erin, for Gerrit's recovery, for Mallory, for special strength…

"That's another thing I noticed about your church." Gerrit's hoarse whisper nearly launched her out of her chair. "Everybody prayed out loud and long. No silent stuff, the way we do at First Church."

"Gerrit Appeldoorn!" She caught her breath. "You nearly gave me a heart attack."

"Join the club."

"Oh, I mean, no, I didn't mean it quite like that."

Gerrit just smiled as he finally opened one eye then the other. "I hear they have some pretty good heart surgeons if you need."

"I suppose you should know. But rest. You don't need to talk."

"Suits me. They woke me up three times last night to take my pulse and blood pressure. I told 'em I'm used to 3:00 a.m. milkings, and this was pretty close to that."

She couldn't help laughing and hoped she wasn't making too much noise.

"So if you want to talk," he said, "I'll just listen to you. Why don't you start by telling me what time it is."

Joan consulted her watch. "Eleven thirty, Monday morning."

"Monday morning, right. I knew that. Triple bypass Sunday, on your feet Monday. How long you been here?"

She explained about the ride in with Liz, and Warney's plans to join them later.

"Well, I'm glad you didn't have to ride that big tractor of Warney's all the way down the highway. And I'm glad you're here now. But don't you have to get back to your students?"

"Not today. Classes are cancelled today."

"On account of the bad weather?"

"That, too."

For the first time in a long time she knew she was in the right place at the right time. No, she didn't have to be anywhere else, and no she didn't need to feel guilty about it. After a few minutes she apologized for going on and on, but did he understand?

"Sure I do. And did I tell you you're the best piano teacher in Nooksack County?"

She caught her breath when he reached out and covered her hand with his own. But she didn't move.

"You don't know what you're saying, Gerrit Appeldoorn."

"Do too."

"No, you should rest. They have you on some pretty strong medication."

"You mean I'm all doped up? Then you'd better not tell Reverend Jongsma."

"I think he'll understand."

"But when you get a chance, you can keep praying for me and all those other folks you were praying for. Mallory, too."

Joan smiled and shook her head as Gerrit closed his eyes once more and leaned back into his pillow. She didn't pull her own hand away until five minutes later, when he was snoring quietly.

It was sort of exciting and sort of scary. Exciting because Mallory had only ever been to the big hospital once before. She waved her foot in front of the automatic doors and watched them come to life.

It was scary, too, because Grandpa would be lying up in a hospital bed in Room 412, the way Dad had told her. He might be awake, or maybe not, or he might not be able to talk hardly at all. Warney wanted her to be prepared for anything. At least Grandpa was still alive, and Mallory's mom had told them he was doing pretty good, considering. Mallory held on to her father's hand as they went through the front doors and looked for an elevator.

"Hey, there she is!"

Not Mom. Mrs. Horton waved and smiled at them from where she was standing in front of the gift shop, and Mallory's dad looked happy to see her, too. So after Mallory's parents found each other, she didn't mind walking with her piano teacher up and down the long hallways, past the rooms with all the doctor equipment, through the big cafeteria that smelled of coffee and cinnamon rolls. She would have to wait her turn to see her grandpa.

"Are you hungry?" Mrs. Horton looked as if she had been awake for hours, because her eyes reminded Mallory of her father's, puffy with dark circles underneath.

"A little," Mallory replied. "I didn't have time for a snack."

So Mallory picked out a banana from the cafeteria line while Joan bought herself a cup of hot chocolate. Mallory explained how she could hardly wait to get off the bus and get to the hospital.

"I think Missy is sick, though," she said.

"I'm sorry to hear that." Joan sipped her chocolate and studied her student's face. "How can you tell?"

"She just sits on the rug by the dryer, kind of whimpering. Hasn't hardly moved in two days."

"Maybe she'll be better by the time you get back."

"Maybe."

"Your grandfather's doing better though. All he talked about today—when he was awake—was going home."

So Mrs. Horton had already seen Grandpa. They walked down the hall toward Room 412, and again Mallory looked up at her teacher.

"You like Grandpa, don't you?"

Mallory thought she saw Mrs. Horton flinch, only just a tiny bit.

"I like all my students." Mrs. Horton smiled and squeezed her hand. "Especially you."

Mallory had seen something flicker in her teacher's eyes, although Mrs. Horton was pretty good at stepping out of the way of embarrassing questions. Sort of like Gina stepped out of the way of the ball when they played dodge ball during PE. Gina was fast. So was Mrs. Horton, but not quite fast enough.

She didn't walk very fast, either, so as they got closer to Room 412, they could hear Dad and Grandpa talking about something. Discussing, maybe. Mrs. Horton frowned and checked her purse.

"You go ahead." She patted Mallory on the shoulder. "I'll be right along."

But as Mrs. Horton disappeared around a corner, Mallory wasn't sure she wanted to step into the middle of what she heard either. Instead, she made a face at the shiny waxed floor and listened.

"Whoa. SIX cows, Warney? How?" Grandpa's voice sort of echoed down the hallway for everyone to hear. Mallory didn't think he probably realized how much. If he wasn't a farmer, he could probably get a job here at the hospital, replacing the PA system. "How could we lose that many cows in one night?"

Dad's voice was lower, more mumbly and harder to understand, sort of like kids' voices got when they were being yelled at by the Van Dalen

Elementary School principal, Mr. Berkenbosch. He explained about the dead cows, then added something about sparing him the details.

"Listen, Son. What else aren't you telling me?"

"What are you talking about? You act like I'm hiding something."

"Well, are you?"

Dad didn't answer for a little while.

"I guess that's my answer," said Grandpa. "So…"

"I didn't want to tell you until later, Dad. I'm sorry."

Mallory heard a groan, then a few words she couldn't understand.

"Of course I know how many generations it's been in the family." Dad again. "I was raised on that place, just like you. But the real-estate guy says we can get a good price, pay off our debt."

"But you didn't come to me, didn't ask me for advice."

"You've had enough to worry about. The doctor said you shouldn't—"

"The DOCTOR?" Now everybody could hear Grandpa again. "You're taking what the doctor said over your own father?"

"That's not what I said. You're twisting it around, Dad. See? This is exactly why I couldn't tell you. You'd get all worked up, and it's not good for you."

"Shoot. That's about the lamest excuse I heard in sixty years. You know what the problem is here, Warney?"

"Don't tell me."

"Problem is you're listening to the wrong people, the people with suits and degrees, instead of folks who have actually lived through it before. That's the problem. So you get into a bind, and you run."

"Just listen to me for once, would you? We have no choice. Losing the cows was just…well, you have no idea how far in the hole we are. We have to sell the farm, and that's all there is to it."

Mallory could still hear the *beep-beep* of the heart monitor, just down the hall. By that time she could hear her own heart beating too, mainly because she understood every horrible word. Her dad went on.

"So I talked to Will deWeerdt about putting the stock up for auction, even before all this came down. We'll be auctioning most of the equipment, too, and some of the stuff in the house."

"Tell me you're not serious."

"I'm sorry, Dad. Really I'm sorry. I wish I *could* tell you I was joking. We just have no choice anymore."

No choice. Now that she'd heard it all again, she knew how much she hated every word. Hated it even more than practicing the piano. And the tears flooded her eyes so the overhead fluorescent lights turned blurry and she could hardly see.

"Mallory. There you are. I thought you'd be in your grandfather's room." Mallory didn't need to see; she heard the clicking of her teacher's shoes approaching on the tile floor, just as she heard the PA system crackle to life.

"Paging Joan Horton. Joan Horton to the reception desk, please."

Joan quickened her step as she approached the front desk, wondering who would have summoned her and why. She didn't have long to wonder when she saw her daughter waiting, her back turned, the baby resting in her arms.

"Alison?" Joan touched her on the shoulder. "What are you—"

"Oh, Mom!" Alison spun and hugged her mother with Erin somewhere between them. Her sobs made it clear this was no casual visit.

"Alison, Alison, whatever is wrong? Is Erin okay? Shane?"

The answer could not come for more than a minute, as Alison cried into her mother's shoulder. Joan tried to hold her as best she could.

"Tell me what's wrong, dear." Joan couldn't keep from crying herself; she felt her daughter's pain even if she didn't know why. "It's all right."

When Alison finally looked at her mother's face and tried to catch her breath, Joan knew it was not all right.

"It's Randy," Alison gasped, and a thousand fears instantly bubbled to the surface. "I…we got a call this morning from a hospital in New York."

Joan had to keep her eyes open, but the wail began to take shape deep in her heart. No. Don't say it, Alison. Please, no.

"Is he?" Joan could not finish the question.

"He's alive. There's been some kind of accident. They say he tried to kill himself."

Chapter 30

Where the Lord closes a door, somewhere He opens a window.

—MARIA in *The Sound of Music*

*J*oan did her best to sleep, but even with the cabin lights dimmed and her headset tuned to the *Classical Sounds of Peace,* sleep would not come. Peace would not come. Not surprising, given the news about Randy. She glanced at her watch and added three hours, East Coast time. Was he resting? How soon could she get to where he was? Couldn't this plane fly any faster?

Her mind replayed the events of the past several days, starting with her foolish decision to drive to Gerrit Appeldoorn's party in a worsening blizzard. She should have known better, but what could she do about it now? And what could she have done about any of the events that followed?

She supposed it was one more example of how God had a way of turning her worst foolishness to good, and that almost seemed like Gerrit speaking, not her. Because what if she had not been there in the barn to help break Gerrit's fall? Or what if she had not gone along to the hospital? At the end of one of the worst days of her life, she could still smile to herself at the thought of Gerrit reaching out his hand to her from his recovery bed.

Now Florence Nightingale zoomed from hospital to hospital, praying for the man—the men—in her life. She was glad Alison had helped her catch a shuttle to Sea-Tac airport. Never mind what the walk-on plane ticket to New York had cost her.

The plane jostled into a patch of turbulence as she prayed, reminding her how the world always seemed far different at thirty-three thousand feet. Different, even if she could not see the Midwest fields and cities passing below her. And for a moment, despite the bucking of the plane, she actually did drift off into a dream. She was still safely at home on Delft Street, enjoying a bowl of popcorn and a cozy evening of watching the black-and-white classic *It's a Wonderful Life*.

Randy's favorite. Pretty soon an angel named Clarence would appear to help her out of this horrible mess. But instead, she woke with a start and nearly checked her pocket for Zuzu's rose petals—Jimmy Stewart's proof that he wasn't crazy after all, that the strange Dickensian nightmare he'd been shown wasn't real.

Since she'd heard the news about Randy, her life resembled *It's a Wonderful Lie* more than anything else. Everything was not all right, even if she had once given Gerrit the impression it was. And as usual, she had no idea how to refloat the shipwrecks of her guilt-ridden life. So she would not blame Gerrit if he called off the remainder of his lessons after she returned from seeing Randy. He could certainly do without all the emotional baggage she now dragged from hospital to hospital and coast to coast. Gerrit had his own family to care for, people who surrounded him with love. Clarence wouldn't be appearing, and her pockets remained empty.

Randy was also alone, facing his own nightmares without even an angel's help. She should have been there for him. She should not have left. How could a mother not be there for her son when he was going through…what, exactly? What horrible experiences had he been through to convince him there was no more hope in this world?

To her shame, she didn't know, other than what Alison had told her briefly about pills, an overdose, and some kind of accident. She'd been too absorbed in her own self-centered funk to know. Too entangled in her one-year sabbatical escape to do more than just leave messages on his machine, exchange the occasional e-mail pleasantries, and pretend he was okay. Too busy finding herself and losing him. And while she'd been stuck on the rearview mirror of her life, looking at the past, Alison's announcement at the hospital jolted her into realizing she'd collided head-on with the present.

Or rather, her Randy had. And the realization stung more than anything she could remember, salt water on an open wound of regret. If the DWI arrest last year had been a warning sign, how in the world had she ignored it? What could she have done differently? Her mind spun until she could no longer hold her head up. God help her, she just didn't know.

Just as she had not known with Jim. Back then, all she could think of, all she could suggest was that they look into the Word, that he pray about his mood swings. Give it to the Lord.

Good advice? Of course. But in the past year, somehow she'd twisted it into an excuse to avoid facing her problems head-on, twisted until only guilt remained. And, dear Savior, couldn't she leave that kind of guilt behind?

I am so sorry. She brought her hands to her tears, knowing it was only a dress rehearsal for another, more bitter apology to come. *I really don't know what he's been through, Lord. But this time I'm going to be there for him, if You just get me there before anything else happens.*

A touch on her shoulder brought her back to reality. And opening her sticky eyelids brought her nearly face to face with a slender young male flight attendant in a navy blue airline uniform, holding a tray with a steaming Styrofoam cup.

Clarence?

"Hope I didn't disturb you, ma'am. You asked for some tea? Would you like milk or sugar with that?"

She didn't recall asking for anything of the sort, but she wasn't surprised. The way her mind was working lately, she could probably have ordered an entire meal and forgotten two minutes later. In any case, something hot sounded very good right now. So she didn't bother with any questions, just thanked him and accepted the drink. And since no one around her seemed to claim it, she cradled the warmth between her palms, took careful sips, and stared past the empty seats beside her, out the dark window. A cluster of yellow-white lights glimmered in the distance below them. Des Moines? Madison?

She had no way of knowing. But again the plane dipped and shook, and the "fasten seatbelts" sign blinked on with an announcement from the captain that they would try to avoid oncoming turbulence at a higher altitude.

That was fine, though the turbulence didn't bother Joan as much as it usually would have. Perhaps she was too concerned with her personal turbulence to care. She was actually more worried about spilling tea on her lap. And as the plane approached the East Coast, she began to quietly hum "O God, Our Help in Ages Past," hymn number 170 from the Psalter Hymnal, the way they'd sung it in Gerrit's wonderful church, especially the lines about "our shelter from the stormy blast, and our eternal home."

Home. Where was it anymore? Somewhere between Port Hamilton and Van Dalen her heart had been torn in two. Accidentally, on purpose, she wasn't sure, and it didn't matter. And now they'd be expecting her back at Gaylord in a few short months, preparing for next year's program and setting out an entire new schedule of classes. They'd even hinted that she was first in line for the open position of department head, if she wanted it. She could tell them in a few weeks. Yes, she would eventually look forward to the new school year, as always, except that this year she had only half a heart left to give to her work. The other half she would leave behind with students like Mallory...and Mallory's grandfather.

By tomorrow Gerrit would probably be sitting up, certainly asking the doctors when he could go home, perhaps worrying Warner and Liz by not sitting still, maybe trying to talk Mallory into pushing him down the hall. The thought brought a tired smile to her lips, and she wondered how different her life might have been had she not taken this sabbatical. A little less pain? Perhaps. But how else would she have reconnected with Alison or learned what it really meant to be a grandmother?

In the meantime, her plane would bring her to LaGuardia soon enough. The only thing was, Randy had no idea she was coming. And she had no idea what she would say when she arrived.

Chapter 31

The best and most beautiful things in the world cannot be seen
or even touched—they must be felt with the heart.
—HELEN KELLER

The outside of the Long Island University Medical Center bore little resemblance to Van Dalen's little hospital. Joan supposed it was something like comparing a 747 to a hang glider. As much as she had pushed herself down the icy interstate north and then east from La Guardia, now she could only stand and stare at the twenty-story tower— at the entry door opening and closing for doctors and nurses, for gaggles of med students with clipboards, for support workers with billowy blue smocks, and for the occasional family member like her. In the early afternoon light they reminded her of two kinds of people arriving at or leaving an airport: those glowing with the prospect of welcoming a loved one home, or those dragging themselves away from a reluctant good-bye. Here there seemed to be nothing in between, only sweet anticipation or bitter separation. Joan bit her lip, not yet knowing which she was.

At least New York's winter seemed milder than the Pacific Northwest ice she had escaped. Strange, but a hint of spring had quietly invaded the planters surrounding the hospital, with a greening and a hopefulness she could only dream of. But she couldn't just stand here in the drizzle and watch the flowers. With a sigh she pushed toward the door and stepped inside.

This would be, what, her third hospital in less than a week? Yet she feared this one might not contain the body of anyone she recognized any longer, only a stranger. How far had Randy slid to find himself in this situation?

"It's okay, dear. I'm sorry…" She whispered the words over and over as she made her way down one hall, then another, then up an elevator. And as she rehearsed her lines, the obvious questions haunted her: Why? How? For the first time in her life, she wished she had not memorized so many Scripture verses when she was growing up. But still she could not shake the impertinent image of a ten-year-old little Joanie, the one her dear father had filmed with his eight-millimeter Kodak movie camera and showed to their family over and over ad nauseam.

She had a yellow gingham dress on, though naturally the yellow didn't show through in the black-and-white film, but she remembered it all too well. And she stood up on the church platform with her little white gloves on, reciting the dozens of verses that had earned her a red-letter-edition *King James* Bible. Only why did that verse keep coming to mind?

"Numbers 14:18." The squeaky little voice had not been enshrined on the film, only the lips moving. But she still recalled every word. "The LORD is longsuffering, and of great mercy, forgiving iniquity and transgression."

Which would have been fine right there, if she hadn't been so diligent to memorize the last half of the verse: "And by no means clearing the guilty, visiting the iniquity of the fathers upon the children unto the third and fourth generation."

Then the camera panned across the clapping, smiling church audience, dear brothers and sisters who had no idea of the horrible truth. To the third and fourth generation? That would include Randy. But like a mama bear protecting her cub, all Joan could feel right now was a brief, unreasonable fury at Jim for dragging their son into such a pit with him. No, he had not sinned, and depression was no sin. But like the sin that reached to the third and fourth generations, could the echoes of Jim's depression have reached this far without his even knowing it?

Though she had never before quite understood the full implications of that obscure Old Testament verse, she knew now. As she had suspected, this was no matter of fairness, of a wrathful God gleefully snubbing great-great-grandchildren for the mistakes of ancestors they had never known. No, this was about consequences, the power of ugly choices to reverberate across years, touching and twisting and handicapping innocents in its wake. With every step closer to Randy's room, she knew it could not be all his fault, no matter what choices he had made.

Could it?

Somewhere between the elevator lobby and the ICU she had started jogging. "That would be Room 210, ma'am. Second floor, down the hall... Resting comfortably. Past the elevator and to the left. But—"

Joan didn't wait for the rest of the receptionist's explanation.

It's not your fault, Randy.

A teenager pushing a linen cart stared at her as she flew by, but by this time she hardly cared. What would Gerrit have said?

"I don't give a fig what they think."

And she didn't; she nearly bowled over an orderly, but that hardly slowed her down. Past Rooms 220, 214, 212. And finally she grabbed the railing on the wall just outside Room 210 to steady herself, wipe away the tears, and catch her breath.

"Excuse me, you can't go in there!" A nurse with a stethoscope necklace stepped up to intercept, but Joan was ready for her.

"I'm his mother." She did not wait for a reply, just slipped inside...an empty room.

~

"Don't mind if I do." Gerrit slurped another spoonful of steaming chicken noodle soup, not bad for a hospital lunch, but nothing like homemade Dutch *erwtensoep*—green pea soup. At least he didn't have to worry about eating in front of anyone. Warney sat in a vinyl-clad waiting-room chair, eating from a bucket of extra-crispy Kentucky Fried Chicken legs and buttered biscuits.

"What about Joan?" asked Warney, taking a large bite of his biscuit. At least that's what Gerrit thought he said. It was a good question.

"Thought you knew." Gerrit blew on his next spoonful of soup and looked over at a clock on the wall. "She should be at the hospital where they took her son by now. She said she'd call. I'm just a little worried about the way she drives, though. *If* she drives, I mean; she went into one ditch already."

Warney looked back at his dad with wrinkled eyebrows. Huh? Liz stared at him at first puzzled, then with a knowing female smile. She set down her *People* magazine.

"I think we missed something there, Gerrit," she said.

Pardon?

"Warney asked what to do about his *bones,* his chicken bones. And you say you're worried about her sliding into a ditch. Are we talking about the same bird?"

"Oh, bones…I thought you said… Well, forget it. Guess my mind was somewhere else."

Joan could have used a translator to help her understand what the doctor said as he walked her to the room in the psychiatric lockup ward where Randy had been transferred. But she understood most of it: He had been transported from their home in Port Hamilton. The ER doctor had ordered a rapid qualitative urine drug test, then a series of quantitative blood tests for tricyclic antidepressants and benzodiazepines, in this case Elavil and Xanax.

"Are those illegal?" asked Joan. She had no idea.

The doctor shook his head no. "Prescription," he explained, before lapsing back into doctor-speak about inserting the NGT (nasogastric tube) to suck out any pill fragments, then how they poured activated charcoal down the tube to bind to any remaining poison.

Joan winced as she understood too well what the doctors had done to Randy. Was that the same as pumping his stomach?

"We don't do lavage unless we know the time of ingestion was less than one or two hours. In this case, we didn't know. We've had him on a cardiac monitor to watch for arrhythmia. So far so good."

So Randy had made it through the mandatory twenty-four-hour observation period; now his ninety-six-hour hold took effect.

"That means he has to stay here for the next four days?" she asked.

"That's the law, ma'am. You can have him back after that, assuming he behaves."

By this time they had arrived at Randy's *real* room: a small, antiseptic triple room in the tenth-floor psychiatric ward. The doctor nodded and ushered the way in with his clipboard, then he retreated to the hall. Randy was dozing in the first bed of three, closest to the small rest room, while a wall-mounted television blared a game show. Ceiling curtains created three undulating partitions, which didn't offer ultimate privacy, but at least Joan was the only visitor at the time.

"Knock knock?"

He opened an eye as she stepped inside.

"Mom?" Randy's voice sounded thinner than Joan had ever heard it, and were he anyone else's son, she probably would have recoiled at the sunken, unshaved face propped up by a hospital pillow. But this was her little boy, this skinny young man with tubes feeding his spindly arm and a heart-monitor wire taped to his chest.

"Oh, Randy." She reached out to brush aside the sweaty curl of hair from his forehead. And she tried not to wince, but this reminded her far too much of where she had just come from. Only this was not Gerrit Appeldoorn, and the irony of how much better Gerrit had looked did not escape her.

"You don't need to talk about it now," she told him.

So he didn't, and she waited all the way through *Wheel of Fortune* thinking about all the phone messages she had left, all the answers she hadn't heard. *Jeopardy!* was almost over before he finally cleared his throat.

"Mom…" The words barely escaped his cracked lips, and she had to lean forward to make them out. "I'm glad you're here."

"I know, Randy, I'm just sorry—"

"Don't apologize." He held up his hand a couple of inches, far enough to stretch the tubes. "Not for something I did."

"But what did you—?" She clapped a hand to her mouth. Too much too soon. Randy said nothing for a long minute, then sighed.

"You want the long version or the short version?" he finally whispered.

"Either. Neither. It doesn't matter."

He nodded and closed his eyes, as if trying to decide. A long minute later the words began spilling out, slowly at first, then picking up speed.

"Okay, so I take too many…Elavil and lay down on the couch. Pastor Tim comes to the door and starts knocking. He wants to go out for coffee and sees me through the door. So when he walks in and can't wake me, he freaks out and calls 911."

His shoulders shook. "That's the short version."

"The doctor told me all about the tests." She stroked his hair. "I don't know if I understood it all, but what is this Elavil?"

"Antidepressant. The doctor here said I need something else from now on."

"You never told me about that."

"You didn't ask."

Oh. Joan closed her eyes and prayed for words to say, ears to hear. The broken heart, she already had. She sat quietly, waiting and wondering how to reconnect with the son she had once known.

"So…is there a longer version?" She had to know more than just what the police knew. So she listened as he finally told her about first losing his job at the market, then the fiasco at Lou's West End Choice Pre-Owned Autos, then the horrible part-time work at the video store down the street. The stories took them through *Who Wants to Be a Millionaire?* then *Family Feud.* She nodded as he told her of the depression and sleeping. And she cried as he described the feeling of slipping into a pit and not being able to get out, as if it were always raining and nothing was good anymore.

She held on to his hands and listened, just listened.

"I guess my days and nights have just been all scrambled. So I hardly remember when I took the Elavil. I just wanted to sleep forever. I mean, one minute I'm watching *Hollywood Squares,* the next minute I'm waking up here, all hooked up."

He closed his eyes against tears.

"I'm such an idiot. I don't remember hardly anything, so it wasn't like some glorious going-out-in-a-flame-of-glory kind of thing."

"There's nothing glorious about…suicide." She choked out the word. "No matter how it happens."

"Tell me about it. I was determined before I sank down into this swamp that I was not going to be like Dad."

The words caught her off guard, as if she had swallowed wrong.

"I know what you're trying to say, Randy, but I don't know if it's really a good comparison."

He didn't reply.

"I mean to your father."

Actually, she knew the comparison was at least partially accurate. Of course they'd never told Randy everything about his own father's secret depression. But suicide?

"You have no idea, Mom." He finally looked at the wall as he took another deep breath. "Listen, I don't know if now's a good time. All I know is I'm flat on my back, and I can't keep it a secret anymore."

A secret? He wrestled with the words as if they caused him more distress than the tubes and the monitors, and by this time his eyes brimmed with tears. What did he know?

"Randy?" Sitting so close to a horrible *Something* chilled her to the core. What was he trying to say?

"I was only trying to protect you, Mom. You've got to believe me. I thought if you knew what really happened to Dad, you'd fall apart."

Joan closed her eyes for a moment, tried to keep from hyperventilating. No. She knew what had happened. She was the last one to speak to him. She knew his heart better than anyone. Even so…

"Tell me," she said. "Just tell me."

He shook his head no and pointed at the little table next to his bed where a nurse had placed his things: a green nylon wallet, a tin of mints, a small bunch of keys, and a crumpled yellow envelope with Joan's name printed in small block letters on the front.

"Six years. I've been toting that…that note around for six years, Mom. Didn't know what else to do with it but keep it in my wallet. Guess I should have thrown it away when I had the chance."

By then nothing held back the tears coursing down his cheeks.

"It was on the kitchen table when I came home early from snow camp the day he didn't. Only I never showed it to anybody. Especially not you and Alison."

"But why not?"

"Read it, Mom."

Curiosity didn't make her reach out a trembling hand, didn't make her open the note. Only dread moved her hands to unfold the years of wrinkles and read the single page stained by teardrops but still readable.

Jim had always had such neat handwriting. But his words hit her with such force she had to stop.

No! Had Jim really thought such things? Had he really intended to end his life, sitting in their family cabin at Great Sacandaga Lake? The horror slapped her breath away, dragged her back to the memory of his phone call that morning, when he'd reached her at the women's retreat. If he'd written this suicide good-bye, it would have been before the time he'd called to promise her he'd be home, that he'd fix dinner. Because no matter how many years went by, she would not forget the hopeful sound of his voice. She could hear the difference between A-flat and A-natural, for goodness' sake! And he'd never said anything to her about…this. So something had happened to her husband after he'd written this note, before he'd called her from that pay phone in the middle of a blizzard. Only what?

"I'm just sorry, Mom. I didn't want it to end up like this. I'm sorry."

By that time her own tears had soaked his sheet, and she could only hang on to Randy's hand and to the crumpled note. The truth was supposed to set him free, but right now it just broke her heart all over again to finally understand what kind of burden Randy had tried to carry for so long. And to see how deeply it had dragged and pulled at his life.

Now the burden fell at her own feet.

"He never mentioned this note to me," she whispered. "I think he must have been ashamed. But when he called me, he told me he was on his way home."

Randy still shook his head. She wasn't finished yet.

"I knew your father, Randy. I knew he wasn't happy about his job. And he might have thought about ending it all, but when he talked to me, he wanted to live. You have to believe me. He wanted to live. If he went to the cabin to die, the way it said in his note, then he changed his mind. He was coming home to live."

She crumpled the note, wanting both to destroy it and to preserve a horrible piece of family history. He studied her tear-streaked face with a tilt of suspicion.

"I never knew about any phone calls, Mom. I just know what he wrote. And when he died, you can see how I put the pieces together."

She took a deep breath, recalling the horrible day of that other snowstorm: the police, the confusion.

Looks like he must have had to stop for the blizzard, Mrs. Horton.

The snow just plugged the tailpipe, ma'am. Nobody saw the little car in the drift. He probably just fell asleep and...

And never woke up.

We're very sorry.

But Randy hadn't heard all that. She remembered the teenager who had run up to his room and locked the door. And then she understood how he could have missed what really happened. How he had intercepted the note his father had surely wanted to take back but never could.

"It's not the way you think, Randy. I'm so sorry."

She hadn't meant to, but how could she have held back the truth from him, a cure to a deadly misunderstanding? More than that, she hadn't even recognized the disease that had gripped Randy, this depression. Passed from father to son, perhaps, but oh, if she had only known, perhaps she could have blunted its pain.

She tried to remember everything again, tried to explain the hope she had held, while Randy listened. Did it all make sense to him, this upside-down truth?

"I don't know, Mom. I'd like to see it that way, but..."

Maybe he would believe again, or maybe it would take a little more time. She could wait, either way. And when she could explain no more, they just cried together in their shared grief until the tears ran dry. And once again the quiet words of a hymn came to her heart.

Gerrit's hymn.

O God, our help in ages past. She heard the tune as it played in her head, heard the voices singing. *Our hope for years to come…*

And there *were* years to come.

Be thou our guide while life shall last, and our eternal home.

Chapter 32

When you come to a fork in the road, take it.
—YOGI BERRA

his was his place.

Kelsey Creek ran deep and cold this time of year, swelled by the chilled rains of early March, yet half-frozen and still holding respectfully below the bank. Her waters had long ago abandoned the tea shades of midwinter, borrowing instead rich iron red leached from the forest floor and ferrying it downstream to the waiting Nooksack River.

This *was* his place, all right.

Gerrit studied his shattered reflection from the high bank, ankle-deep in week-old snow and far over his head in memories. But they tumbled about like the waters below his feet, none clear enough to float to the surface, all tossed and blended as if they had somewhere important to go and couldn't stop to linger in the eddies of remembering. Here by himself a week after his operation and firmly on his feet, Gerrit just watched the waters and ignored the chill.

Because this was *his* place.

A raccoon worked the far shore, upstream and nearly out of sight behind an overhanging blackberry bramble that still clung to dried skeletons of last fall's fruit. Strange he was out in the daylight like this. Ignoring the statue of an old man, the coon reached down for his supper and found it. He looked a lot like Ray Charles reaching for a note on his piano. But the little guy's fine, black-gloved hands flashed too quickly, and Gerrit could not see whether it was stickleback or crawdad. Either would do.

He supposed it was the raccoon's place as well.

So Gerrit hardly breathed, afraid to disturb his friend's meal. And the raccoon obligingly paid no attention, so he finally relaxed enough to refill his lungs with damp air. This time he smelled years in each breath, and that was how the memories finally came to be measured. How many times had he heard the story?

Gerrit's great-grandfather, Opa Joost's father, had cleared this land with an exceeding strong back, a bucksaw, and a double-headed ax, but he'd left this grove of towering red cedars and Douglas firs alone, left it to shelter the creek as it snaked through what would become prime grazing land. Here the cedars had survived, and the tallest had been saplings when Lummi Indians had hunted and fished here for generations before. Every year the generous trees had grown another rung and drizzled yet another layer onto the aromatic carpet under his feet.

"I'm going to miss you, old girl." He patted the fresh dirt over the spot where they'd buried Missy, let a tear water the little grave, and straightened the little sapling Mal had placed there earlier that day. A memorial tree, she'd said, and everyone had thought that was a good idea. Several of the sapling's big brothers had met their end during the storm and now lay dead on their sides with upturned roots gasping for breath. The thought made him shiver, not the cold, as he felt the tug on his own roots. Another cold sleet began to soak through Gerrit's Mariners cap, but he hardly noticed. The raccoon paused and looked up, but looked right through him. Maybe he was already somewhere else.

Growing up, Gerrit liked to think his great-grandfather had left such a greenbelt here by design, that he intended to create this riverine monument to God's glory. Maybe the old pioneer had envisioned a prayer retreat or a place to escape from the unending chores, a place where a man could come for a few minutes to catch his breath.

If he had, though, he hadn't told anyone about it. The pictures Gerrit had seen of the man made him look like a mean son of a gun, with a glare cold enough to freeze water. Of course, that's how they took pictures those days. Serious and straight-backed, without a lot of foolishness or teeth showing. That was just the way it was.

But this place? More than likely Great-Grandpa had simply run out of steam after slashing and burning enough acreage for his growing family. He would have been beat after carving out a clearing in these tall quiet woods, yanking out stumps and roots with only a mule to help, roughing out a place to build their home and run their livestock. For sure, Great-Grandpa knew nothing about the setback regulations and riparian zones Warney had learned so much about in college, and that kind of ignorance would have been one great advantage to living back then.

But no, he'd probably just reached the end of his day and quit, shucked the harness, and let the mule rest down here by the creek. Probably he was just plain tired of cutting down trees, just plain tired of fighting. And as Gerrit's bone-tired sigh turned to a prayer, he guessed he knew the feeling, though he wished he did not.

I've had enough fighting, Lord. The words slipped out in a whisper, and he couldn't have stopped them if he'd wanted to. But it was true.

And I don't want to fight Warney, especially.

The creek gurgled in reply. A sad sort of smile crossed his lips, as if it felt good to say "uncle" to the God of Kelsey Creek and the God of the universe. Even at his age? Fact is, it felt good, mighty good, this cutting loose these roots that had maybe run a little too deep. Hadn't they? Is that why it hurt at the same time?

Go ahead, Father. He paused, but he knew what he had to say. He stared at the lifeless tree trunk with the outstretched roots and took a deep breath. *Okay, cut. Cut the roots already, would You?*

No, he couldn't recall ever talking to the Lord quite like this, but he had waded into this prayer and it was no time for changing his mind. If what he had believed all his life was true, God had had this moment planned for a long, long time.

So whatever it takes. Before these old roots rip apart in this storm.

Over on the other side, the raccoon must have finished his meal. He wiped his little hands one last time, sniffed the air, and shrank back into the bush to rejoin his family, leaving Gerrit alone to finish his odd conversation with the Almighty.

And well, he'd more than said his piece, maybe said too much. God didn't necessarily need an amen, but Gerrit added it for good measure, the way they'd said amen at Joan's church. And as he stared at the rippling waters once more, the memories surfaced, but only for a moment, like a flash of silverfish scales from the water below or a dream half-remembered in the still of a morning after the milking but just before breakfast.

Now he knew what he was leaving behind. For that briefest of moments, Gerrit remembered himself wading in the creek below, chasing king salmon with his hands in October, falling in and thrashing about like a spawning fish. He remembered skipping stones in the quiet waters of April, trying to see who could beat Lenny Hekkema's seven skips. He remembered swinging by a long-forgotten rope into the cold July swimming hole, leaving his clothes piled in a heap on the bank. He remembered the times he had come here to pray, mostly for the kids, but for other things, too, for the tears of childhood past.

Then the memories washed away for good, leaving him with his own tears, dropping one by one into the pool below his feet, joining the musical melody of a steadily increasing rain. The tears came not just for yesterday but even more for today, for the sudden empty ache that had pounded in his chest since Joan had hurried off. And he wondered if she might not come back or if he might not again hear her music, the way he had heard it last year from across the farmyard.

Honest, now? It was one thing to let God cut his roots, as much as that would hurt. But it was quite another thing to step out alone.

So as he watched the ringlets on the water, he imagined how his salty tears would join the sweet waters of the creek for only a few short miles before joining the salty bay. And he imagined that if he stood there long enough, those tears might return again to rain and soak his head and…

And shoot, that sounded way too much like some kind of New Agey school lesson or half-baked newspaper exposé in the *Seattle Times* about recycling or evil polluting dairy farmers and how they needed to be more environmentally conscious. Shoot. He was getting soft in the head. He'd find a new place to live and that's all there was to it. With a grunt he scooped up a handful of slush and flung a half-melted snowball into the creek. Not such a bad arm for an old guy.

He stooped to gather another, packing it into a second globe. A twig snapped somewhere behind him—probably an ice-laden branch falling to the ground, maybe another crow. They had been out in force for the past several days, scrounging food through the worst of this nor'easter. Liz had even felt sorry for the scavengers, and she had tossed a pile of bread crusts out on the ice to be gobbled and squabbled over. And sure enough, a pair of skinny old crows had landed on the log just below him. So he took aim, wound up, and changed his mind. That surgery, remember? Besides, they weren't hurting anybody, just being themselves. Instead, he wiped his nose on his sleeve, tossed the slushball underhand into the trees on the far side of the creek, and turned to see his granddaughter standing at the edge of the woods.

"What are you doing here, girl?" he called out louder than he might have, just to be sure he cleared his throat of any remaining frogs.

"Mom said to call you in for dinner, but nobody knew where you were. I thought maybe you'd come back to say good-bye to Missy again."

"Dinner?" He shoved his hands into the pockets of his jeans, and they felt good and chilled, actually numb. "I was just going to fix something for myself."

"Those ready-to-eat things you buy are gross, Grandpa." She shook her head. "Mom and Dad want you to eat with us tonight. So do I."

"So you tracked me down."

She pointed at the slush.

"You have big footprints, Grandpa."

She turned and sprinted through the woods back toward the house, losing one of her boots in the slushy snow before picking it up again. Gerrit was just about to follow when he had to choke back a major-league case of déjà vu. Who had said that before?

You have big footprints. Joan. Of course, Joan, the night she came for his party. And it occurred to Gerrit as he left Kelsey Creek that he was following another set of footprints too. Only they were definitely not his own, and he was glad the Lord wore such large boots.

Thing was, he wasn't sure where these new prints were leading. All he knew was this was not his place.

Not anymore.

Chapter 33

If music be the food of love, play on.
—SHAKESPEARE, *Twelfth Night*

Randy swished the water around in the kitchen sink a little more, watching the suds dissolve into lukewarm water. He looked through the kitchen window at his mother's little overgrown yard and actually smiled at a sparrow hopping around their empty bird feeder.

Step by step.

First, take the new medication, the right dose. Promise everybody who will listen that you're not going to do anything stupid again. Smile a little. Answer e-mails.

The days had passed. Had the long winter fog really begun to lift?

His mom must have thought so. Otherwise she wouldn't have left him alone while she ran to meet somebody from the college. Back in a couple hours, Randy. There are cookies in the pantry, Randy. Are you sure you're going to be all right, Randy? When the phone rang he grabbed a dishtowel and lifted the receiver.

"Horton's. And I'm all right."

The guy on the other end *umm*ed and *ahh*ed before he finally asked for Joan.

"Oh, sorry. She's won't be back for a little while. Can I take a message?"

"Well, sure, I guess. It's Gerrit Appeldoorn from Van Dalen, er… Washington. Washington State."

"The famous Gerrit." Randy scribbled circles on the back of an envelope with a dry pen. "Heard all about you."

"That right?" The guy sounded surprised.

"I mean, the piano playing mostly. Mom says you're really good…" He paused, wrestling with the foot in his mouth. "…for a beginner."

"Oh, well, that's about all I'm ever going to be, I guess. But…uh… I'm speaking to Randy, right?"

"Oh yeah." Randy tossed the pen aside. "Sorry—"

"No, I didn't mean it that way. It's just that your mom, she's…uh… always talked a lot about you."

Randy swallowed and wondered if that was a good thing.

"No kidding?"

"Yeah." Gerrit paused. "So…ah, you'll tell her I called?"

"Sure. She has your number, I think."

"Yeah, I think so. But look, Randy. Your mom hasn't been telling me more than…I mean, she's just been concerned about you is all."

"Can't say I blame her, after…" How much did Gerrit know? "…after the last few weeks."

"I suppose the good news is you and your mom probably had a chance to talk while you were laid up. Without playing phone tag, I mean."

"Huh." Randy almost chuckled. "I haven't talked to my mother so much in my whole life as I have in the past few days."

"Well, glad you connected. I can think of better places to hang out, though. I mean, the hospital."

"Me, too. Psych wards are…"

His voice trailed off when he realized what he was saying.

"That's okay," Gerrit almost whispered. "I felt like dirt when I was in the hospital too."

"Oh, that's right. I…ah…hope you're doing better."

"Thanks. The important thing is we're both out now. And I'll tell you what, I am not going to miss those…hospital gowns, are you?"

"Oh, those!"

They both laughed at a memory shared while Randy peeked out the front window to make sure his mother hadn't yet returned.

"Anyway, I'll tell Mom you called, soon as she gets home. She went out to coffee with somebody from the music school. I think they're talking about making her a department head in the fall."

Gerrit sounded like he swallowed hard. Either that or their call was cut off.

"Hello?" Randy tapped on the receiver.

"I'm still here." Finally. "That's...that's great. Department head."

"Yeah. I told her to go for it."

"How 'bout that."

"I mean, what an honor. Not every day you get an offer to be a department head at Gaylord, right?"

"Not every day, right."

"Yeah."

"Uh-huh."

The second hand on his mom's kitchen wall clock worked its way up for another go-round. Time to wrap it up.

"Well, anyway," Randy began, "I will leave Mom a message." (What was that, the third time he said that?) "And sorry. I didn't mean to go on with my life story."

"Not at all. Glad I finally got a chance to talk to you. You never used to answer your phone is what I hear."

"No excuses." Randy scratched his head and sighed. "I know a jerk when I see one in the mirror."

⌒

Gerrit pulled down another sack of goat feed from the shelf, ripped open the top, and tossed the scoop to Mallory. Now he *really* wasn't supposed to be doing this sort of thing. Good thing Warney wasn't around to see.

"I wonder how many more weeks." Mallory stooped down to see how big her goat had become.

"She's going to be there awhile. Her son needs her help. He was a nice guy, though, on the phone."

"Her son?" Mallory looked back and forth from her grandfather to the goat, then giggled. "I was talking about Lilbit. You're talking about Mrs. Horton."

Gerrit grinned. "Guess I am."

"Do you think she's going to cancel the spring recital?"

"Not a chance. She'll be back."

Mallory groaned.

"Don't you want her to come back for a while before she moves home to New York?"

"Sure, Grandpa. It's just that…"

She paused.

"It's just that I'm not going to play in the recital."

So there. The ten-year-old had put her foot down. But here came that stupid déjà vu thing all over again, the past pretending it was the present. What was it, the first sign that his mind was out to pasture? But sure enough, he and Warney had had a conversation exactly like this, years ago, when he'd offered the farm to his son.

"I just don't know if I can handle it, Dad." Warney had stood here in the barn, almost in the same spot as his daughter.

"What do you mean, 'not handle it'?" Gerrit remembered delivering his best argument right to his son's strike zone. "Your great-great-grandfather handled it, and your great grandfather handled it, Opa Joost. For goodness' sake, even *I* handled it. And you're the smartest in the family. With all your college learning, don't tell me you can't handle it."

Besides, who else would take on the family tradition? Not Gene, Bruce, or Patti. That left it to Warney. Besides, added Gerrit, this had to be God's will.

Well, maybe it was…and maybe it wasn't. Because a funny thing had happened to Gerrit's thinking over the past few months, ever since he'd met Joan and especially ever since his operation. He wasn't even sure he could put a finger on what had changed. All he knew was that while he was still knee-deep in it, Gerrit never thought he'd been twisting Warney's arm. Only with a few years between then and now did he see it more clearly.

And look where all the arm-twisting had gotten them.

In the end, Warney had hated working the farm. And Mal hated playing the piano. Same thing?

"And it doesn't matter how much I practice," Mallory went on. "I just can't get it."

Gerrit sighed and searched for a Solomon-like answer. Maybe he'd blown it with Warney. So did he really have to repeat all his mistakes? After raising four, it seemed like he ought to get extra credit for grandchildren.

"Okay, then I suppose you could quit," he blurted out. "That would be fine with me."

Mallory's eyes widened, like "quit" was cussing.

"You're just being sarcastic, Grandpa. Dad said you shouldn't be that way."

"Oh, so he taught you that word, did he?" Gerrit had to laugh, and if it weren't for the still-tender scars on his chest, it would have felt real good. "Well, tell you what. If you don't quit, then I'll stop being sarcastic. How's that?"

"Huh." Mallory crossed her arms. "I dunno if that's such a good swap."

"Oh, come on." He tossed a handful of hay at her hair. And as Mallory counterattacked, he thought he heard a yell from the house. Phone call from New York? Forgetting his scars, he vaulted over piles of slush on his way back to the house and finally grabbed the receiver from Liz.

Hello? (followed by heavy breathing). No, he wasn't doing anything. (Take another breath.) And yes they were all just fine. What about her? How about her son?

"I was able to bring him home after the ninety-six-hour hold." Joan's voice sounded far away, maybe because it was. "The doctors were more or less happy with his progress, and he's on a different medication now. I think he's going to be okay."

"Glad to hear it." Gerrit pressed the receiver into his ear so he wouldn't miss her words. "We've been praying. I've been—"

"Thank you. I wondered how you were doing too."

Liz leaned his direction from where she stood over the stove, heating up dinner. So he pulled the cord out as far as it would go, out into the front room, closer to the piano.

"Me?" He waved off the question. "Never better. The way they did it, that EVH stuff, really was slick. Who'da thought I just had a heart operation? I'm back on my feet. Well, pretty gimpy for a while. Slow and everything. But not bad, considering. You getting any rest yourself?"

"Not really, but that doesn't matter. Randy and I have had a lot of time to talk, to catch up on things."

"Oh yeah, well, speaking of catching up, we sent you a copy of the *Sentinel* the other day. Had a bunch of ice-storm photos. Mal thought you'd enjoy them."

"Tell her thank you for me."

Liz banged a pot in the kitchen, and he figured she heard just about every word, at least from his end of the conversation. But it didn't matter a fig. And this wasn't about him, either. He took another breath.

"But listen, you want me to do anything else?" he asked. "Maybe call the rest of your students for you? I could tell them when you'll be getting back."

"That's sweet of you to ask, but I'd best contact them myself. I have one of those calling cards."

"That's good. Sure. But…" Oh, well. He might as well be straight with her. "But really that was just a sideways way of asking *when* you were getting back."

"Oh!" She sort of giggled. "Well, I'm still not sure. Perhaps a couple of weeks. It depends on how he's doing."

"He sounded real decent when I talked to him. Don't know if he told you, but we had ourselves a good talk. Like I said, pretty upbeat too, considering—"

"Considering how much he's been through."

"Right." Gerrit thought he heard Joan take a deep breath.

"Gerrit, I don't suppose he told you he's been carrying around a suicide note from his father for the past six years?"

"Suicide? No." Gerrit sucked in his breath. "I mean, I can't imagine. But you didn't know, did you? Or...shoot, it's none of my business."

"It's all right. I wouldn't have mentioned it if I didn't...trust you."

So she finally told him how Jim had died of carbon monoxide poisoning, buried inside his little car in a snowbank along Highway 30. She told him about the phone call, and she told him what she had learned most recently: how Randy had believed it was a suicide, and how it must have weighed on him. Had it pushed him to do what he did? She wasn't sure. Gerrit nodded quietly, asking the occasional question but mostly listening. And what had she thought when she heard about the note?

"The note hit me pretty hard too, but only because of what it did to Randy, not because I believed Jim had followed through on it. I keep going back to that phone call."

"So where does that take you now?"

She sighed. "Back to where I started, I suppose."

"Yeah. Randy told me about the promotion. Congratulations."

So now it was her turn to listen as he told her how he felt, how he wished her the best. That this sounded like the opportunity of a lifetime. That the timing had to be God's will, even.

Was it? She would miss her students, she said. All of them. He assured her that he would keep up his practicing at least.

"I hope so," she said. "You have a real talent."

Oh. Well, by this time Gerrit was wondering how to say good-bye without sounding too sappy. Joan beat him to it.

"I don't care what anybody says, Gerrit Appeldoorn," she whispered. "You're a gentleman and a good listener."

Even if he was, he thought, that didn't change the fact that Joan was leaving Van Dalen.

Chapter 34

I married the first man I ever kissed. When I tell this
to my children, they just about throw up.

—BARBARA BUSH

O ur ad's in the *Sentinel* again this week." Warney said as he leaned over his dad's shoulder and pointed at the computer monitor. "See it?"

"Saw it." But Gerrit sure wasn't going to get excited about a stupid farm-auction ad. Nothing to get hopped up about since he knew everything that was for sale in the ad anyway. His trusty Deere, a bunch of plowing equipment, tools, supplies, you name it. His life, piece by piece or the whole lot. Maybe somebody would want to buy one of his kidneys while they were at it, or a liver. How much for a patched-up heart in fair-to-good condition?

He thought about it for a second, the way people think about what they would do if they won the lottery. But no, selling hearts was probably illegal. And no, the auction was nothing to get excited about. So he scrolled to the online classifieds and clicked on a couple of help-wanted ads for things he could have done if the doctor would've let him. North Wash Farm and Garden Supply needed a salesman. He could do that. And Van Dalen Ag Services needed a driver. How hard could that be, driving around to farms, emptying milk tanks? Except that they probably wanted a young guy, not a sixty-year-old ex-farmer.

"Looks like you're starting to get the hang of this." Warney straightened out while his dad navigated through the site. "Try—"

"I'm way ahead of you, Warney-boy." *Click, click, click.* "Know how much they're selling tractors for on eBay? We could've made a fortune."

"I don't think so. We'll stick to the in-person auction."

"Well, how about this health online thing? Shows how you can change your diet and add years to your life."

"This is not my dad speaking." Warney shook his head. "They switched you with somebody else at the hospital, right? Since when are you interested in adding years?"

"Not past what the Lord has for me. But I was just thinking if we put all this money into a heart operation, maybe I shouldn't waste it by being in too much of a hurry to leave."

"You mean 'leave' as in placing your name in the *Sentinel* obituaries."

"Yeah. And speaking of the *Sentinel,* if somebody had told me it was online, I wouldn't have had to mail the printed thing all the way to New York. Buck thirty-nine just for that envelope. Why does anybody read it on paper anymore?"

"I can't believe you. Last month you were ready to give your computer away. Now you're an Internet junkie. But I still don't know what made you change your mind about all this."

They heard a soft chime and a pleasant voice announcing, "You've got mail."

"Aha!" Gerrit clicked at his mail icon like a hungry steelhead taking the bait. "Probably junk mail. I get more junk mail. Diet supplements, investment advice, Nigerian millionaire scams…"

"Junk from profhorton@gaylord.edu? So you're e-mailing outside the faith, huh?"

Gerrit moved his head to block Warney's view.

"Makes me nervous, people looking over my shoulder."

"Aren't you glad I finally showed you how this all works?"

Joan stopped by her son's room upstairs four hours and that many cups of coffee after dinner. She leaned on the doorjamb, head spinning as her eyes adjusted to his flickering television nightlight. The color was all wrong, so the hosts looked like Smurfs. Were they selling a pearl necklace this time or a special-purchase Pentium system?

"He's a nice guy, Mom."

She jumped, though by this time she should have expected it. Randy always started conversations with a bang.

"I thought you'd be asleep by now," she whispered and wiped at her puffy eyes. Maybe in the darkness he wouldn't be able to see how much she'd been crying.

"What, and miss the three-in-one blender, slicer, and CD player? You should see the price on this one. But it's only until midnight. Thirty minutes left."

She smiled and shook her head as she lowered herself into her chair by the bed. The Smurfs wheeled out a dramatic new breakthrough in fax technology.

"Besides," he added, "I couldn't fall asleep while you were still out on your online date."

"Randy Horton! What kind of drugs are they giving you now?"

"No, no. That's what you always used to tell *me*, remember?"

"I remember. But it seems to me you used to stay out a bit later than 11:30."

"You have my permission to e-mail your friends as late as you want." He put down the newspaper he was reading, only how he could read by the light of the television, she wasn't sure. "It just surprises me that Gerrit is e-mail savvy."

"Warney showed him."

"Warney. Now there's a farmer name. But Gerrit surprised me."

"What were you expecting? Jed Clampett chewing a piece of hay?"

"Uh-uh. I just never knew any farmers before. He was a nice guy, that's all. At least he sounded like it on the phone."

She nodded as she recalled their latest flurry of e-mails. Was it just her, or had he softened his fatalistic edge even as she had come to understand him better? Could a brush with death change someone that way? As she mentioned Gerrit's offer to help her move when the time came, she still couldn't stop her hands from shaking.

"It's okay, Mom," replied Randy, leaning closer. "We're going to be okay."

"That's what I told you."

She buried her face in Randy's shoulder—gently—and sobbed one more time, perhaps not so much in remorse. Now the stinging tears had changed to relief, a spring rain that slowly melted the worst ice from this bitter winter. Randy stroked her shoulder and said nothing, just let her cry, until finally she gathered enough breath to speak again.

"Are you really going to be all right?" she asked.

"Mom. Don't stress about it. Just enjoy your life. Look forward to the promotion. Even your buddy Gerrit is fine with it."

"My *buddy* Gerrit." She picked up the newspaper, which had a couple of holes torn out of one of the pages. "Is this the newspaper he sent?"

"Yeah, did you know Wilhemina Hekkema came to Van Dalen with her family when she was four, and that she lived all her life in your town?"

"Who's Wilhemina Hekkema?"

"Don't you read the obits? She was ninety-four, lifelong member of Third Reformed. The Klompendancer Club meets Tuesdays and Thursdays at the Senior Center. And the Young Calvin Club is selling little trees to help raise money for a missions trip to Tijuana."

"Oh yes, I'd heard about that."

"How did you know?"

"It was online."

"Well, I didn't know there were places like this anymore. Even have a couple of halfway decent-looking jobs."

She smiled as he picked up the paper and held it up to the light.

"And check this out: Farm sale and auction. Includes a 1955 John Deere Model 50 tractor—always wanted one of those—plus implements, tools, fifty years of blah blah… Okay, here it is, antique upright Steinway piano, circa 1870. Sounds like a really nice old instrument."

She stiffened, then grabbed the paper.

"Let me see that."

Chapter 35

Twenty years from now you will be more disappointed by the
things that you didn't do than by the ones you did do. So throw
off the bowlines. Sail away from the safe harbor.
—MARK TWAIN

I remember something like this in a movie once." Warney looked around at the garage-sale crowd that had already gathered to inspect their castoffs, their farm implements, their life. They'd put up an awning for Will deWeerdt, the auctioneer—which was the only prudent thing to do in mid-April. *April showers bring...* and all that. But though the sky had threatened to unload last night, so far the Saturday morning gray had only proven to be an empty threat. So far.

Warney yawned and crossed his arms. Not that he wasn't used to rising early, but this was another kind of work. And they'd been at it since before five that morning, pricing items and setting fifty years of memories out for the world to cart away. They'd be glad when it was all over.

"What movie, Dad?" Mallory gripped her father's arm.

"Your dad's thinking of one of those disaster flicks he likes to watch," said Gerrit. He had to laugh, or he knew he'd cry at the sight. Had his life been reduced to this? "The ones where a tornado comes and wipes everything out, or maybe God is going to have Mount Baker erupt in the middle of all this..."

"That wasn't the film I was thinking about." Warney steered his father across the yard with an arm around his shoulder. "I think it was called *Country.* Mid-'80s. I was telling Herm at the bank about it. There's this

farm auction in Iowa where all the neighbors come, but they all refuse to
bid, like a protest. So the auctioneer just has to give up and go home."

"Oh, you mean a fantasy." Gerrit chuckled. Yeah, that would be a fantasy plot all right, and he knew they would have plenty of bidders this
morning by the way the vultures were already circling. Good thing this
wasn't a foreclosure sale, or the fur would really fly.

As it was, the drive was lined with pickups, and Gerrit did his best not
to scowl at people he had known all his life. Like Winnie Vranken, whose
bumper sticker tells the world that she stops for garage sales. Thanks for
taking a break from the Velkomvagen, Winnie. How's Earl doing?

Gerrit greeted everyone else, too, of course. People who were all too
willing to pay pennies on the dollar, but he guessed it wasn't their fault.
They were as Dutch as he was. Not Warney's fault, either. This sale was
nobody's fault, or maybe his own, if he really wanted somebody to blame.
But he was done crying, since there was a time to weep and a time to
laugh, a time to mourn and a time to dance.

No plans for dancing today, though. The auctioneer tapped on his
portable microphone.

"Testing, *phtt-phtt*, one-two-three."

The tall bald fellow didn't need any loudspeaker, but he was welcome
to do things his way, of course. Gerrit had seen him off and on at livestock
auctions. Will deWeerdt could get his lips moving as well as anyone.
Maybe better.

"God's in it, brother." An older fellow from Liz and Warney's church
clapped Warney on the back, and Gerrit supposed he was trying to be
encouraging. But from where he stood it sounded to Gerrit more like one
of those hollow comments people make at funerals.

He's out of his pain now. He's in a better place. It's all for the best.

All true, maybe. But saying so never helped. And this was as close to
a funeral as he had ever been without a body to take center stage.

"I know, Wes." Warney didn't look at Gerrit when he agreed with the man, which was the proper thing to do. "But it's all happening pretty fast."

"I thought you said you'd been talking to your buddy at the county ag board for months."

"Yeah, but still." Warney nodded. "It's all coming together at the same time: Selling, moving to town, the new job. And what do I know about being an agricultural lobbyist anyway?"

"That's what we're going to have to call you now? You'll do great."

Gerrit had already told Warney as much. But still this Wes fellow insisted on heaping the encouragement pretty high. A little would have been fine.

"And the way Larry Kroodsma is taking over your acres. You won't have any problem selling the house separate."

"Already had two offers."

Warney needed to stop adding comments like that, or the guy would never give it up.

"See?"

"It's just so fast, too fast." Warney still shook his head, and Gerrit said nothing, just agreed with his son. Six weeks to sell everything, including the livestock. Well, that would happen in a matter of hours, the way the auction was going. But still, they only had a month and a half to clear everything out. Sell the house to some nonfarmer who would want to live in a quaint old farmhouse. Shoot, maybe they'd come up from California, pay cash for the building on its new scalped lot, keep a couple of horses in the barn, run a bed-and-breakfast, and pretend they were country folk. People like Joan Horton could come out and visit, ride horses, and feel as if they had spent time at a real homestead.

And he could have kicked himself for thinking of her. Didn't do any good to make friends with people who come and go. Fly in with their pianos and fly out with your heart.

But of course God had things under control. Gerrit could say that, even if he would let no one tell him the same. See? Warney had already helped him find a nice two-bedroom condo in town, bigger than he needed, really, but close to the new golf course, which wasn't too bad maybe. They told him he wouldn't have to do any yard work, so maybe he could talk the groundskeeper into letting him take a turn on the riding mower.

Gerrit found a place on the back stoop behind the house, watching the auction out of the corner of his eye but staying well enough away so as to avoid talking to anyone else. Wasn't in the mood, thanks. He whistled for Missy, but then remembered. And the clouds finally began spitting as the auctioneer sold off their '55 John Deere Model 50 tractor for way less than it was worth. Shoot, he didn't even listen to the final price; it hurt too much. Good thing his grandmother's piano was safely under the awning, the last item before the friendly vultures moved on to the barn.

But he wasn't sure he could watch this part.

A fleece, that's all it was. A test, and Joan wasn't at all comfortable with it. Fundamentally disliked the idea, in fact. But as she felt the two letters in her purse, both to Dr. Adelstein, but each with a different answer, she didn't know how else to do this.

"I apologize, God." She whispered as she parked out on Vanderkrans Road behind two rusty pickups. "But I honestly don't know what else to do."

She hoped the Lord would understand. She knew He understood the horrible tug of war still going on between her heart and her head. And now here at the Appeldoorn farm, where she would no doubt run into him, her heart was gaining a clear edge.

She came armed with a promise from a piano dealer in Seattle. He would take her student Baldwin off her hands as a favor if she would also give him a good price for the more coveted Yamaha baby grand. The package deal would provide her with quick cash. Not accounting for the considerable sum it would take for a full refinishing and restoration of an antique Steinway, she would have ten thousand to bid, no more.

Her fleece? Simple: If she could win this auction with the proceeds from selling her two pianos, she would stay in Van Dalen and turn down Dr. Adelstein's offer. If not, she would be on a plane to New York in three weeks, or as soon as she could put her things in order, leaving behind what her one-time colleague had called her "heartland-of-America pilgrimage thing." She winced at her impertinence, presuming on God. But how else could she decide? And where was Gerrit in all this?

She wasn't sure, but she stayed close behind a couple walking up the driveway. By the way they were talking about udder capacities and ligaments, they were going to bid on some of the livestock. Let them. Joan slipped past the deep tire tracks where she had slid into the little ditch and joined the growing crowd under the canopy.

She counted forty or fifty bidders, each holding their own number, and most were obviously interested in the generator or the manure spreader or some such item. But on the far side, a gentleman with round spectacles and an ugly gray toupee looked to her like an antique dealer. And across on the other side, a well-groomed woman in a red dress looked as out of place as a...well, it was fairly obvious. Joan would not be the only one bidding on the Steinway, and she did not have long to find out.

"We got something completely different here." A half-hour later the auctioneer paused to take a sip from a cup of steaming coffee before going on. He adjusted his glasses and checked his program. "I'm told this here Stainway and Sons upright Victorian piano was brought to the property by the owner's grandmother somewhere around the turn of the last century, but it dates from around 1868. Extremely rare, a piece of history. Looks a little rough around the edges, but it's been partially restored on the insides, so it plays like the day it was built."

Well, an auctioneer might be expected to employ a bit of hyperbole. Nevertheless, it was a special instrument to be sure, with as much character as any piano could claim. Joan noticed the gray-haired man and the woman in the red dress had taken notice and held their numbers ready. So did she for that matter. Everyone's attention turned to the fine old piano perched on the plywood platform at the center of the tent. It would have been far better if they'd left it in the house, but Joan supposed farm auctions didn't often handle valuable old pianos.

"So we're not going to mess around with garage-sale pricing, here, on this Stainway."

Steinway. Joan corrected him silently, but it didn't matter, as the bidding between her two competitors quickly passed five thousand and then six.

"Sixty-five, sixty-five, sixty-six—" He looked back and forth in the two-way bidding battle, using a slower cadence by far than he had used for the farm equipment. And when the two bidders paused at eighty-two hundred, Joan raised her number and cleared her throat.

"Ah, a new bidder over there in the back." Their auctioneer brightened at the prospect, showing a flash of a gold crown in his smile. He likely had no idea what the instrument was truly worth, since it wasn't painted green and lacked a starter button. But again, no matter. "Eighty-three hundred, says the young lady in plaid."

Young lady, indeed. But that must have alarmed the other two, as the high bid leapfrogged from eighty-four hundred to ten thousand in a blink. And in a blink Joan's hope melted to her shoes. She stared helplessly at her number, dumbfounded and blinking back tears. One bid, and her fleece had been blown away? She glanced over at the house to see Gerrit disappear inside, not watching but perhaps hearing.

In that moment her tug of war ended as abruptly as it had begun in Randy's room when she'd read the auction ad. Without another thought she abandoned her fleece in the mud, exchanging it for her heart. It had been a dumb idea anyway.

"Thirteen thousand!" she shouted, and the auctioneer turned to her with wide eyes. They'd been slowing at ten and a half, eleven thousand, obviously nearing the top end. The fellow with the toupee turned as red as the woman's dress.

Don't lose your hair, sir, Joan silently advised him, and she chewed on her lip to keep a smile from breaking out. Meanwhile, the woman in the red dress nibbled on her bidding card, obviously fuming, before she shook her head and made a petulant about-face exit.

"You, sir?" The auctioneer wanted to make sure before he triple-repeated the top offer, then banged his gavel with obvious relish.

"Sold! Thirteen grand for the grand. To number..." He squinted to read Joan's card, which she had dropped to her side in the excitement. A woman next to him leaned over and whispered in his ear. "Oh, okay," he continued. "Sold to the piano teacher. You gonna be giving some lessons on this fine instrument, ma'am?"

Joan didn't hesitate. "You bet I am."

⌒

Gerrit had figured they'd get a few thousand for it at least. Hopefully more than five, what that fellow had once offered him. But he really didn't feel like knowing, not now, so that's why he'd slipped inside for a drink of milk. Or water. Whatever. The price would be what it would be. He gulped down the milk, popped another Dubbel Zout, and finally returned outside to wait for the auction noise to die down and the crowd to move on to the barns. Only then did he dare look over to see if they were going to try to move his Oma's piano out of the yard.

And there it was, of course—or the back of it, anyway. But not for long. The auction company had said they'd hire a real piano mover and get it out of here immediate-like, assuming the buyer's money was good. The folks who had been hovering around the piano and some of that stuff under the tent were moving on.

Fine. He assumed maybe the buyer would have been able to play the thing, unless they were taking it for some kind of investment or maybe as an antique to wheel and deal. You never knew, and he didn't really want to know. Bottom line was Warney and Liz needed the cash, so that was all there was to it.

Sold. Just like everything else, right down to his grandfather's old hay scythe and toolboxes. And though the lesson tore at the moorings of his heart, he supposed he was learning to get rid of things he could not really keep anyway. And he supposed it probably reminded Warney of some movie.

But he wasn't prepared for the music coming from the tent, a sound that hit him with a sweetness that made him catch his breath. What?

Debussy.

There could be no doubt who was playing it.

～

"You're back?" He leaned over the top of the piano as if he were just saying howdy or "Play it again, Sam," but the sad question in his eyes betrayed him. And her fingers tangled the second movement as she nodded a weak yes.

"I heard about the auction, so I…"

"Pardon me, Mrs. Horton," interrupted one of the young auction clerks. "How would you like to arrange for payment?"

Gerrit stared as she fished a check out of her purse and handed it across, and she did her best to keep her hand from shaking more than it did.

"So you stopped by to pick up a piano," he said.

"I'm sorry." She studied her hands. "I thought it would be better to keep it here in the community."

"Okay, now I'm really confused." He looked at her sideways. "You're leaving, but the piano is staying? How does that work exactly?"

"It's staying in my living room." She reached into her purse once more and handed him two envelopes. "But I want you to do something for me. Rip up one of these letters for me. Please?"

He pulled out his glasses as he sat on the edge of the piano bench.

"They're both to Dr. Herbert Adelstein at the Gaylord School of Music," he told her. Obviously. "You want to explain?"

"The one with the stamp says that I'm not coming back to the school, even after my sabbatical is done. That I'm staying here in Van Dalen. The one without the stamp says I'm packing up, and I'll be there by June 1."

She paused. The drizzle had stopped. And she took a deep breath.

"I want you to tear up the one without the stamp."

"So this one says 'thanks.'" He held up the unstamped envelope in his left hand as a smile crept across his face. He understood.

Then he held up the twin envelope, stamped, in his right. "And this one, 'no thanks.'"

"That's right. Now would you please tear it up, or shall I?"

He extended the unstamped "thanks" envelope to her with a dare in his eyes.

"Make a wish."

Oh, so that was the game now, was it? She grabbed the end of the envelope and tugged, like a wishbone, and the acceptance letter tore down the middle with a satisfying rip. He yelled at Mallory as she ran by, waving the surviving letter at her as he did.

"Mal! Do me a favor. Joan—Mrs. Horton—has an important letter to mail. Run it down to the mailbox before Mrs. Pietersma comes by to deliver, would you?"

Sure she would, but what now? Gerrit turned to her.

"So that means we don't have to carry on an e-mail relationship."

She nodded and felt a grin playing at her lips.

"And," he added, "you're still going to be here for the recital."

"I wouldn't miss it for anything, Mr. Appeldoorn. In the meantime, why don't you play me something on your grandmother's piano?"

"You bet." He chuckled and slid a little closer on the bench, paused for a moment to pop another piece of Dubbel Zout into his mouth, and began to play a simple tune. She grinned along with him when she recognized the old Johnny Cash standard and added her own harmony to weave in and out of the melody.

"You know this one?" he whispered.

"Sure I do. He was one of my favorite composers."

By that time even the auction helpers had all stopped to watch. The city girl and the farm boy concentrated on their duet, following the same rhythm, blending two melodies into one. He even managed a few of the words.

"I keep a close watch on this heart of mine..."

Great Sacandaga Lake, Upstate New York

$\mathcal{F}$rom the passenger seat Randy leaned forward and nearly poked his nose through the windshield of his mother's rental car to see better. She had already flipped her headlights on as the May afternoon slipped into evening. Just off to the left the lake glimmered golden with the last shreds of the day's sunshine.

"You gonna miss the place?" he asked, studying her face. Once, he didn't know much about his mom, the piano player. Now, since she'd come back, he'd been introduced to a whole new Joan Horton.

She shook her head no. "I thought it would be harder than it was. But it sold so quickly. Just like the farm."

"And just like the house, too. I don't think you guys asked enough. Or maybe I should go into real estate. Let's see, six percent commission, that's more than they pay at the market, right?"

She laughed. "You could. I doubt all sales are that easy, though."

"Really, though, Mom. With all those memories at the lake?"

He glanced at the cardboard box on the seat behind them, the one filled with framed pictures.

"No." She still sounded sure of herself. "I realized today I'd already said good-bye to that place a long time ago. Now we have new memories to make."

"New disasters to plan."

"Oh, don't talk like that. Moving to Washington isn't a disaster and you know it. You have a place to stay with Shane and Alison as long as you want, a new job…"

"Yeah, I know. I can handle screaming nieces. But you're sure my job is going to work out with your buddy Gerrit?"

This time she nodded without hesitating, even as a grin threatened to hijack her mouth.

"You're going to want to call him *Mr.* Appeldoorn. But he did say they had a place for you at the John Deere dealership. As long as you can manage not to blow up the tractors on your test drives."

"Aw, Mom! You told him that story? I didn't think you were going to blab to the whole world."

"Gerrit Appeldoorn isn't the whole world. Just your new boss. And he's learning the ropes too, so you might even teach him a thing or two about sales. He thought the story about your test-drive disaster was funny, by the way."

"Yeah, well, what do *you* think?"

This time she paused as she glanced out across the big, darkening lake.

"I think…God is in control."

He looked at her as if she had never said such a thing before, and maybe she hadn't. They drove on in silence for several miles until they could no longer make out the lake, only what lay ahead, illuminated in the car's headlights.

"Do you still carry mints everywhere you go?"

"You remember." But when she reached into her purse with her free hand all she came upon were the remnants of one of Gerrit's rolls of Dubbel Zouts. Well…

"Try these." She held them out to her son with a grin. "You might like them."

Acknowledgments

*P*aul the apostle once wrote to his Roman friends that "none of us lives to himself alone and none of us dies to himself alone." That's nowhere more true than in the sometimes solitary writing process, one in which writers like me depend upon the expertise and perspective of others. These personal connections serve as our lifelines, so I'm grateful to a number of people who helped make this story possible.

Chip MacGregor, my agent at Alive Communications, was probably the first to catch a vision for *The Duet,* and he championed it at the earliest stages. Forgive the analogy, but Chip served as an expert literary midwife. I also appreciate the enthusiastic support and wise advice of Dudley Delffs, my editor at WaterBrook Press, as well as Don Pape, Steve Cobb, John Hamilton, Laura Barker, and so many others at WaterBrook, from proofreaders to sales and support staff. Each one approaches his or her work with energy and a servant's heart.

I value the daily online support of fellow Christian fiction writers, members of the fellowship called Chi Libris. Each one demonstrates the scriptural principle of how "iron sharpens iron." Yet I would surely not have been able to write this story without the willingness of so many helpful friends and neighbors. Henry Bierlink at the Whatcom County Ag Preservation Committee helped pave the way with referrals and a farmer's perspective. Henry steered me to the farm of Larry Stap, who raises and milks beautiful Jersey cows. Larry allowed me to tag along during his daily rounds and patiently answered all my questions. He even let me try my hand at milking. In addition, Dave Buys offered numerous creative suggestions and valuable background from a dairyman's perspective. He helped me understand more clearly the struggles of passing along a farm to a new generation.

Mel Hodde, MD (along with his wife, Cheryl), provided detailed help with the treatment of depression from an ER doctor's perspective. Thank you, Mel, for your to-the-point explanations. Pastor Jon Aldrich gave me advice and counsel on the finer points of theology. My friend Bob Fraser gave me a quick lesson on how a banker in a farm community works. Roxanne Lawson and Gladys Van Beek graciously read the first draft and offered valuable feedback. Carol Eickmeyer, a talented piano teacher with a heart for God and music, helped me imagine the world of a piano student—particularly the challenges that would face a beginner or an older learner. And I can't neglect to mention how Mrs. Martha Helder provided the ultimate inspiration for this story (though she didn't know it at the time). The idea for *The Duet* came as my daughter, her piano student, was playing during one of her recitals. What if the roles were reversed, I wondered, and the grandfathers watching from the pews became the students?

I should mention one other thing about the setting and characters in *The Duet.* Though the fictional town of Van Dalen might resemble the real town of Lynden, Washington, it is not at all meant to fully or accurately represent a real place. In the same way, the Dutch Reformed church in the story is fictional and is not meant to accurately represent today's Christian Reformed churches. I only used the Dutch Reformed label because of its historical and ethnic significance, and in doing so only meant to describe a generic church in the Reformed tradition. In every instance, I did not mean to imply any one-to-one correspondence. So, as they say in legal circles, any resemblance to actual persons or places is purely coincidental!

In the end, no one helped more than my wonderful wife, Ronda, whose name could legitimately appear on the cover as a coauthor. She has offered endless plot suggestions and helped flesh out the characters. She has read and reread every draft, offering valuable improvements. She has struggled through the difficult passages and helped bring *The Duet* to life, knowing that our ultimate audience is not just you, the reader, but God Himself.

—ROBERT ELMER
Lynden, Washington

About the Author

ROBERT ELMER is the author of thirty-two youth novels, including the Young Underground series, the Adventures Down Under series, the Promise of Zion series, and AstroKids series. A certified teacher, he speaks at schools and homeschool groups all over the country. He is also a veteran advertising copywriter and a former pastor and news editor. Robert holds degrees in communications and Bible. He and his wife Ronda are the parents of two college students and a high-school senior. They live in Washington State.

If you'd like to learn more about Robert's books,
please visit his Web site at www.robertelmerbooks.com.

To learn more about WaterBrook Press and view
our catalog of products, log on to our Web site:
www.waterbrookpress.com